I'M A WALKING, TALKING BRUISE. Every muscle is in some stage of soreness. That's how I like it, because that's how muscles grow. After you destroy them with resistance training, they repair themselves and get bigger.

Destroy and build. Destroy and build.

ALSO BY FRED ACEVES:

The Closest I've Come

THE NEW DAVID ESPINOZA

FRED ACEVES

Quill Tree Books
An Imprint of HarperCollinsPublishers

Quill Tree Books is an imprint of HarperCollins Publishers.

Library of Congress Cataloging-in-Publication Data

Names: Aceves, Fred, author.
Title: The New David Espinoza / Fred Aceves
Description: First edition. | New York : HarperTeen, [2020] |
    Audience: Ages 14 up | Audience: Grades 10–12 | Summary:
    Obsessed with the idea that he is not muscular enough and
    tired of being bullied, David, age seventeen, begins using steroids,
    endangering his relationships with family and friends.
Identifiers: LCCN 2019026614 | ISBN 978-0-06-248988-3
    (hardcover) | ISBN 978-0-06-248990-6 (paperback)
Subjects: CYAC: Body image—Fiction. | Bodybuilding—Fiction. |
    Steroids—Fiction. | Drug abuse—Fiction. | Bullying—Fiction. |
    Latin Americans—Fiction.
Classification: LCC PZ7.1.A216 New 2020 | DDC [Fic]—dc23
LC record available at https://lccn.loc.gov/2019026614

Typography by Fine Design and Catherine San Juan
22 23 24 25   PC/LSCC   10 9 8 7 6 5 4
❖
First paperback edition, 2021

For all of you struggling with a silent hurt. You matter.
You are not alone. You are loved. I see you.

PROLOGUE

IT SUCKS being the skinniest guy at Culler High. If kids rag on me when I'm fully clothed, just imagine their joy when I whip my shirt off, exposing my stickman physique. That's why I rush to PE and change before anybody shows up. It's why I volunteer to be ball boy every semester. After Coach Carlson's final whistle sends everybody else running to the locker room, I take my time herding the soccer balls in the Florida heat.

Today, the last day of my junior year, it's no different. By the time I'm carrying a net bag of soccer balls through the doorway, the locker room is mostly abandoned. The last of the boys are turning in their uniforms and padlocks to Coach.

I swing the bag off my shoulder and drop it into the large metal basket. Then I walk deep back into the last row of lockers. Nobody's around. Lucky me. I spin the combination into the lock and open the metal door for the last time this year. I grab the bottom of my sweaty Culler High Cougars T-shirt and start peeling it off.

The moment it's almost over my head, pain explodes inside the left side of my face.

Someone punched me! What the hell?

The vented blue doors around me go blurry and the T-shirt falls to the floor.

I tip sideways, then back, then forward, my legs trying to find balance. Next thing I know I'm on the floor—my stomach, chest, and half my face cold.

The stench of teenage sweat and feet is way stronger down here.

There's a high-pitched cackle—Ricky's trademark laugh. I could pick him out from about a million idiots, just from that sound.

I strain to lift my head and catch a glimpse of Ricky's grin through my blurry vision before he turns to leave.

Though Ricky might lift weights, he's not what you'd consider muscular at a wiry 5'8". He's not even the in-your-face bully who puts hands on you, from what I've seen. He just makes fun of people, like when he cracks on Ricardo's fat rolls when we change. He nicknamed me Fuckstick that one time he saw my bony torso which got others in PE using that nickname. But from that to punching me?

I mean, sometimes I get shoved against lockers and kicked and punched in the arm real hard, but never by Ricky, and never in the face.

As the bell announces the official end of school this year, I check for blood. Nothing on my fingers.

I push myself up off the floor and stand, still dazed and super confused. A real guy would shake it off and go after Ricky, beat his ass good. What can I do though? Not a damn thing.

I'm not saying that to seem less like a wimp or anything. It's just that, at my size, all I can do is shake it off. Forget the whole thing and try to move on with my life.

I remember what my mom used to say whenever we had a bad turn of luck: *things could always be worse*. So even though my head is wobbly, my cheek stings, and my shoulder somehow aches, I can find the silver lining.

At least it was only one punch.

At least there's no blood.

At least I don't gotta deal with more bullying for three months.

At least nobody saw it happen.

HOURS LATER, in the safety of home, I still haven't shoved the whole Ricky incident outta my head. Enough worrying about it, I tell myself. Technically, Ricky punched me *last* school year. Now it's officially summer: three worry-free months ahead of me. I get amped about that, about tonight especially, the fun that begins just as soon as I change into formal clothes.

I put on my black slacks and take in the bare torso in the mirror. A recent four-inch growth spurt has put me at six feet. Tall is good, but that upward stretch has enhanced my skinniness like when you pull apart taffy. Why couldn't I have grown the other way too?

I slip my arms through the sleeves of my white dress shirt, covering up my knobby shoulders. I button it from the top, hiding my bird chest and pokey ribs. My twig arms are also hidden—I love that about long sleeves.

I consider my reflection. My girlfriend, Karina, often wears black because she says it has a slimming effect, so I figured this shirt, the opposite color, would help me out some by giving me the illusion of bulk. Nope.

That's right. I, David Espinoza, have a girlfriend. Me, the guy who, as of today, has experienced every known form of bullying known to man. We've been going out for four months now.

The other miracle of this year is that I'm going to my first real party. You know, the high school kind—with alcohol and fun, not cake and parents. It's a big deal, the end-of-the year party the whole school has been talking about.

Actually, it's Karina who got invited, by her friend Emily in drama club, and I'm tagging along with Karina, just like my best friend Miguel is tagging along with Karina's best friend. But still.

If only I can figure out how to knot this tie so it's the right length.

"Come on," I tell myself, "the third time's a charm."

Nope. Too short. I give it a fourth, more careful try. Really take my time.

The damn thing droops two inches past my belt.

I take a deep breath to keep my anger at bay. Most of the time, I catch it before it grabs hold of me.

Fifth try, here we go. I grit my teeth as I tighten the

knot and slide it up to the collar: about three inches too short again. I could sell used cars like this, but it's not okay for a party.

"Stupid fucking tie," I say under my breath.

I pull it over my head and fling it across the room. It twists in the air and lands on my small bed.

What a stupid invention! A bit of fancy fabric to dangle around your neck, serving no purpose. And why have a dress code for a house party? I mean, who *does* that? We're not actors going to the Oscars.

And why am I even *going*? If I get harassed at school when adults are nearby, supposedly watching out, what might happen when it's only kids around?

Right away Ricky pops into my head again. My blood simmers and I start pacing.

Ellis comes to mind, this brace-faced guy who flipped my food tray over last week. The ketchup on my face and shirt entertained the hell out of everybody who saw it, their laughter loud enough to draw the attention of half the lunchroom. When Mr. Trevors walked over to ask what happened I told him I'd tripped.

I remember last month in history before the teacher showed up, when Julian hit me in the head with a marker from across the room. "Bring it back to me, or I'll beat the shit outta you." I did, walking all those steps while every eyeball in the room followed me.

This is how it happens. A horrible thought or memory

drifts into my head. Another attaches to it, pulling another one behind, and so on, until I'm clenching my teeth and fists, pacing and wanting to kick some serious ass.

That's where my thoughts end up every time.

I come to a stop and find myself facing the *Nightchaser* movie poster hanging on my door. Van Nelson, the star of the movie, has a fierce scowl on his face. Plus muscles to back it up. He uses them in the best fight scene of all time, at the end of the movie when he gets revenge on those guys who tried to frame him.

So when my thoughts land on Ricky again, the sucker-punching bully materializes right here in my room. He's standing above me, cackling like the idiot he is.

You messed with the wrong guy, Ricky.

I throw two left jabs to his face followed by a hard right hook. A strong kick to the chest splats him against the wall.

When he wobbles toward me I finish him with a round-house that knocks him out cold.

"Whatcha doing?"

The question makes me jump. Puts an end to my triumph. Once again I'm in my bedroom, alone.

Okay, not alone. My little sister, Gaby, is in the doorway. I turn. Confusion is bunching up her face, making her round cheeks even plumper.

Well, *this* is awkward. You don't want your eight-year-old sister thinking you're some weirdo.

I need to remember to shut my tricky door hard enough. Yet again it has clicked away and swung open. So it's my bad. Gaby actually respects my knocking rule. I finally got Dad to start knocking too, which wasn't easy. He's a small-town Mexican who struggles to understand the concept of privacy the way the rest of us struggle with physics.

"Me?" I ask Gaby. "I was dancing."

"For real?" Gaby's eyes go wide. "What kind of crazy dancing was *that*?"

I snatch up the tie in case she wants to jump on my bed. "I was trying some moves for the party."

She takes a seat on my desk chair instead and swivels, considering what I said.

With Gaby around, the anger has drained from me. I'm back to being chill, ready to give this tie another attempt.

"I've never been to a night party," Gaby says, "but you should probably *not* dance like you were dancing."

That makes me smile. "How do you suggest I dance?"

She stops swiveling to think this through, hands clasped to the sides of the chair.

She says, "You should look at how Karina and others are dancing, and dance that way."

I stop messing with my tie to look at her.

"Good advice," I say, putting out my fist.

Her four small knuckles press against mine.

Hanging out with Gaby is the best. Over the years, little by little, she's turned into a real person. Gone from clueless and whiny to smart and fun.

We cook together and play games and watch enough animal documentaries and Pixar movies to qualify as buddies. Sometimes I wonder if she isn't my actual best friend. If not, she's a close second to Miguel.

Dad calls me a good brother for how tight we are, but the truth is I need her as much as she needs me. More than ever since Mom died fifteen months ago.

Cancer—a thought I push outta my head right now. Tonight, I'm all about positive thoughts.

I slide the tie knot up again, feeling good about it.

Yes! The bottom points to the top of my belt, as Dad says it should.

I turn to face Gaby and punch my fists high in the air, like I won a marathon or something.

"You look fancy," she says.

"I *am* fancy," I tell her. "Dad's the one who fired the butler, sold the mansion, and moved us to this part of town."

Gaby smiles and says, "At least we still have the yacht!"

I laugh, but Gaby cracks up for a good ten seconds, slapping her knee and everything. She's the only person I know who laughs hardest at her own jokes.

As she takes a slow spin in the chair, her single thick rope of black hair trails behind her. Despite a few loose strands, the French braid I did for her this morning is holding up. What can I say? My braiding game is tight.

Gaby stops. She hops down from the chair, croaks "ribbit," and hops onto the bed, landing on all fours. Frogs are her thing—learning about them and sometimes, when she's in a goofy mood, hopping like them. After a hard rain, I sometimes take her to Collins Park to look for some.

Her favorite shirt is one with this cartoon frog face on it. Her second favorite is a solid green T-shirt, which she calls frog-colored.

I don't know why, but silly stuff like that coming from her weird brain makes me love her even more.

I sit on the chair to put on my shoes.

Dad walks in, sees me, and asks in Spanish, "Has anybody seen my son, David?" Pronounces it Dah-VID.

Though his English is near perfect, it's always Spanish with him. Gaby and I switch when he's around.

Gaby points to me. "I think that's him dressed up all fancy."

Dad and I are now the same height and we both have short, barely combable hair. That's where the similarities between us end. I have brown hair instead of black, lighter skin like my mom had, and the skinniness that runs deep on that side of the family.

He's brought me his suit jacket, which is my last hope to appear bigger, but the shoulder pads curve down the sides all clownish.

"I'm way too skinny," I say, handing it back.

"Skinny or fat doesn't matter," Dad says, setting a hand

on my shoulder. "Being a man has nothing to do with how you look. A real man is honest, hardworking, and takes care of the people he loves."

Ever since I turned seventeen two months ago, he's been talking about what it means to be a real man.

"I still think I should go and meet the parents," he says, sitting on the bed.

"Nobody does that here, Dad."

"Fine, but you're going to come home if there's anything weird going on at this party," he says, in a way that makes it sound like a question.

"Straight home," I assure him.

I probably got permission because I made the honor roll again this semester. It also helps that I'm going with Karina, who my dad seems to love as much as me.

"Be careful driving," he says, starting to launch into a lecture. "Check blind spots and remember to park on—"

"I remember, Dad."

The trick for his ancient Pathfinder is to park in such a way that you don't gotta put it in reverse. The noisy transmission, grinding for months now, is pretty much shot. You'd think a mechanic with his own auto shop would have replaced it. Dad, however, is broke. He's paying off the house, most of the shop equipment, and there's the rent of the place, of course.

If I hadn't created a GoFundMe account when Mom died, the small funeral would have put us on the street.

Dad runs down the list of instructions.

I'm to use the center lane, which is the safest due to the choice of lanes if you need to steer to avoid an accident.

I'm to park along the curb, the front end of the car almost at the corner so nobody can block me.

"Be polite to everybody, especially the parents, and don't slouch."

It's true I slouch a lot. Like right now, for instance. I straighten up.

The whole time Dad talks, Gaby is standing behind him on the bed, mouthing the words and wagging her finger. If I look directly at her I'll laugh.

Dad's always lecturing *her* on what to do or not do, so she gets a kick outta witnessing it happen to me.

Helicopter parent is a term I caught on the TV this one time and it describes him perfectly. Whenever I hear a helicopter overhead, the propellers beating the air around, I picture him up there with binoculars pointing at me, his grease-stained mechanic clothes ruffling in the wind.

"And no drinking!" he says now, lifting a calloused finger.

Gaby has stopped imitating him to put both hands on her hips and look at me. "There's going to be *beer*?"

"There won't be beer," I assure them. "And I wouldn't drink alcohol anyway."

I'm totally drinking. Just enough to fit in.

I remember the creative ways some idiot kids consume

alcohol, the ones Dad learned from the evening news and freaked out about.

"However," I deadpan, "if people start *eyeballing* or *butt-chugging*, I'm all in."

Dad doesn't crack a smile. His face is harder than concrete.

"Butt-chugging." Gaby giggles. "What's that?"

"If you see any alcohol," Dad tells me, a severe edge to his voice, "you come home."

"Relax, Dad. It was a joke."

"I don't care if it's beer, whiskey, or liquor-filled chocolates. I don't care what hole they're putting it in."

"A *joke*, Dad," I insist. "You know, ha-ha?"

I get up to look at myself once more. These sharp clothes don't make me any less goofy. What does Karina see in me?

She's probably home by now, getting into her new dress after doing her hair and makeup at her friend Janelle's house. Karina's mom had to wait until today, payday, to buy her dress. Picked it up before heading to her second job.

There's a knock at the door.

Gaby rushes there first, asking "Who is it?" Dad and I follow behind.

No response. I look through the peephole. It's Karina. Her face is flawless under much more makeup than usual. Her normally long black hair is swept up and styled all elegant.

I swing open the door to reveal the rest of her: she's in the same T-shirt and cutoff shorts she wore to school, plus she's holding a Macy's bag. Her bright purple Nikes are wet because of the late-afternoon rain. You wouldn't believe the number of pond-sized puddles in the twelve blocks between her house and ours.

"When the invitation said formal," I say, "they probably didn't mean just the neck up."

"You didn't answer your phone," she says, not smiling. "We have to take an emergency trip to the mall."

2

IT TURNS OUT the perfect dress, the one Karina and her mom agreed on after an extensive search, is not the dress her mom bought. Instead, she bought the one Karina hated.

"It really is the worst kind of ugly imaginable," Karina tells me once we're inside Macy's, at 8:41. We have nineteen minutes before this place closes.

She grabs a simple black dress from the rack and checks the tag to make sure it's the right size.

A saleslady is going through receipts at the register. As we head over, my formal shoes click and Karina's sneakers squish on the floor.

"It can't be *that* ugly," I tell Karina.

But when she pulls it outta the bag and sets it on the counter for the woman to inspect for return, I see I'm wrong. *Ugly* might be an understatement.

It's long and unrevealing the way moms probably like, but why is it blueberry-colored? And what's up with the roundish sleeves and shiny stuff around the collar?

The lady eyes the receipt and asks, "What's the reason for the return?"

"It makes me look like a piñata."

"Hey," I tell Karina. "You know how much I like piñatas."

She gives me some side-eye.

Serious situation = no jokes. I need to remember that.

The woman accepts the return. Minutes later Karina emerges from the fitting area, mouth slack with disappointment.

I don't get it. Is that not the right dress? It should be. *Please* be the right dress. She looks so amazing.

The way it hugs her completely, from the breasts down to mid-thigh where it stops, showing off her legs.

"Dayum!" I say, louder than I wanted to.

My girlfriend is a straight-up stunner, despite the frown on her face.

"What's wrong?" I ask.

"It's my legs," she says, without averting her gaze from the mirror. "I hate them."

"I've always loved your legs."

Back when we first met she considered herself fat—a ridiculous idea. It's why she wouldn't let me see her naked the first two times we did it. I switched the light off and called her silly, but I was actually grateful for the dark. Because I didn't want her to see *me* naked.

That's only because I'm *supposed* to have some bulk on my body. Hell, I'm supposed to defend her with force if it comes down to it.

"How thin do you wanna be?" I ask.

Karina doesn't answer. She's staring down the mirror as if it's a person she doesn't trust.

I encircle Karina's shoulders with my arm. Our eyes meet in the mirror reflection. For the millionth time since I've met her I wonder, how can someone so pretty worry about her appearance?

"You always look amazing," I tell her. "Today you look extra hot. Lava hot. Surface-of-the-sun hot. You look Tabasco-sauce hot." I pause to consider what I just said. "I know my examples make no sense but I can't compare you to other girls. That's how hot you are."

"You're just being nice."

"No. I'm being real. And you're sort of being a spoiled brat," I tell her, trying to keep my face straight.

Her eyes dart away from the mirror and onto me. "*What* did you say?"

"Rather than appreciate all your beauty, you just want more." I shake my head in mock disappointment. "It's an injustice how sexy you are. You should spend the whole day apologizing to every girl you see."

She laughs, breaking loose from my embrace. Seconds later she's still smiling when she pulls me close for a kiss.

"Okay," she says. "Let's get the dress and get out of here."

3

WE'RE SITTING at one of the six outside tables in Emily's back-yard, among the supertall palm trees, cords of dotted light swirled around the trunks. As EDM plays from two large speakers, people come through the side gate or the house, boys and girls in ties and dresses, red Solo cups in their hands.

The glass door slides open and two more formal kids come out. Neither of them bullies. The punch from earlier still has me on edge. I told Miguel about it because I tell him everything.

He gets picked on almost as much as me, being fat with those wild curls on his head and all. Yet he emerged from the house with a drink, unscathed. He's certain nobody will mess with me.

Our table is made up of three girls, and the three guys they brought along—a sort of triple date. One side is girl-talk: Karina and her two friends are desperately catching up after being apart for a whole three hours. They're wearing nice dresses and have their long hair all swept up and close to their heads. I don't know what it is about fancy parties and dances that makes girls hide most of their hair.

On this side it's Miguel, Enzo, and me. I've been friends with Miguel since the summer before fifth grade. That's when our dads, sick of us being in front of all kinds of screens, forced us out into the sun. There we were on our front yards, Miguel across the street and four jacked-up houses over. He walked over and we sat in the shade of my porch, talking about video games and Marvel vs. DC. We're still into those three things.

Enzo I barely know. He's Janelle's boyfriend, who's Karina's second bff. Today's the first time I've said more than *wassup* to him.

"This tie is killing me." He loosens it by tugging it back and forth. He unbuttons the top button of his shirt and looks around. He's been looking around a lot, as if he's not sure he belongs either.

Enzo is about 5'8", neither tall nor short, neither fat or skinny. Too average to stand out to bullies.

"So what do you think?" he asks. "Do you think Emily wanted a fancy party because juniors can't go to prom?"

"Maybe," I say, and pop another barbecue chip in my mouth.

Miguel tells Enzo, "Maybe it's because Emily thought

that dressing more formal would make everybody act more civilized."

If so, it's working. Nothing has gotten smashed, though after some people have a few drinks that all might change.

The popular guys aren't tormenting anybody either. Then again, I've seen only two of them, briefly, when they stepped out here real quick. For all I know, they've set up a torture chamber inside.

Miguel lifts his almost brimming cup to his nose. Cringes when he takes a whiff.

"How nasty can it be?" Liliana asks. "You barely put rum in it."

They've been going out since two months ago, when Karina and I each brought our best friends to the movies with us. Nobody was playing matchmaker or anything. It just happened.

"Super nasty," Miguel says. "The rum ruined the taste of the whole soda."

We all wait for his second attempt to take a swallow. He sips from the cup and winces. A second later he spits it out on the grass.

"I told him not to put rum in his Coke," Liliana tells the girls.

Miguel sets down the cup. "I didn't know it would be this bad." He pushes it to the side.

"Give it up, man," I say.

"I'm no quitter," he says. "Also, I heard this TV chef say

that we gotta taste new stuff three times before deciding if we like it."

I really wish I had something to drink, anything without alcohol. Since nobody's drinking at this table, there's no pressure. With certain guys around, you don't do something they're doing and you lose your guy status.

Enzo starts talking about *Nightchaser*, which is one of his favorite movies too. Miguel and I have watched it about a million times.

"With all the special effects," Enzo says, "I thought maybe that wasn't Van Nelson's actual body, but he really is that big and ripped."

"Why wouldn't it be real?" I ask.

"Did you see his last movie?" he asks. "He played this regular-sized dude, some corporate lawyer."

I didn't see it.

Miguel points out that back in the day action heroes weren't that buff. "James Bond was skinny as a pencil. Or how about the TV Batman and Robin? I could've kicked both their asses. Like, at the same time."

"Yep," I say. "Back in the day superheroes didn't even wear muscle suits underneath."

"Actors who wear muscle suits are lame," Enzo says. "If you get paid a zillion dollars, you should make the effort, you know?"

"Why get all muscular for one role?" I ask. "What if the

next role you want doesn't require big muscles?"

Enzo shrugs. I guess he doesn't take his opinion too seriously. I'm the same way. How cool that we can disagree without turning it into a huge competition, like some guys do. Enzo is alright.

"*The Ovato Mission* is out next week," Miguel tells Enzo. "David and I are going. You should come."

"I'm down for that," he says.

Maybe we could all hang out this summer and, more importantly, sit together during lunch when school starts. It's just been Miguel and me since our other friend Tommy moved to Kansas because of his mom's job.

"Third and final attempt." Miguel is staring down the cup like it personally challenged him.

"You can punk out if you want." I smile, a total instigator. "I won't tell the whole world you couldn't swallow even a tiny sip of a drink you prepared for yourself."

"Thanks."

"I'll tell only the people we know."

The girls have stopped talking to watch him again.

Miguel takes a deep breath, lifts the red cup to his lips, and takes a swig. Actually holds it in his mouth for more than a second, cheeks puffed and lips pressed tight. It's going to happen. He's going to swallow.

But then he ducks his head under the table to spit it out.

The girls make grossed-out noises.

Miguel pops back up, face scrunched. "Nobody can say I didn't try."

He gives his head a vigorous shake, as if taste vanished that way.

He turns to Liliana. "I hope I still have your respect."

"You never had it," she jokes.

After a few more laughs, Enzo says "Duuuude" to nobody in particular. "Just remembered there's a new *Nightchaser* ride at Universal Studios. It's supposed to be awesome, and there's a discount for Florida residents."

Though Orlando is only an hour away, I haven't been to any of the theme parks there. Gaby is forever asking to go to Disney World and Dad tells her what he used to tell me—that we'll go when we have extra money.

The closest thing we've ever had to a vacation trip is when we went to Mexico for my abuelo's funeral three years ago.

Miguel says, "Count me in." He turns to me. "What about you, Big Money?"

"I'm down," I tell Enzo. "And I'm *not* Big Money."

"I have almost two grand saved up," I explain, "because I wanna buy a used car. I've earned it by mowing lawns in the neighborhood and helping my dad at the auto shop."

I'll be helping out more since the part-timer Diego moved back to New Jersey. I won't feel bad about spending money on Universal Studios. Summers are all about having fun.

"Universal Studios sounds awesome," Karina says.

The girls look at each other and Janelle shouts, "Triple date!"

"It sounds cheesy if you say it like that," Enzo says.

Cheesy or not, I love the idea. Friends packed into a car, a short road trip to Orlando, where we'll have a blast. Maybe we can go for the whole weekend to hit another theme park while we're there!

Miguel says, "I'll be in the Dominican Republic for six weeks, so it has to be before or after."

Enzo starts telling us his favorite rides and shows at Universal. Then, all of a sudden, I hear something that puts a stop to my good time.

"Ricky."

The sound of that name makes me snap my head to the left. Liliana said it.

"What about Ricky?" I ask, heat spreading in my chest.

"We're talking about what he said to Karina today."

Enzo busts out laughing. I guess Janelle already told him.

Miguel and I eye each other.

I must look confused because Janelle turns to Karina. "You didn't tell David about rapping Ricky?"

No, she didn't. Why the hell not?

Karina sets down her Diet Coke, red nails bright against the silver can, and says, "It happened during PE."

PE today = the punch

"After class, when we were going back inside to change, he goes up to me all," she says, and makes her voice dumb and deep: "Hey, girl, you look good. Let me rap to you for a bit."

My jaw clenches. Shitbag Ricky knows we're going out! I force a smile to fight back the anger.

I guess he figured that if Karina could like someone like me, she would like him even more. You know, since in his mind he's much cooler and better looking than the dork he named Fuckstick.

My brain goes to the dark place of wanting to inflict pain—nonstop punches, kicks, and body slams.

"As if that were a smooth line," Karina says. "Who talks like that?"

"Then what?" I ask.

"I told him that I had a boyfriend, and even if I didn't I wouldn't give him the time of day."

"Cool," Miguel says.

Janelle says, "You forgot the part about him calling you a bitch."

"Oh yeah." Karina shrugs, without looking at me. "There was that."

It all makes sense now. She didn't tell me before because there was nothing I, her weakass boyfriend, could have done. And Ricky, who got shot down, punched me because he wanted to take his hurt out on somebody.

Miguel leans closer to me. "If you have a hater, you must be doing something right."

That actually makes sense, to my surprise. It hurt Ricky to learn he wasn't above my level. So I forget all about Ricky, who's old news anyway.

All of a sudden, one of my favorite songs comes on. "Uptown Funk" will never get old. It's one of Karina's favorites too.

When Karina's eyes catch mine, she breaks into a smile.

She stands up and calls out to everybody at the table, "Give us some toast, bitches."

I stand up and add, "Because this is our jam!"

I take Karina by the hand as her friends try to get their guys to join us. I wind through the tables and standing bodies in the yard until Karina and I are on the reddish tiled patio.

Over a dozen people are dancing, more girls than boys, Karina the sexiest of them all.

Okay, maybe I'm biased. But she's stunning tonight, and dances really good. She flashes me a smile, liking how I move too.

I'm not James Brown or anything, but rhythm does run on both sides of my family. Dancing is an obligation at family celebrations, whether it's a baptism, quinceañera, or a wedding, and I've been doing it ever since I could stand on two feet.

To my left Enzo is giving the minimum effort, shifting

with the music just enough to qualify as dancing. Janelle in front of him doesn't notice, with how into the song she is, eyes closed as she sings along to the hook.

Miguel can't dance—something I learned at his older sister's quinceañera three years ago. But what he lacks in ability he makes up in energy. He's all smiles and sort of hopping up and down, like he's the mascot at a school pep rally. Liliana, both embarrassed and entertained by this, sways with slightly less energy.

Karina takes her phone from my front pocket to snap group selfies. Tries to get all six of our moving bodies in the shot.

By the time the next song drops the crowded patio has me turned around. I'm facing the backyard again.

The too-many-bracelets girl from Language Arts is pointing me out to a friend. When they look away, I check my shirt and zipper. Everything seems fine.

Maybe she's shocked that stickboy can dance.

Seconds later a guy over by the snack table points to me with a Dorito as his two friends gawk at me.

I glance around to make sure—yep, at me.

My heart drops and I freeze up. Why didn't Karina tell me I looked ridiculous?

"What's wrong?" she asks me now, oblivious that I've become entertainment.

"Nothing," I tell her. "I'm getting something to drink."

I'm thirstier than ever and now the inside of the house

seems like the right place to be. At least nobody in there witnessed me making an ass of myself on the dance floor.

I leave Karina dancing with her friends and head over to the patio door, feeling eyes on me every inch of the way.

As soon as I slide the glass door open, the smell of weed hits me hard.

A smoke cloud is dissipating above the coffee table. A bunch of cool kids are gathered under the smoke, on the furniture and floor, passing around a joint. They're cracking up at something on the TV. I can't see it from where I'm standing, but I bet it's a big screen, top of the line, just like everything else in this swanky place.

The kitchen to my right is so crowded, like it's a second party. That's where my cold drink awaits. I can already feel it in my hand. I slide the door shut behind me. It dulls the music out there and amplifies the laughter in here.

"That's not funny," a girl in cat-eye glasses says.

"No, it's not funny," a girl sitting on the rug says, her voice heavy with sarcasm. "It's *hilarious*. Play it again, Jared."

Jared Ross, as douchey as he is popular, sits facing the TV. I move toward the kitchen.

"It's David!" somebody shouts—a voice I don't recognize.

"Holy shit!" That's Jared's voice for sure. "David, wait, is that you?"

I stop and turn around. His pink eyes have gone round. Jaws hang open and silent. A second later there are surprised comments like "No way" and "Oh my God!" partly drowned out by loud laughter. Aimed at me this time. Real laughter, not that kind bullies force to make you madder. If it's possible to literally laugh one's head off, heads will be dropping to the floor soon.

What's going on? How do these popular people know my name? And how am I funnier than whatever they were watching before?

The sarcastic girl sitting cross-legged on the rug catches her breath to say, "Come here, David."

The nervous jitters hit me all over. Especially in the stomach—a steady tingling in there telling me something bad is going to happen.

I've picked up some keys to survival over the years. For instance, you avoid eye contact when entering a room or walking down the hall.

But I haven't yet mastered the whole "walking-away" thing, though it should be easy. Why do I go up to bullies when they ask me to? I'm hopeful, I guess. As if being a good sport might make them like me better. All I do is prolong the bullying.

"You gotta see this," Jared tells me, wiping happy tears from his face with the back of his hand. He slumps back into the couch, exhausted.

"I'm tripping hard." This is from Stacy Rivers, who's wedged between two cheerleaders on the loveseat. "I can't believe David actually walked in just now."

Others shout at me to "Come on" and "For a second," but I know that trick. Being nice is a trap they set so they can be mean.

Or maybe this time it's not a trick? Everybody is in total chill-out mode, eyes bloodshot from weed, totally harmless. Just having fun, and I wanna know what the joke is so I can laugh too.

I fix a smile on my face and walk over. "What's up?"

That's when the large TV comes into view. I see what's paused on the screen—*me*.

When I realize I'm on YouTube, panic clenches my stomach and my heart pounds in my throat. That's me wearing a PE uniform and about to open my locker. Am I really *that* skinny? My next question—What the hell is happening?—is answered a millisecond later when I remember the punch. Someone else was there to capture it on video.

No fucking way. No fucking way. No fucking way.

I need to get outta here. *Now*. No time to tell Karina.

I cut right between the asshole kids and the TV, then walk through the foyer and out the front door, laughter trailing me as I make my escape.

4

EVEN THOUGH it only makes me feel worse, I keep watching the video. I refresh the page on my computer screen, my insides bunching up every time. *David Gets Bitchslapped* has 8,507 views. Over thirty more since I checked a few minutes ago.

Once again I click *play*.

00:01: Even after so many viewings, the first image still has the power to shock me. That's me in the locker room. Calm and unsuspecting boyish face. Stick limbs poking outta a blue-and-gray PE uniform.

00:04: I take off the shirt, revealing the skinniest teenage torso the world has ever seen. That's when Ricky, edited into a blur, rushes in to swing an arm and land a loud slap across my face. A *slap*, not a punch. Turns out my weakass got knocked out by an open hand.

00:05: My head whips to face the camera while my T-shirt, barely off and over my head, falls to the floor. My eyes glaze over as I wobble like a stripped Jenga tower. I sway right as if pushed, put my foot down to steady myself, tip forward, and keep stumbling until I end up in the same spot.

00:08: My legs give out and I drop to my knees. My head hangs as if in solemn prayer before I topple forward. My shoulder bounces off the narrow bench before the side of my face thuds against the floor.

00:13: The camera zooms closer to capture my head lifting, eyes struggling to fully open and figure out what happened.

Offscreen, Ricky and his buddy burst out laughing, the sound echoing throughout the empty room.

Then it's the first frame again, signaling the start of the slow-motion version. I have mercy on myself and click *pause*.

I've reported this video to YouTube, flagged it, and checked the *Violent or repulsive* option. A message informed me that someone would review my complaint.

Does it even matter though? In the meantime, people keep watching and sharing. Besides, anyone who has down-loaded it can upload it again. Soon my fifteen-second clip will be featured on compilations. Best of the month. Best of the year. Any day now I can expect GIFs and memes—I'll be the joke used for other jokes.

How many times have I laughed at embarrassing videos or shared them? What was wrong with me?

This one beats them all, and not just because of how hilariously goofy I look at every moment of it, from the slap to being dazed on the floor.

It's also the high quality. Usually these types of videos are shaky, blurry even, recorded from a distance. Not this one. Ricky's sidekick has a steady hand and a talent for framing shots, could practically work for Steven Spielberg or something.

The whole world will know me: a guy so skinny you can see the contour of every bone. A guy so weak that a slap knocks him out cold.

This shit's going viral for sure. It has . . . I click to reload the page . . . One hundred more views than minutes ago. 1,843 likes. 1 dislike. Mine.

It might have millions of views by tomorrow!

My throat tightens as I scroll down to look at the comments for the first time.

what a loser

I love how his face wiggles in the slo mo

the stumbling around looks like country line dancing

Comments accompanied by laughing emojis. Heart emojis. The applause emoji.

I remember TrashTalk and feel a cold pang in my heart. I open the TT app on my phone. Wait as the Culler High School page loads.

TT is where you go to comment anonymously about someone's outfit or new hairstyle or who's fat or who's not as pretty or cool as they think. It's mix of mostly disses and rumors.

The TT logo stops spinning and the Culler High page appears. My video is on there. Plus comments as dickish as the ones on YouTube. It might as well be renamed the *Take Shots at Bitchslap David* page.

That's what everybody is calling me. It's as bad as the YouTube comments but hurt so much more because I will definitely see these "anonymous" people again.

What can I do? How can I ever leave this house? How can I go back to school after the summer? My head buzzes with these and a million different thoughts.

I close TT and go into my other apps. Remove the Facebook account I rarely use. Deactivate my Instagram I always use and then remove that app. I move on to Snapchat and find a message from Miguel.

u ok man? i'm worried and you won't pick up

I'm not taking any calls. Can't even talk to Dad, who's knocked on my door twice to find out why I'm back from the party so early.

I delete Snapchat.

There. No more social media. I'm officially cut off from a big chunk of my life. What next? With nothing left to do I feel useless. My stomach starts to rumble for real. If it's possible to get physically sick from humiliation, it's happening to me.

I wanna believe that things aren't as bad as they seem,

but hell no. This isn't something that will seem teeny-tiny in retrospect. I won't be laughing about this in months or years. My loser status is fixed. I'm forever Bitchslap David. And I thought the few dozen people calling me "Fuck-stick" was bad.

Then I get an idea. What if I change my features? Surgeons give narcos new faces so they can hide in plain sight.

Yeah, right. I'd have to *be* a narco to afford a surgery like that.

A text lights up my phone: *missing u here*

Karina is still at the party with the others. The second I got to the car, I texted her to explain why I was leaving and needed to be alone. She's been checking up on me ever since, downplaying the gravity of my situation, trying to cheer me up.

A selfie comes in. She's beautiful, her smile bright underneath a lit-up palm tree.

She sends other pictures she took while I was there. In the last one all six of us are on the dance floor, Miguel in mid-jump. Not all of our limbs are visible, but the joy on our faces is clear.

Crazy how fast life can change. There I was, having fun and making friends at the party of the year. Setting up summer plans and, beyond that, my senior year stretching before me. Now I'm at home on a Friday night, counting views on a video that destroyed my life just as I was starting to live it.

So I can forget new friends. Forget my girlfriend too. Though Karina is sweet and awesome, she won't want me as a boyfriend. She's Karina of the drama club, Karina the honor roll student. She's not trying to be *Karina-who-goes-out-with-Bitchslap*.

The greatest thing to ever walk into my life is going to walk right on out. Sprint is more like it, just as soon as she realizes how the slap will affect her.

How am I supposed to face everybody back at Culler High?

I won't. Dad will have to accept me dropping out. I'd rather work or something. From home. I can't set foot in public.

I'll stay safely inside this house forever, ordering groceries and anything else I need online.

But I know that my dad won't have that. No way. He's still expecting me to get a scholarship. Even gifted me an SAT prep book this afternoon, a present for my last day of junior year.

Transferring isn't an option, unless I can somehow find a town without internet. I can't go to another school and I can't go to Culler and I don't know what to do.

I'm used to thoughts rushing one after another. The problem now is that they stay stuck, unable to escape, crowding up my brain.

This must be how people end up in straitjackets.

Video games! Yep, that will take my mind off things.

I click open *Call of Duty* on my computer. Slouch in my chair and try to loosen up. I shoot down enemy combatants with skill and avoid bullets. But it gets boring after a few minutes.

So I give *Mortal Kombat* a try. The character chart loads. There they are, twelve muscled fighters to choose from. Even Cassie Cage is crazy buff, her arms thicker than my legs.

I select my guy, Kano with that fierce red eye, and start kicking ass. But I can't get into this game either. This alternate world isn't shutting out the real one or soothing my reeling brain.

Although I'm winning, it's like I'm not even playing. It's like I'm watching somebody else kick ass.

I thumb the joystick and press the right combination of buttons for the finishing move. Watch as Kano kills off Trooper with a fatality.

Kano won, not me.

I *was* watching somebody else kick ass. That realization hits me harder than the slap from earlier. In video games I pretend to be all big and tough. That's how I spend my time. Pretending.

Fuck this. I turn off the monitor and push myself up from the desk in a hot rage. It's sizzling in my blood, making me pace around my small-ass room, hating myself and wondering what to do about my shit life.

When there's a knock at the door, I damn near jump outta my skin.

"Come on, mijo," Dad says, louder than the last two times. "Open up."

Maybe Dad will know what to do. He *is* older and wiser. He *does* live for giving advice. Over an hour after getting home, I'm no less scared or confused than before. I have nothing to lose.

"I know what happened," he calls in softly.

Yeah, right. He probably figures it was everyday teasing or something. My dad doesn't go on the internet, doesn't have a computer or tablet or smartphone. His dumb phone might be older than me.

He gives the door two more light taps. "Your aunt called and said she saw it on the bookface thing."

Shit. I wonder which asshole cousin discovered and shared it.

I open the door.

There's a sad worry showing in Dad's eyes as he steps inside and sits on my bed. He's wearing sleeping clothes—old shorts over thick calves and a faded gray T-shirt covering up a bit of belly. The rest of his body is muscle even though he's never set foot in a gym.

"Who hit you? Why didn't you tell me?"

I start from the beginning, when I walked into the locker room carrying the soccer balls. Every word I speak makes my face burn with more shame, as if I'm living it all over again.

"Basically," I explain, "the slap was recorded and posted on YouTube. They were watching it at the party. By now, the whole world has seen it."

He doesn't understand and will keep insisting so I let him watch the video. I open it on YouTube and turn away.

When the horrible fifteen seconds are over, Dad spins back around at me, his brow creased.

"Pinches malcriados," he says, breaking his own no-cursing rule. But Ricky is so much worse than a fucking brat.

After shaking his head he says, "You should've told your coach or principal what happened."

I say nothing. I'm waiting for him to get to the point.

"Why don't you change with everybody else so you aren't alone?"

What the hell is Dad talking about? I need some help here. A fix-it for my life or at least some clarity. Instead he tells me I should've done things differently. I *should've* changed around more people. I *should've* told somebody what happened.

There should be a rule about *should've*. Anyone who says that needs to lend you a time machine so you can zoom into the past to take their advice.

I'm done with Dad.

"I'm tired," I say, though I've never been more awake. "I need to sleep."

"We'll talk to the school." Dad gets up carefully and straightens his back with a groan. "That Ricky kid is going to get kicked out."

At the doorway he turns back to look at me. His expression has gone sad.

"Listen, mijo," he says, fixing his gaze on me. "It's not a big deal."

He doesn't say it in that cheering-me-on way. He says it like it truly is not a big deal. Nothing to overcome.

The last bit of hope I had shrivels to nothing.

Why am I surprised? Dad thinks I have everything so easy just because my life is different than his was. He married my mom almost twenty years ago, so his papers are all in order and everything, but he sure had it rough for a while.

At my age he dropped outta high school to cross into this country. He survived the Rio Grande, then the sweltering Texas desert before hitchhiking to Florida. Here he worked construction in the middle of the summer. At night he slept under an I-275 overpass. All so he could support my sick grandmother and his two younger brothers.

And me at seventeen? I'm barely surviving high school.

But I also have struggles I didn't ask for. He doesn't know what it's like to slink through the halls, eyes on the floor, nervous about being spotted by one of the cruel kids. When has he ever been shoved or kicked or slapped in the face?

When it comes to bullies, *he's* the one who's always had it easy.

"You don't know how lucky you are to be big," I say.

Dad studies my face. "What do you mean?"

"Remember when the new neighbors moved in last year?"

The burly man next door parked his truck half on our lawn, so his wife's entire car could fit next to it on their driveway. Dad sent me over to ask the neighbor to move it so it wouldn't damage our grass, just as it was getting green.

The man's eyes swept me up and down and then he closed the door in my face. The truck stayed put.

So Dad went himself. From the porch I heard Dad say the words I did minutes before and saw him come back. A moment later the man walked out to park the truck along the curb.

"Remember that?" I ask.

"Yeah," Dad says slowly, not getting it. I guess some people really don't know how good they have it.

"You're lucky that guys never mess with you."

"You're smart," he says. "Your dedication will take you to college and far in life. That's better than being strong or anything else."

He's trying to make me feel better with words because he can't actually help me.

I sigh. "Whatever."

He gives me a weak smile. "You'll be fine, mijo. You'll see."

When Dad leaves and I close the door, Van Nelson is staring at me from the back of it. Another lucky man that bullies would never mess with.

On second thought, luck had nothing to do with it. Enzo mentioned earlier that Van Nelson wasn't even muscular in the movie before *Nightchaser*. I guess he put in hours at the gym to make it happen.

Why didn't I start lifting weights long ago? I could be the biggest guy in school. Getting respect instead of getting bullied.

I sit at my desk to find out how Van Nelson did it and luck out—there's a short video online of his six-month transformation.

Holy shit! I can't believe my eyes! He really was a regular guy. Without these before and after pics side by side like this, how would you know they're the same person?

In the three months before school starts, I could grow about half as much. Talk about *insane*. Nobody would ever call me Bitchslap or mess with me ever again.

For a second I think steroids, but then I play his video. He's in a private gym, talking directly to the camera. As if reading my doubtful mind, he mentions he's completely steroid-free.

"I got these results by giving my workout one hundred and ten percent. A lot of you have been asking for the exact diet and workouts I did to prepare for my new role. Click below to check it out."

It's a calendar PDF, the days marked with a numbered workout. A bunch of exercises I've never heard of, including the sets and repetitions, fill several pages. At the very end is a list of muscle-building foods to eat.

The information I need to make this happen is right here! I'm going to join a gym and transform this body!

Dad can't say no. Why would he?

I search for more transformations. Teen bodybuilders get my attention, especially the results they share after three months. Eye-popping, jaw-dropping results.

Kids at school take way longer to put on size. What's up with that? They must not be training the right way, like Van Nelson does in the video. They damn sure aren't eating lean meats, egg whites, oatmeal, and green veggies. They wolf down pizza, nuggets, and vending machine junk like everybody else.

That's not me anymore. My protein-packed diet will be on point and I'm going beast-mode in the gym, giving each set my all.

I get up and take off my shirt for my *before* photo. Looking in the mirror, my first thought is that I hate my pathetic body.

That's okay, I remind myself. I'm finally doing something about it.

I snap away, taking pics from various angles, hitting the

same poses as the other guys online.

Then I stare myself down one last time. Make a pact with myself.

You're really going to do this, David. For the next three months you'll eat clean and be all about your goal. You'll become so unrecognizable that people won't even believe you were that scrawny kid in the slap video.

This summer you will become the new David Espinoza.

5

Eighty-six days until school begins

MY MOM started a Saturday breakfast ritual that we've kept up after her death. During the week our morning routines were, and are, too hurried for us to sit down to eat.

On weekdays I do Gaby's hair and serve her cornflakes—always pouring the milk because she's a spiller and I don't have time to clean up. Dad handles Gaby's school stuff. Makes sure she has her homework, packed lunch, and everything else in her My Little Pony backpack.

On weekends we have time to ease into the day.

While Dad takes a shower, Gaby and I are making French toast. After she dips both sides of the stale bread slices into the egg and milk mixture, I drop them to sizzle in the big pan. The cinnamon and vanilla, the sweet smell of my favorite breakfast, is really torturing me.

My first muscle meal ever is in the microwave. Eight raw egg whites in a ceramic bowl and a large mug filled with half a cup of oats with one cup of water. According to Van Nelson, they can be cooked all together that way.

Lucky for me we happened to have those ingredients at home already. I gotta buy more, including stuff our kitchen has never seen: lean steak and skinless chicken breast. Vegetables like kale and broccoli. Carbs like brown rice and quinoa.

The diet plan calls for eating double. Normal portion sizes, six meals per day instead of three, to feed the muscle. Stuffing my face all day, plus the gym membership, is definitely going to put a dent in my savings.

I flip the French toast and press *start* on the microwave for my own breakfast.

Dad comes in showered and ready for work, T-shirt and cargo jeans stained with grease streaks and splotches. "Did you join a new weird religion?"

Gaby looks at me and cracks up.

Since I can't afford face surgery or walk around in a mask, I did the next best thing. Got rid of my hair with Dad's mustache trimmer.

"Somebody recognized me this morning," I tell him. "You were wrong about *it* not being a big deal."

As always, he made me mow the lawn early, in full view of passing traffic. Jaime down the street, riding shotgun in his mom's car, yelled "Bitchslap!" loud enough to hear over the mower. His mom smacked him upside the head for cursing.

"I think he sort of looks like a baby bird," Gaby says, and cracks up again. "Big head and tiny body."

"Good one," I tell her, glad she's not pressing for details about why I wanna change my look.

She can't find out about the video. I need at least one person whose image of me is not tainted by that slap.

I set down their plates and go back to get my meal before joining them.

"What is that?" Dad zeroes in on the white, gelatinous disk on my plate. It sort of looks like shiny plastic and is perfectly round. Only the steam rising from it makes you think it might be food.

I explain, and Dad sets down the syrup he was pouring to say, "Let me get this right. You used eight eggs for your breakfast and threw out the yolks?"

"I've read that this is the perfect meal before a work-out."

By "workout" he's no doubt thinking about my weekly run with Karina—another Saturday-morning ritual for me. But this morning when she called I reminded her I'm not ready to be that exposed in public unless it's necessary.

"I'll buy more eggs with my own money," I add, so Dad doesn't lose his mind.

He doesn't believe in throwing food away. Gaby can get away with leaving a few bites because Dad finishes it for her.

"This kid, throwing out food." He shakes his head, still

incredulous. "Your *own* money, Flaco."

I wonder how many weeks until I outgrow that nickname.

I slice banana onto my oatmeal, the only sweetness I'm allowed. Banana is excellent for my glucose reserves, which need to be full for an effective workout, according to what I read last night. I spoon some into my mouth. It's not horrible.

"I wanna join a gym today."

Dad chews and considers me with interest. Then, instead of saying no right away, he takes another bite of food.

Weird.

In this house, new ideas are met with resistance or at least a barrage of questions.

He swallows that second bite before saying, "If you want to, that's fine. It's summer and you have extra time."

What just happened? That was way too easy. As if he's been waiting for my announcement. Maybe he's *wanted* me to bulk up and stop being flaco.

Dad lifts another forkful to his mouth, syrup dripping from the bite of French toast.

I ask, "Can Gaby go with you to work today?"

"Of course. During the week you can go early and get back by seven forty-five, before I go to work. Or go when I get back from work."

My plan this summer was to drop Gaby off at the

auto shop whenever I wanted to hang out with Miguel or Karina, which would be most of the summer. Now I'll be hanging out with Gaby more than anybody else.

The last few summers, Mely took care of Gaby, along with her own two kids. She was Mom's best friend, a stay-at-home mom and seamstress who lived on the other side of our backyard fence. Gaby played with her neighbor buddies all day and it didn't cost us a thing.

But ICE came for Mely, her husband, and kids last November, and weeks later deported them.

I finish with the oatmeal and move on to the egg white disk.

"Are you sure that's safe to eat?" Dad asks.

As they watch me expectantly, I put the first bite into my mouth. It's a bit tougher than regular eggs, and gross. Not gagging gross, just the regular, offensive-to-taste-buds gross.

They watch me chew, which I do quickly. To get this slimy yet chewy grub down.

"It's good," I lie, and prepare for another bite.

I need to get used to this. From now on, mealtimes are nothing more than refueling for my muscles. When you're eating tasteless food every two and a half hours that might be the only way to see meals.

When I leave my house a little while later, my cap is so low it covers my eyes. I zip up my hoodie and throw the hood over my head so it touches down almost to the tip of my cap's brim. As long as my face is covered, I don't mind sweating bullets.

Then I hop onto my bike to pedal off, just as Karina pulls up to the driveway in her mom's car. I feel a pang of shame so hard I almost close my eyes. She's seen the video. If I could choose one person to unsee it, I'd choose her.

She gets outta the car, sporting running shorts and a purple sleeveless shirt that matches her sneakers. "I thought you weren't leaving the house for anything."

"Except for work or to go to the gym."

And to the supermarket, I think to myself, remembering I gotta drop by on my way home.

She closes the door with her hip. God, she's cute. I really hope she hangs around long enough to see what I'll become.

"The gym?" she asks. "I was going to try to convince you to come out to the trail with me."

I tell her about my plan for the new, muscular me. It seems arrogant to say out loud, like Babe Ruth pointing to the fences, but it *is* going to happen.

"If going to the gym makes you feel better, great," she says. "But what's the deal with that hoodie?"

"It's so nobody notices me."

"*Riiiight.*" She likes to stretch out words right before being sarcastic. "Because a guy wearing a *hoodie*, in the *summer*, in *Florida*, won't draw attention. David, you're going to either die of heatstroke or melt."

"I'll be fine," I say, and let my hood drop.

The truth is my skin is already popping with sweat under this thick fabric.

"What did you do to your hair?" She lifts my cap off, and her jaw drops. "You chopped it off!"

I shrug. "It will grow back."

She nods. "True. But in the meantime you look like . . . What do you look like?"

"Like a baby bird, according to Gaby."

Karina laughs, and runs a hand over the bristles. "That's it. Which is to say this isn't an attractive look for you." She puts the cap back on my head and kisses me. "Do your thing and I'll text you later, okay?"

"Yeah," I say, surprised how normal she seems.

Like she never saw the video. Like the video doesn't exist. Maybe Karina is even cooler than I thought.

I'm tearing down the street, pumping my legs as fast as they'll go as the bright sun scorches my hoodie. Air-conditioned cars cruise past, inches from my elbow.

Good thing the gym I found online is only eleven and a half blocks away, behind the Wash & Save. That's where we used to do our laundry before we bought our second-hand Whirlpool. I had no idea there was anything behind that Laundromat.

I pull into the parking lot, the familiar scent of fabric

softener from the hot air vents hitting me all at once.

I bike behind it, along the tall wooden fence. The ruddy, unpaved road slows me down. I bunny-hop over a pothole, ride past a dumpster, and there it is—Iron Life Gym in big letters.

The sign seems as old as the brick building and neither are well kept. With how the sun slants down this early, the glass façade temporarily blinds me with its silvery brightness.

There are only four cars in the parking spaces. Few people working out means fewer possibilities of being recognized. I love this place already.

Please let there be at least another newbie among the experienced guys. *Please*. I don't need a bunch of super swole guys making me feel worse than I already do.

And let them be mostly older people who are less likely to come across stupid YouTube videos. I checked in on my video before I left and it's up to about 533,000 views. It hasn't even been twenty-four hours yet, for fuck's sake.

After I lock my bike up I push through the door. Classic rock plays out of small mounted speakers, barely louder than the rattling AC.

The cool air feels great on my face, hands, and bottom half of my legs.

I take in the wide-open space. It's the size of a basketball court, with mirrored walls and exposed wiring dangling from high ceilings. Rubber mats here and there protect the concrete floor.

Besides the few old machines, it's mostly free weights. A long barbell is at each station. The smaller dumbbells are paired by weight on two-tiered racks. Round plates are strewn all over. The red-padded surfaces of the benches and seats are raised on iron legs. Everything is as practical and unadorned as the tools in Dad's auto shop.

Awesome. This is why this gym is cheaper than the others.

I'm about to take off my sweat-soaked hoodie until I get a good look at the two monsters working out in front of their reflections. It's like I shrink to the size of an M&M. I've never in my whole life felt tinier.

This hoodie is staying on.

A tatted white guy, about twenty-five, is wearing a stringy white tank top with a black Superman *S* on it. His hair is shiny black and parted, sort of like Clark Kent with a receding hairline.

The guy sits upright, the bar racked just behind his head, and pounds his chest twice before gripping it. As he presses the weight overhead, the muscles in his shoulders shift.

The black guy in the corner is maybe 6'3" and even more jacked. He grunts with the effort of every squat. The bar across his upper back curves from the weight of four large plates on each side.

Don't stare, I tell myself. As I stand next to the reception desk, waiting for somebody to notice me, I turn my attention to the hand-painted quotes on the wall.

EVERYBODY WANTS TO BE A BODYBUILDER,
BUT DON'T NOBODY WANT TO LIFT NO HEAVY-ASS WEIGHTS

LIFE'S TOO SHORT TO HAVE SMALL ARMS

Okay, so these aren't profound quotes. This is a gym after all, not the public library. But at least the words are spelled right.

THAT WHICH DOES NOT KILL ME MAKES ME STRONGER

I like that last one, which could be the motto for the two meatheads working out. With how they groan and struggle through their reps, it really does look like they're willing to die for their muscles.

The only other wall décor are the posters of steroid-pumped bodybuilders arranged into a circle. A young Arnold Schwarzenegger poses gloriously in the middle like he's the leader—the only bodybuilder I recognize.

The size of these guys is unreal. It's no wonder that pro bodybuilding is open about drug use. The guys working out here are pretty close to that size, so they must be on steroids too.

A waist-high glass case holds about a dozen trophies, short and tall, with a tiny gold bodybuilder flexing in various poses on top.

A man built like a middleweight boxer stops on his

way to the drinking fountain and smiles when he sees me. "Alpha will be right with you."

Was that a funny look he gave me? Nah. It could have been just because I'm wearing a hoodie while everybody else here is either sleeveless or with short sleeves.

I need to chill. Not everybody will have seen the video.

As he slurps from the drinking fountain I check him out. He has the kind of body I'd kill for. Strong and chiseled, without overdoing it. Damn impressive for somebody who looks close to forty.

I turn back to the trophies. The name *Alfonso Richardson* is engraved on all the gleaming brass plates, sometimes with the nickname "Alpha" in the middle. Every single one of these trophies belongs to a guy named Alpha who will be right with me. An actual bodybuilder working here. How cool is that?

The names of these competitions are new to me until I come across the trophy that says *World Muscleman Championship*.

Holy shit! That's the most important bodybuilding competition on the planet! The Super Bowl of muscles! And Alpha got fourth place this year? This is almost too good to be true.

Don't get me wrong. I'm not into beauty pageants for muscles. Bulking up with steroids and shaving everything from the neck down, tanning and greasing up to flex while 98 percent naked on a stage? No, thanks. But a top pro working here means I've come to a hardcore gym. I'm among guys as passionate as me about their goals.

The picture above the case has Alpha's name on it, and his age: twenty-three. Just look at that physique! Oh. My. God.

Alpha is a *gigantic* white guy. I'm talking muscles on top of muscles. Flexing in tiny red underwear, he's as big and ripped and shiny as anybody on that wall. Biceps as big as my head.

His smile really stands out too, with a gap between his two front teeth similar to Arnold's and a few other body-builders.

"Wassup, bro?" booms a deep voice, startling me.

I whip around. The image has come to life. Except the guy is clothed, wearing shorts and a white Iron Life T-shirt with one of the wall quotes: *Life's too short to have small arms.*

"Can I help you?" he asks with a smile.

Why am I nervous? He's not going to eat me or anything. "I'm looking to join the gym."

"Cool." He goes behind the reception desk laptop to take my name, my thirty bucks for the first month, and my information.

"There's a waiver for your parents to sign," he says, still typing.

Stupid me. Of course there is. But I can't have Dad drop in. If he sees the size of some of these guys he'll think *steroids* for sure and won't let me train here.

"I'm almost eighteen," I say, though my birthday is ten months away.

Alpha eyes me. "Almost, huh? I'll tell you what. We can forget the waiver on one condition."

"Sure," I say, so relieved I'll agree to any conditions.

He turns not just his eyes to me but his whole body. "You have to promise to be safe and follow the rules. And always get a spotter when you lift super heavy or try to max out. You can ask me or anybody else who's around."

A spotter. Gym talk. That must be the guy who helps you lift in case you can't anymore. *Max out* must mean lift as much as you can.

I'm learning the language of my new life.

Van Nelson suggests not going super heavy anyway, just lifting what you can comfortably, and never going until exhaustion. I won't be bothering Alpha or anybody else with anything.

"I promise," I say.

"It's a deal, then. So what are your training goals, David?" he asks, searching among papers in a folder. "Endurance, weight-loss, muscle-building?"

To get as big as possible this summer, I wanna tell him. What would be a better way to put it?

He bursts out laughing. "I'm fucking with you, bro."

"Nice one," I tell him, laughing along.

He puts out a fist for me to bump, and I do.

Of course the skinny dude wants to gain size.

He slaps a printout on the counter titled *Feed Your Muscles*. "To pack on muscles, you need to eat enough calories and the right kinds."

The list of foods is the same as the one on Van Nelson's plan. Egg whites and oats are featured often in the sample breakfast.

Alpha points a thick finger to the bottom of the printout. "That's the formula to figure out your caloric needs, depending on your weight. If you ain't eating enough, no amount of lifting will give you results. Muscles are made in the kitchen as much as in the gym. Got it?"

"Cool, thanks."

Alpha hands me another printout with a routine. I tell him I have my own workout.

"Does your coach give you a routine?"

My coach? I guess my coach is the guy who played Nightchaser. "Something like that."

"Cool, bro. Do your thing and if you wanna go heavy or max out, holler for me."

I head to one of the benches covered in red vinyl and patched with duct tape. I'm ready to blast my chest and triceps, the parts highlighted for Van Nelson's workout.

The long bar is heavy all on its own, maybe fifty pounds. I warm up by bench-pressing it without additional weight, hoping the three other members here—all lifting big—don't look over at me.

For my first real set I put a small plate on each side.

I lie back on the bench and slide under the bar. Grip it a bit more than shoulder width apart, like Van Nelson did in his video. I'm going for one rep less than exhaustion.

I lower the weight to my chest and push it out, careful to keep the bar even with every lift. After some struggle with the ninth rep, I rack the weight.

There's a tightness in my chest that I sort of love. It burns, as if the muscle growth has already begun. The clock ticks off the seconds. In sixty I go again.

"That ain't heavy!" Alpha shouts.

For a moment I think he means my bar, but he's shouting at the huge guy squatting in front of him. "One more rep, Tower, you pussy!"

The drill sergeant motivation is working. The squatter's—Tower's—face twists angrier as he stands up again, letting out a monster grunt. He's definitely going extra heavy, maybe even maxing out.

"Hell yeah!" Alpha helps him rack the bar. "That's what I'm talking about!"

Tower, wincing and breathing heavy, says nothing back. He picks up the small bucket by his water bottle and lifts it to his face.

Is this really happening? I tell myself *no way*, but a second later he quivers, so the answer is clearly *yes*. I hear the gag over the music, which can only mean vomit. He spits three times into the bucket before setting it back down.

When he glances over his shoulder in my direction, I turn my eyes to the clock. Not smoothly at all. I damn near gave myself whiplash.

I consider what just went down. A guy at this gym, *my* gym, lifts so hardcore it makes him sick. I like it. How cool to be among such dedication.

"Insanity," a voice says behind me.

The middleweight boxer guy slides a large plate on one side of the bar.

"Yeah, these guys are freaks," I say.

After we do our respective sets, he introduces himself and I do the same.

It turns out Rogelio is a real estate agent with two kids.

He asks, "Are you in high school?"

"Yeah, one more year left."

"Nice." He searches for another plate. I guess his previous set was a warm-up. "If they have a gym there, that's probably where you should work out when school begins."

"Throw some wheels on that bar!" Alpha shouts from across the room.

"On it!" Rogelio shouts back, and smiles.

I may hit the school weight room when classes begin. Who knows? It would save me time and money, though I also may be bulked up enough by then.

Rogelio slides a plate on the other side to even out the

bar. Two large plates and two medium-sized ones against my two tiny ones. I wanna disappear.

"Why would the school weight room be better?" I ask him.

Across the gym, Tower starts another set while Alpha barks encouragement.

Rogelio smiles and says, "Let's just say there's a lot going on in this gym that has nothing to do with fitness or being healthy. I only come here because I live down the street."

I nod. He's nice and seems worried that I'm impressionable. As if I'd ever do drugs. I've never even taken a puff of tobacco or weed.

"Four hundred and five pounds ain't shit!" Alpha shouts at Tower, who's doing deadlifts. "More reps! Let's go!"

Tower lifts the bar back up from the floor, straightening out one last time, and lets loose a wild sound in the gym, something between beast and machine. A chill runs through me.

Right away he reaches down for his bucket.

I turn to Rogelio, who's already shaking his head in disgust.

An hour and a half later I'm totally wrecked. My weekly trail run with Karina has nothing on this. I feel the throb of the post-workout pump. That's the warm blood swelling around my worked-out muscles. My chest and triceps burn with a sweet intensity. I've never been more aware of my body in general. How muscles cover all my bones, stretching from joint to joint. How you can actually make them bigger by lifting weights and setting them back down, again and again, and eating right.

Vomit-bucket Tower, chest-pounding Superman, and Rogelio have left. Fine for them, but I'm gonna start on the workout meant for tomorrow. Double the effort might double my results. I could gain even more than twenty-five pounds of muscle this summer.

Alpha, one of the greatest bodybuilders on the planet, wouldn't give up after twenty-eight sets.

But when he notices me about to sit down at the lat pulldown machine, that's what he tells me to do.

"You're done, Little Man. Don't add back to your chest and triceps day."

Little? At least he called me a man.

"I have some energy left," I say, hoping to impress him with my determination.

"You're going to burn out. You can't hit too much in one workout, because muscles need days to fully recover. If you work chest and back and legs today, what muscle group will you work tomorrow, or the day after?"

Good point. I thank him.

"I love your determination though." Alpha puts out his fist for me to bump. "Now it's time to go feed your muscles and get rested so you can do it again tomorrow."

I take a superlong drink from the fountain, over-whelmed with pride and joy.

Then I put the hood over my cap and step into the midday heat outside, hoping nobody spots me while I bike back to the safety of home.

6

Eighty-one days until school begins

FIVE DAYS into my twelve-week transformation I'm a walking, talking bruise. Every muscle is in some stage of soreness. That's how I like it, because that's how muscles grow. After you destroy them with resistance training, they repair themselves and get bigger.

Destroy and build. Destroy and build. The aches I feel, even if I'm just getting outta bed or scratching the back of my neck, are a constant reminder that I'm putting in the work.

Today sucks, though. It's a rest day, which means zero gym time—a day off so my entire body can fully recover. Tomorrow I go full force, starting with the chest and tris workout again. Tomorrow seems so far away.

I'm hoping Dad needs lots of help at the shop today so I can keep busy. He's called midafternoon every day this week for my help, but the work was done within two hours.

Though I don't wanna be out in public, I need money badly. Who knew trips to the supermarket, and whey protein for shakes and two important supplements would cost so much?

I'll have to wait even longer for my used car. That sucks, but I remind myself what matters.

Karina calls. "Guess where I am," she says. "Guess who with."

I don't have to guess. Miguel called earlier, trying to get me to go to the movie we talked about seeing last week. I keep telling him we'll hang, but that hasn't happened yet. Karina has only come over once since this whole mess started. She ate chicken and brown rice with me, because she's likes to eat healthy anyway, while my dad and Gaby ate enchiladas. The whole time I felt shame, looking at Karina. Because she'd seen the video.

She's keeping plenty busy these days. A sleepover at Janelle's, a trip to Clearwater beach, another one to the Dalí museum in St. Pete. Plus working part-time at the retirement home with her mom, just like she did last summer.

"Is everybody there?" I ask.

"Janelle, Liliana, Miguel, and Enzo. I'm the only one without a date. Miguel says he hasn't seen you at all, so I'm not taking it personal."

"Come over tomorrow if you want. It's not so bad hanging out here at home, is it?"

"I worry about you," she says. "Stuck at home doing nothing."

"Doing plenty, actually. There is something called the internet, with lots of articles to read and videos to watch. Don't worry about me."

The articles and videos are all about bodybuilding. Plus every 2.5 hours there's a meal, which I have in front of the computer screen while a weightlifting YouTuber talks about an aspect of my new lifestyle. This nineteen-year-old guy who goes by Natural Nathan is my favorite.

I'm so *not* bored, so busy with this new world, that I haven't hung out much with Gaby either. When I leave my bedroom for more food, she comes to the kitchen to talk while I heat up a container of my prepped meals. This morning she asked to go with Dad to work because it's "too boring at home now."

"I got my mom's car today," Karina says. "I can come pick you up real quick and we won't even miss the trailers. Come on, David. That video is old news."

"Not true. I took your advice and didn't search for it since the weekend, but yesterday . . ."

I was weak. I couldn't help it. I explain that YouTube took the original slap video down but two other people, at least, uploaded it. Exactly what I knew would happen.

What surprised me was the video entitled *Bitchslap David Remix*.

"Have you seen that one?" I ask her.

"I'm not going to watch it, and you shouldn't be watching that crap either."

"In that video, Ricky slaps me across my face to a Kanye West beat, over and over again for almost three minutes. I used to love that song."

"You can still love the song if you want."

I swear, sometimes her optimism crosses into crazy.

"Karina, that's not the point. Just come over tomorrow, okay?"

We hang up.

Two hours later my phone alarm beeps. Time to eat again. I press *pause* on Natural Nathan.

In the kitchen I heat a container of chicken breast, broccoli, and brown rice. I have three of those left in the fridge, about eight more meals in total. I cooked a few different things in bulk the other day.

Some meals it's tuna instead of chicken, sweet potato instead of brown rice, spinach instead of broccoli. But lean steak, quinoa, and asparagus are too expensive.

It's all about packing on muscle, which I assume is happening. I see no difference in the mirror—yet. They say a watched pot never boils. Well, apparently a watched physique never grows.

The microwave beeps. I take out my fourth meal of the

day, at 2:31, and take my meal back to my room, happy to have the quiet house to myself.

I chew the food quickly, wishing the video could completely distract me from the blandness in my mouth. Eating has become a chore.

When I'm close to the final bite, my phone rings again. Dad's calling.

I swallow and answer. "Hello?"

"I'd like to speak to Mr. Boring, please." It's Gaby, the comedian.

I laugh. The truth though? It sort of hurts. Before my life became all about gains my sister thought I was the coolest person in the world.

If only she could understand that it's not normal for a high school senior to spend so much time with an eight-year-old. Besides, I'm becoming a better version of myself. I don't really have time for silly games and other kid stuff.

"This is Mr. Boring," I say, playing along. "How can I help you?"

"Dad needs you."

"I'll be right there."

Espinoza Auto Repair is on Bautista Street, across from a furniture factory and next to a run-down sandwich shop. We're small but impossible to miss. Used tires on a tall rack are displayed in front of the passing traffic, and a large banner advertises 25 percent off oil changes.

Dad and I even put up the long streamers from the shop to the tall street sign, the triangles in red, white, and blue. Dad says immigrants are the true patriots. "You want to know what makes this country great, ask an immigrant," he likes to say. "Not those ignorant racists who wave the flag like it's a symbol of hate."

Rather than put up a flag, he thought the American colors streaming over the lot would be a nice touch. It definitely draws attention.

I roll up on my bike hoping Dad takes care of the tire repair and replacement work if it comes in. I normally prefer the easy tire work, love that customers often slip me a dollar or two as a tip. But now that I'm world-famous Bitchslap, I'd rather stay in the back.

Dad won't let me wear my hoodie—says it's tonterías—so I take it off before I roll my bike inside. Sweat streaks down underneath my moist T-shirt.

"Hi, Dad."

He's lying on a creeper under a Kia. One day we'll have one of those professional hydraulic lifts that raises the car over your head. Un día, he always says. But with business so slow he sometimes waits with nothing to do. We're barely scraping by. Months ago he still had a full-time employee helping him out.

"Your sister has been bored all day." His voice comes out muffled from under all that metal.

I leave my bike along the back wall, about ten feet from

where Gaby is playing with off-brand Barbies on the patch of grass.

"Hi, Gaby."

She barely lifts a hand to wave a wild-haired doll at me.

"The Ford truck has a leaky radiator," Dad calls out.

At work he speaks in orders. It's never please, and rarely thank you.

"On it," I say.

I'm uncapping the radiator when I hear a car pulling up outside. I turn. It's a small, newish two-door Chevy, no troubling noises coming from the engine.

"Tire work, Dad," I say. "Do you mind? I don't want to be out there."

"Tonterías," he says. "Nobody is going to recognize you."

Dammit. I head out into the bright afternoon again. Enzo hops outta the driver's side, and Miguel outta the other side. Double dammit.

I feel a tingling of shame in my stomach. This is why I don't wanna see people, even friends, until I become the new me. How can they look at me without remembering that video?

Though I see the Chevy has a small spare on in the front, I ask, "What are you guys doing here?"

"Flat tire. It's in the back," Enzo says, and goes to open it.

I talk to Miguel quickly, and in a low voice. "I told you I don't wanna see anybody until my transformation is complete. There are other places to fix a flat."

"I thought you'd appreciate the word-of-mouth advertising," he whispers back, one eye on Enzo, who pulls out the wheel from the trunk.

Then Miguel's voice goes sunny and loud. "You're welcome! You know I'm always glad to bring you a new customer."

I take the front wheel from Enzo, feeling an ache in my biceps and shoulders.

"We just saw *The Ovato Mission*," Enzo says. "You totally missed out."

Miguel agrees that it was awesome.

They say nothing else, eyes watching me. Am I supposed to be sorry I missed it? I made plans with them to see it *before* my life got destroyed.

"Cool," I say.

In that silence, all I imagine them thinking is, *Poor Bitchslap.*

To locate the puncture, I start with a simple visual inspection. Ever so slowly, I turn the tire in the sun. A dot of dull metal is stuck in the black rubber. I pull it out with the nose pliers—it's a broken, half-rusty nail.

"I leave for the DR this weekend," Miguel reminds me. "If you're busy the next few days, we'll have to hang out in six weeks when I get back."

"We should all go to Universal Studios then," Enzo tells me, "or you and I can hang out before, if you're around."

"Maybe," I lie.

I jam a rubber plug into the puncture with a twist of the tool. Once I fill the tire with air I carry it back to the car, wondering if it feels lighter than a thirteen-inch wheel normally does. Can't tell. Tomorrow I'll test my new strength at the gym and confirm, without a doubt, that all my hard work is paying off.

After I swap out the spare for the fixed wheel I bring down the car with a twist of the hydraulic carjack handle.

I take my cap off to wipe the sweat from my forehead and face.

"Oh my God!" Miguel says.

"You buzzed your hair off," Enzo says.

I'd forgotten about my head. "Does it look weird?" I ask them.

"No," Miguel says. "The haircut looks fine. *You* look weird."

"Thanks."

He studies me close and then steps back to take me all in again. "How is it possible that your head looks bigger when you chop off your hair?"

"I'll be growing into my head this summer."

When Enzo pulls out his wallet, I tell him there's no charge for friends.

Dad does the same. What's a tiny piece of rubber thread and a few minutes of labor?

"Hey, Bitchslap!" a voice calls out.

I stiffen. This is exactly why I don't wanna be outside. My two friends turn to the street.

A blue Honda Accord is slowing down. The open windows reveal three just-graduated seniors with nothing better to do. The car keeps cruising, emitting wild laughter.

Come back at the end of the summer, I think to myself, and I'll kick all your asses.

That thought helps keeps my anger down inside. Also knowing that the shout was loud enough to reach Dad.

Now I shout to him in Spanish. "Did you hear that?"

"Yes!" he shouts back.

Good. Maybe he'll stop thinking the tragedy is all in my head.

"Thanks a lot for the hookup," Enzo says. "See you soon, I hope."

"Sure thing," I say.

I'll see him in the lunchroom on the first day of school, when I'm no longer the stick he talked to at the party or the bitchslapped kid on the video.

"Six weeks without you." Miguel opens his arms wide. "Bring it in."

My best friend's idea of fun is making things awkward. Most times it's funny.

"We don't gotta hug," I tell him. "Don't be weird."

"We've been friends since fifth grade. It would be weird *not* to hug."

Maybe he's right. His whole family is huggy, the men too. My dad became more huggy when Mom died, but I'm not used to touching guys with my whole body that way.

Miguel keeps his arms splayed all *ta-da*, like he just pulled off a magic trick. "You're leaving me hanging."

Enzo is cracking up. Most school guys would. Around here, you're more likely to find teenage boys fighting than hugging.

"I'm not even sure you wanna hug. It's like you get a kick out of making me uncomfortable."

"We love each other, don't we? So of course I wanna hug," Miguel says. "Are you afraid it's not manly or something?"

Well, according to lots of people, it isn't. I guess that's why I'm so uncomfortable. It's like ever since I was seven or eight, when girls became gross and supposedly too beneath us to mix with, I've been trying to hang onto my boy status.

It's so easy for guys to strip that status from you. Just be too scared or weak to do something, like hop a fence, and you're not a guy anymore.

But me and Miguel aren't that way with each other. So here I go.

I hug him real quick.

"See?" Miguel says. "Was that so bad?"

"No, not bad." And it's true. Miguel grabs me by the

shoulders and looks intensely at me. "Now look deep into my eyes and tell me that you love me."

Enzo cracks up. It sort of makes me smile too.

I do look Miguel deep into his eyes, but I say something else entirely. "I can't believe I'm saying this, but I'm going to miss your weirdness."

7

Eighty days until school begins

STEPPING INTO the gym is a huge relief, and not just because today is the hottest day so far this summer. It's because the weight I lift will finally prove I've gotten stronger.

Mirrors and other reflective surfaces have been useless but numbers don't lie.

I give Alpha and Tower a quick nod as I walk past them. The gangsta hip-hop in my headphones insulates me. Helps me forget about who might be watching me, lifting more than me, looking down on me.

Plus there's no better gym music than a hard beat with braggy and angry lyrics. Rappers talking about doing what they want, getting what they want, and what could happen to you if you try to get in their way.

I head to the same duct-taped bench as last Saturday. For the warm-up, I start with just the bar like last time.

Damn, this thing is heavy. The fifteen reps I do feel pretty much the same.

No biggie. The warm-up is just to get the blood flowing into the muscles, loosen them up to do real work. I add the same small plates, one on each side. If I did nine reps last time, I'm thinking fifteen today. Fifteen easy ones, because overdoing it is a bad idea. For my next set I'll add even more weight. Van Nelson and Natural Nathan on YouTube both recommend this, pyramid sets.

With Eminem screaming over a beat, I lie back on the bench, slide under the bar, and grip it. Raise it off the rack.

Fuck. This feels as heavy as last time. I ignore that. Count off the reps to the beat of the song. By the time I get to four, I'm pretty sure I won't see fifteen. The ninth rep is brutal, has me panicking. For the tenth I grit my teeth, channeling all my anger into my trembling arms to push this bar up.

One more rep than last time? My brain tells me to rack this weight hovering over me, but fuck that. I'm doing fifteen. Even if I gotta grunt through the reps. Even if I gotta throw up from the exertion afterward. I'm hitting fifteen no matter what.

I need more anger. Instead of beating myself up like the chest-pounding Superman before every set, I beat myself up mentally. Think back to Ricky's slap and that high-pitched cackle on that video that went viral, the video everyone has seen and will remember unless I get stronger and bigger.

My knuckles go white from squeezing the bar.

I lower it, my chest tensing as it touches down above my nipples. Then I push it out, inching it up halfway. The bar wavers and trembles above me. Without Alpha shouting insults at me like he does for Tower, I think them to myself.

Come on, Bitchslap David! You pussy! You loser!

But my arms give out, and the bar comes slamming down on my chest.

"Don't do that!" I hear over my music.

Alpha snatches the bar up with one hand and racks it.

I sit up and slide the headphones down around my neck. Feel myself go red from both humiliation and rage.

"*Always* get a spot when you do sets to exhaustion," Alpha says in a stern voice. "*Always*. You don't wanna get hurt and I don't want a liability."

"I *wasn't* going until exhaustion. I was gonna do fifteen easily."

I get up, more interested in the weight I've lifted than in Alpha. What the fuck is going on? Where is the bar I used last time? The lighter one. Because there's no way that was the same bar as last time.

I inspect the one on the incline bench. It's the same length with the same thick cyclindrical ends. I lift it an inch off the rack. Yep, it weighs the same too. My eyes roam, searching for the right bar.

"You have to follow the rules if you wanna work out here," Alpha says. "Hey, where are you going?"

I weave through the equipment to look at the barbell angled on the corner of the wall—which also looks the same. It must be hollow, which means it weighs less, which means it's the one I used before. That's the only explanation. But it feels the same in my hands. A deep ache settles in my stomach.

Alpha asks, "Are you even listening, Little Man?"

I whip around to face him and Tower, who have both followed me over here.

"Sure, Alpha," I say. "Sorry about that. I just didn't realize the bar I used last time was lighter." I can't let go of hope.

"They all weigh the same."

"They *can't*," I insist.

I've been doing everything right at the gym. At home, I've been getting enough calories, hitting my macros, the right ratio of carbs, fat, and protein.

"It's true," Tower says. The bandana wrapping his skull is so tight I'm surprised it doesn't cut off his circulation. "Forty-five pounds, bro. I've used them all. Here or in any gym, Olympic barbells weigh forty-five pounds."

I go completely stiff.

So I'll be lifting one more rep each workout? At this

rate, there's no way I'll get big enough this summer.

What the hell has all my effort been for? All that money spent on a gym membership, at the supermarket, and the supplement store.

I've been eating six times a fucking day, putting down double the calories, going hard at the gym and sleeping eight hours every night.

I mean, what the actual fuck is going on?

"Breathe," Tower says. "Come on, bro. Take it easy."

I'm staring at the weight I should've lifted at least fifteen times.

"What's wrong?" Alpha asks.

"I can't gain muscle! What a bunch of bullshit!"

I didn't mean to say that out loud, but now that it's out there I don't regret it. Maybe they have an answer for why this is going so slow. A piece of the bodybuilding puzzle I've missed.

Tower is fighting back a smile. Alpha is straight-up grinning at me.

"You joined the gym last *week*, bro," he informs me, like I've forgotten. "What did you expect?"

"To do way more reps than last time," I say. "If I'm going to gain twenty-five pounds of muscle by the end of summer, I need to get way stronger each workout."

Alpha full-on laughs now and Tower, unable to contain himself, joins in. Like I'm a stand-up comedian who's just told one of my best jokes.

They quiet down when they notice my unamused stare.

"Sorry, bro," Alpha says. "Talk to me though. What gave you the idea you could gain twenty-five pounds of muscle in three months? That would take *years*."

"There's this Van Nelson video online where he talks about his transformation. Explains his workouts and diet regimen."

Tower drops the smile and his dark eyes flash. "Fuck Van Nelson!"

He's pointing a finger at me as if I'm supposed to pass on this message to the actor myself.

He turns to Alpha. "See what I mean? When those Hollywood fakes deny using gear they not only make it look like we're cheating, they also put crazy ideas into people's heads."

Gear? That's steroids.

"Here's the thing about Van Nelson," Alpha tells me, with the tone of a doctor with bad news. "He took a shit-ton of steroids to get that big that fast."

It's all a lie? I'm frozen from the shock.

The guy who played Nightchaser punked me.

I ask Alpha about the YouTubers I've been watching, all those before and after pics, and Natural Nathan.

"He's natural and getting swole so quickly," I say.

Tower contemplates me as if I just spoke a language he doesn't understand. "Everybody claims to be natural because steroids are illegal and taboo as fuck."

Alpha shrugs. "If people get results that fast, they're not natural. It's as simple as that."

"But don't worry about them," Tower says.

"That's right!" Alpha perks up. "Don't compare yourself to anybody, Little Man. Just do you and focus on getting stronger day after day. Alright?"

No, it's *not* fucking alright. My goal has been totally crushed. I don't know whether to scream, punch, kick, or just die. I can't even be here right now.

Fuck the rest of my workout.

I clamp my headphones on, put my hood over my head, and get the hell outta the gym.

8

VAN NELSON is far from the only fake-ass celebrity who takes steroids. The proof is right there on my computer screen. In the before and after pics of actors in different movie roles.

I move on to the scientific studies that explain how people gain muscle mass naturally, with normal levels of testosterone.

Every expert agrees with Alpha and Tower. There is no fucking way to get so big so fast without the help of anabolic steroids.

I think back to the action movies I've seen, the extra-swole tough guys and the superheroes without the muscle suits. As I sat in the theater, munching popcorn and slurping Coke, it never occurred to me that those physiques were because of steroids. That those stars were popping or injecting illegal drugs.

I get up from the chair to look at the movie poster on

my door. I've seen *Nightchaser* like a million times and this image every day since I hung the poster up.

Why did you take steroids and lie about it, Van Nelson?

The movie comes back to me, every action-packed scene, especially the glorious ending at the shipyard. *Nightchaser* was one of the biggest-budgeted movies of all time, a total blockbuster that turned Van Nelson into a major star almost overnight.

And there's my answer. He did steroids because that's what it took to play the *Nightchaser* role. He did what it took to reach his goal.

Now I wonder, clinging on to the last sliver of hope: Am I willing to do whatever it takes to reach *my* goal?

Is taking steroids *really* out of the question?

They may not be as dangerous as I think. Or dangerous at all.

What about all that propaganda back in the day about marijuana being dangerous? How a few puffs could make you crazy and criminal to the point you might kill your parents.

Google brings up a list of websites about steroids. I click one that ends in *.org*. It's a medical institute website. The article is written by Jonathon Weber PhD, who says he's been studying anabolic steroids for twenty-two years.

He explains that anabolic steroids are synthetic variations of the male sex hormone, testosterone.

That doesn't sound so bad. Steroid users give their

bodies more of what they already produce. That sounds different from drugs.

Thank you, Dr. Weber, for cheering me up.

The following section is about the potential side effects. It mentions aggressive behavior, severe acne, prominent breasts, premature balding, heart disease, liver damage, infertility, impotence . . .

I stop reading. Damn, Dr. Weber. What are you doing to me?

What if he isn't really an expert? Some doctors turn out to be quacks. I scroll to the bottom, where there are links to the studies he's referencing. Too many to count. After another ten minutes of clicking and reading studies that back him up, I know he's legit.

I slump in my chair, still unable to accept defeat. Van Nelson seems fine. Same with all the actors who have taken steroids. The hardcore guys at the gym too, even though they're so much bigger.

Me, I don't wanna take steroids for years. Not even months. I'm talking *weeks*. Twelve weeks in total, from now until when school starts.

To achieve my ideal size and then give them up forever.

A boost is all I need.

After a few minutes of searching, I find out that a typical "gear cycle" lasts anywhere from ten to sixteen weeks. Sweet. The price is a little harder to determine. Black market prices differ all over the place, but the ballpark cost is in the hundreds.

Sorry, used car. You'll have to wait. I'd much rather be swole on a bike than a skinny twerp in a car.

So it's settled. I won't worry about the horrifying thought of injections. I'll buy the pills instead. And I won't worry about where to score steroids, like these guys on the bodybuilding forums.

I know exactly the place to get hooked up.

9

Seventy-nine days until school begins

YOU DO NOT go up to the biggest man you've ever seen in real life and just straight up ask him for steroids. Besides, Alpha's eating now, shoveling food into his mouth as Rassle, who just finished his workout, chats him up.

Rassle's skin is almost as red as his hair. He's an alligator wrestler who spends most of the day in the sun. A few days ago he showed me the half gator tooth lodged into his bicep. Says he's waiting for his body to reject it naturally.

He, Alpha, and a few bodybuilders on the posters on the walls have that little gap between their front teeth. I've learned that it's another potential side effect of steroids—a long-term one. Your jaw may grow wider.

So I can ask either guy. As far as size, Rassle is less intimidating. Plus, Alpha may not love the idea of hooking up a minor in his place of business.

As I finish my third set of pulldowns I hear, "Later, David!"

Rassle lifts the arm with the tooth in it and waves. Dammit. Through the glass wall I watch him get into his truck.

I'm not waiting one more day to start my cycle. Nothing to do but ask Alpha for the hookup. He's been so nice and helpful with everything else, I remind myself. Not that it makes me feel any less nervous.

Alpha spoons the last bit of brown rice into his mouth, his square jaws chomping. He sets the container behind the reception area and heads over this way. The gym was busier than usual when I came in and he was occupied, renewing another month for one member and then spotting a few others.

Now it's just him, an older man doing barbell curls, and me.

"Glad to see you back today, David."

He looks at where I put the pin on the machine. I'm working with three rectangular plates.

"You keep eating and training right, eventually you'll be doing that whole stack of weight."

"How soon you think?" I ask.

Talking about progress and time. This is good. We're easing into the conversation we need to have.

He shrugs, his volleyball-sized shoulders moving up

and down. "Depends. Everybody's different. It's also about genetics. A hundred people eating and training the same will grow at different rates."

No doubt. Some guys are bulky without ever lifting a weight or doing manual labor.

"So it will take me forever to make gains." I hope he catches the deep disappointment in my voice and will wanna come to my rescue.

My palms are sweating and I got a knot in my throat. We're getting closer to my big question.

Alpha shrugs again. The distance between his thick neck and where his arms begin is ridiculous. You could set dinner plates on his shoulders.

"Not *forever*," he says. "Besides, everybody has a different idea of what big is."

True. Let me show him what *small* is in my case. I unzip my hoodie, the first time I've done so in the gym.

I slip it off, feeling naked in my short-sleeve T-shirt.

"These are my genetics right here, and I'm trying to get as big as possible by the end of the summer. Got any advice?"

A subtle question. I'm not flat-out asking for illegal drugs.

"Just what I already told you, bro. Eat right and train hard. There are no shortcuts."

Yeah, right. Is he trying to make me laugh? He's *all* about shortcuts. The guys on the wall of champions, his heroes, took shortcuts too.

I say, "*Some* guys take shortcuts."

Perfect. Not the least bit accusatory.

"Yeah, well." He turns his head, as if suddenly shy, and speaks with a lower voice. "I don't know about that."

He starts to walk away.

"Do you know where I can buy steroids?"

I didn't mean for that to come out. What's wrong with me? That was the *opposite* of subtle. The knot in my throat has gotten bigger.

Alpha stops. The stringy tank top shows some of the definition in his wide back, all those ridges of muscle. He turns around and there are his pecs again, big and thick and jutting.

He points to the wall of champions. "If your goal is to compete at that level, you might fuck with gear one day. For now though, get as big as you can on your own. Don't be lazy."

The knot slips down my throat and becomes hot rage in my stomach.

Lazy?

As he heads to the bathroom and lockers, I aim all my hate at the back of his head.

He called *me* lazy! Don't I have a 3.4 GPA? Don't I work at the shop, do my chores, and take care of my sister? I'm reminded of the bullshit stereotype about Mexicans being lazy, which only pisses me off more.

Why am I shocked though? Big guys can talk shit. And when you're Alpha's size, you can do whatever the hell you want.

Usually. Not with me. I don't take shit from anybody. Not anymore.

I stomp across the gym to follow him, the fury in my blood propelling me.

He has gone into the large dank room in the back, the one I try to avoid. It's essentially a big bathroom, lined with two urinals, a stall, and two small showers. On the other side are the lockers, with benches in front, like our PE locker room at school.

The flimsy door bangs against the wall when I push through it.

"Go easy with the door, please," Alpha says.

He's peeing with his back to me. His round bulging calves cast a shadow over his high-tops.

It hits me how crazy this is. I'm confronting the biggest guy I've ever seen. With no backup or witnesses around.

I'll stay by the door in case I gotta run.

"Who the fuck did you call lazy?"

My voice booms in the emptiness. The adrenaline rushing through my veins has me extra alert. I'm both invigorated and shit-scared. Why am I stepping to the biggest guy in Florida?

"Sorry, bro," Alpha says, with a true gentleness in his voice. "Didn't mean to offend you."

"I don't give a shit how big you are," I tell him, my heart racing. "I'm sick of you guys thinking you can do and say whatever you want just because you're bigger than me."

"Whoa, hold up." His voice echoes, punctuated by the zip of his fly. He turns around to aim squinted eyes at me. I swear he's the size of three people. "What are you saying?"

"I'm saying there's more to life than muscles and that maybe—"

"No, no. You said 'I'm sick of *you guys*.' Are you talking about bullies?" He takes a small step forward. "Are you calling me a *bully*?"

An honest answer might get me killed, so I say nothing.

My stomach twists when he walks across the room, brushing past me. He opens the first locker. "Come here."

I join him, my hands trembling.

In the locker is a small towel, wrist wraps, and an enormous tub of protein. Or maybe the tub contains the ashes of people who've offended him.

"You see that?" he asks.

"Yeah." I try to keep my voice even as I read the label. "Chocolate-flavored protein powder. Twenty-eight grams per serving."

"Not that, dumbass." He jabs a finger onto the inside of the metal door, causing it to bang against the adjacent locker. "*This*."

A bunch of photos, each one with a different shirtless guy flexing, who all seem related. That's my guess at first, until I see the final photo: Alpha, recently. These are all photos of him. This is his transformation.

Alpha taps the photo on top. "That was me as a high school senior," he says in a faraway voice.

The kid, bony as me, is flexing biceps that just aren't there. Pimples cluster both cheeks. And those dark brown glasses! They're the thickest, ugliest frames I've ever seen.

"Zit-faced and rocking bifocals. I was so fucking skinny I practically had to run around in the shower to get wet." Then he adds, "No offense."

"None taken."

I step closer to the photos, too shocked to say anything else. If Alpha went from what I'm seeing to what's standing next to me now, I'm more sure than ever I can hit my goal of twenty-five pounds of muscle.

"So don't call me a fucking bully. Bullies are the reason I started lifting. I got picked on every day." The hint of pleading in his voice surprises me. "I wasn't interested in becoming 'as big as possible,' as you say. It was about self-preservation."

He understands me! Hell, he used to *be* me.

"That's exactly why *I* wanna get big," I say. "So people stop fucking with me. I just wanna live in peace."

He slams the locker shut with a flick of the wrist. "Nah, bro. You don't get picked on like I used to." His eyes take me in from head to toe, lingering on my exposed arms. "You're skinny as fuck—ain't gonna lie—but you're an okay-looking kid. Coming across an occasional bully is just part of being a teenager."

"I get picked on *all* the time," I correct him. "Also, sometimes once is enough," I say, remembering the video.

Not that I ever completely forget it. It's always on the edge of every thought I have, ready to drop into my brain and take over everything.

Alpha shakes his head, and starts to walk away. Just when we're getting somewhere. How can I get him to understand?

By showing him the video, which is still on YouTube. After all, he showed me his goofy high school picture. I hate the idea of one more person seeing my humiliation, but it might change his mind.

"Wait," I tell Alpha.

He stops reaching for the door and turns. "What?"

"Give me a second," I say, searching for the video.

Right away it pops up. Fuck me. The video posted by *another* user days ago has almost 1,673,000 views. In total, about four million people have seen me get slapped.

I hand the phone over.

Alpha looks at it in his palm as if it's a foreign object. "What's this?"

"Proof that I have it worse than you ever did."

He starts the video. As he watches with the sound on, I watch his face. In my mind, I revisit the details that are stuck in my memory.

Alpha winces at the loud slap. Seconds later he winces again as Bitchslap David drops to the floor like a bag of laundry.

"The whole world has seen it," I say. "Including everybody at my school."

"Fucking hell, bro. That's brutal." He lets out the hugest sigh I've ever heard and hands me back the phone. "Point made."

"So you'll hook me up?"

His eyebrows raise. "With gear?"

"Yeah."

"Hell no. Are you crazy? First, you're a minor. Also, most people get as big as they can on their own before fucking with gear."

"I don't have time to get big on my own. Come on. I'm trying to become a new person so I can separate myself from what you saw in the video."

He's listening, so I continue. "My senior year of high school can either be the greatest year of my life or the worst. It's up to you."

"Don't put this on me," Alpha says, shaking his head.

"But it *is* on you."

Alpha takes a deep breath and looks away before sort of looking at me again. "My senior year was the worst. Not that I got bullied more, necessarily. Just that everything I wanted became more important and was just as unattainable. A girlfriend, self-confidence, friends."

It just might happen. I don't know how else to nudge him in the right direction, so I repeat myself. "I don't have time to get as big as I can on my own."

"You *do* go hard as fuck in your workouts," Alpha says, considering me with a calm gaze. "No doubt about it. I shouldn't have called you lazy."

"I'm totally dedicated," I say, barely able to contain my excitement. "All I need is a boost this summer."

"A high school senior," he says. "To be seventeen again. You lucky bastard."

It's like he'll be doing it for the both of us. Giving me the chance he didn't have when I was his age. Whatever helps him say yes is fine with me. I'm vibrating with nervous anticipation.

"Okay, I'll hook you up," he finally says. "I got some extra gear at the house."

My heart pounds with excitement. I gotta contain myself so I don't start screaming with joy or something crazy.

Physically I'm here in the locker room, among the urinals and lockers and general stinkiness, but actually I'm above it all, soaring through the sky like a fucking bird.

10

ALPHA'S HOUSE is about twenty blocks away in a nicer neighborhood than mine, the houses about the same size but in better shape. I roll up in Dad's puttering Pathfinder, under a darkening sky that is streaked purple.

When Alpha opens the door I ask, "Is that a dog?"

A huge pet is behind him and I wanna make sure. If you focus on the face, it looks like a Rottweiler alright. The body is way bigger though, lumpy with muscles.

Alpha laughs. "Yep. I gave Crockett his last injection a few weeks ago. I wanted to see how big he could get. But he was getting out of control, trying to hump my girlfriend Mindy and all her friends."

A dog on steroids? That sounds dumber than stoners blowing weed smoke into their dogs' ears to get them high. I've heard of kids doing that, but Alpha isn't some kid from school.

"Come on in," he insists. "It's okay."

Crockett eyes me, muscles tensed and tail wagging. He lets out a low murmur. Though I normally pet dogs, I don't feel like losing a hand today. When I move quickly past him he follows me.

"Can you put him outside or something?" I ask Alpha.

"He's been outside all day and wants to hang out with his best friend." Alpha bends down to kiss the dog between the ears. "Isn't that right, boy? You wanna hang out with me?"

It almost makes me laugh, a big guy like Alpha kissing and baby-talking a dog.

"This dog is a sweetheart," Alpha says, and points a finger away from us. Crockett takes a spot on the couch.

Mindy must have decorated this place. Everything matches. The dark blue in the striped throw pillows that go perfectly with the curtains, for instance. Leave it up to Alpha and he might have put muscle posters all over the walls, with pseudo-inspirational quotes like in the gym.

A photo of him and his girlfriend hangs on the wall. She's hot.

Mindy's due home in an hour, which is why I came as soon as Alpha called, when the evening trainer showed up at the gym to cover him. We gotta do this before she shows up. I guess she might get mad at him for giving gear to a kid.

"Stay right there," Alpha says at the entrance to the

kitchen. "The light is perfect for a *before* pic."

He takes a few steps back to size me up. I cross my arms, wishing I had my hoodie on. I feel like I'm under a microscope right now.

"I've taken *before* pics already," I say.

"I wanna track your progress too."

Cool. It's like he's not just selling me gear but also taking me under his wing.

It puts me a bit at ease.

I take off my shirt.

He snaps three pics and pockets the phone. "People think we cheat, but we train harder than anybody else. You know why?"

"No," I say, putting my shirt back on. "Why?"

"Because we're doing whatever it takes to be great. Most people never try to achieve greatness."

I'm totally with that. It's exactly how I see myself, as someone aspiring to greatness.

He climbs onto the kitchen counter looking more gorilla than man. Grabs the long cardboard box that was pushed out of view on top of the cabinets and brings it down.

"First rule of Gear Club is you don't talk about Gear Club." He pauses to consider something. "Actually, that's the only rule. Gear is taboo only because people think it's drugs, so don't tell anybody you take them. And *definitely* don't say where you got them."

"My lips are sealed."

"This is important," he insists. "Don't. Tell. Anybody. Not even the girls who'll be all over you like white on rice."

I laugh at the idea that I might become what girls call *hot*. Not that I'd break up with Karina or anything. It has to feel pretty good though, for girls to see you in that way.

"For real," he says. "And whether you play the field or finally get a girlfriend, you say nothing. I don't care how close you are, how cool you think the girl is."

"I have a girlfriend," I say.

"Really?" He raises one eyebrow, and I totally get it. A kid with this physique isn't supposed to have a girlfriend. If he met Karina he'd be even more shocked at how cute she is.

"I mean, okay," Alpha says. "But don't tell her."

Of course I wouldn't. If Karina or anybody else wonder how I got my gains so fast I'll just say it's thanks to the supplements I'm taking: the protein powder, creatine, and glutamine.

He lifts the lid off the box. Dozens of tiny packages are inside: ampoules, bottles, boxes of pills, and individually wrapped syringes. All with pharmaceutical logos and unpronounceable names, the dosage labeled ml or mg.

I shiver at the idea of getting poked with one of the syringes. By superstrong Alpha no less. But he insists it's a must for big gains.

"How does your girlfriend not know you're on gear?" I ask him.

"She knew when we started dating three years ago, and it caused problems," he says, poking around the box. "She asked me to stop and I told her to give me one more year to win the World Muscleman Championship."

As he continues his search, he explains that he just wants to win once, to know what it's like to be a champion, and with that title he'll have recognition, use it to start a chain of high-level gyms.

"Iron Life I bought from a friend who moved away, with the money I inherited from my grandparents. It's okay, just not as nice as it could be."

He sets a small box marked Dynabol aside. "So anyway, a few weeks ago Mindy said no more chances, and that if I continue to take gear, we're done. So I told her I've given it up."

"And that's going to work?"

"She'll come around. I've convinced her before and I'll do it again. I *have* to take gear. Without gear, there's no way to be big enough to compete in the World Muscleman Championship. And all my years of hard work can't be for nothing."

He sets down a rubber-topped transparent bottle about the size of his thumb. It seems to be full of water. "There's your stack. Dynabol and Suspension." He turns to me. "Listen, David. Girls are always trying to change us, but we have to resist and be who we are."

I think of how Karina has tried to change me but come up with nothing. Well, this week she's been on me to leave the house, believing it will cheer me up, but that's just her being nice.

I turn away as Alpha unwraps the syringe. I can't look. Alpha said he'll inject me at the gym for a while, whenever I go to work out, until I can do it to myself. But I can't imagine that ever happening. He'll need to do it for me all summer.

I say, "I really wish I could just take pills."

"They're not as effective, bro, unless you combine them with an injectable. Besides, too many pills are hard on your stomach. Didn't you notice Tower throwing up after each heavy set?"

I move my eyes from the fridge to Alpha—not a good idea. I feel my spine go cold. The needle looks about as long as half a pencil. He jabs it into the bottle and draws the clear liquid into the cylinder. This is what will get shot into my ass muscle every other day.

"Exactly how long is that needle?"

"An inch and a half." He sets the bottle aside. The needle glints in the kitchen light. He presses on the tiny plunger until a single drop oozes out of the pointy tip.

"No air bubbles, so your muscle doesn't get injected with oxygen."

"Thanks?"

I guess that's good. I'm so nervous right now I don't know what's good or bad, what's up or down. All I know is that this is the only way to hit my goal.

Alpha holds the syringe behind his back. Is it that obvious I'm freaking out?

He smiles and asks, "Are you ready to start your journey toward monster gains?"

"No monster gains," I remind him. "It's just this one cycle. I'm not trying to hurl cars at people or scare small children."

Alpha laughs, his gigantic shoulders going up and down. "That's the best compliment ever, when kids point and stare." He gets serious. "Alright, bro. Which is the lucky ass cheek? Left or right?"

My heart is really racing now. I pull down my shorts and boxers enough to reveal my right cheek. Here we go. No turning back. I ready myself by taking a deep breath.

I turn around to place my hands on the kitchen counter by the sink. Crockett watches from the living room couch. I almost forgot he was there.

These injections will help me transform into muscular David, who will get respect. That exciting thought brings me some calm.

"I'm going to add twenty-five pounds of muscle by the end of summer," I say out loud. Anything to focus on the positive instead of the horrifying needle about to stab me.

"I didn't mention it before," Alpha says, "but Suspension

is the one steroid that is water-based instead of oil. That means it's fast-acting."

"Awesome."

"It also means it burns like a bitch going in, so I'll inject it slowly," he says. "Don't freak out."

Those are probably the worst three words to hear when you're on the verge of freaking out. My heart pounds and my neck starts sweating.

All of a sudden, the needle stabs me. A pain flashes, then disappears. Next the hot liquid oozes in, dripping down, burning.

The fire spreads more as I squeeze my eyes and also my lips together—so I don't whimper from the pain. I open my eyes to see Crockett standing on the couch, way too interested. Looking at me like he's starving and I'm a big steak.

"Ow," I say, suddenly feeling the metal needle among all that burning.

"Stop clenching."

"Your dog's making me nervous."

Crockett hops down from the couch and trots over, moaning like he's in heat.

"It's attacking!" I shout.

I fight the impulse to run. The needle is still in.

"Done," Alpha says, pulling it out before Crockett runs into the kitchen.

He leaps toward me. I jump back, tugging up my shorts.

I hold my palms out and walk in reverse until my back is pinned against the wall.

"No, Crockett!" Alpha tries to grab the collar as the dog keeps lurching for me.

The liquid heat burns in my glute and hamstring as I slide along the wall. "Keep it away!"

"No, Crockett!" Alpha shouts.

Alpha throws himself on the dog, a tackle in front of the fridge. He clutches the collar with one hand and helps himself up with the other. Crockett tries to jerk away as Alpha stands still, completely out of breath. Alpha is actually panting, his big chest rising and falling.

"You okay?" I ask him.

Alpha nods and says something I can't understand. He's too winded to make any sense.

"Damn, bro," I say. "Don't you ever do cardio, like running or something?"

Did I just say *bro*?

After a few more seconds to regain his breath, he says, "Fuck cardio. Running doesn't make you big. It only makes you susceptible to getting hit in the head with an empty bottle of Muscle Milk when I'm driving down the street."

He laughs and drags the still-manic Crockett to the back door.

I take a few steps around the living room to bring back the feeling in my steroid-soaked muscles.

Alpha comes back, no longer panting. "Crockett must have thought you were one of Mindy's friends. No worries though. You'll be built like a real man in no time."

The burn now feels like a warm glow in the back of my leg.

"An injection every other day, and thirty milligrams of D-bol daily." Alpha opens the tiny box, takes out the bottle, and tosses it to me. One hundred tabs, says the small print, ten milligrams each. I rip the top open and pop three, barely bigger than dots, into my mouth. Swallow them without water.

It seems like the manly thing to do.

Alpha does his gorilla crawl onto the counter to put away the large box and comes back down.

"Gear only works if you keep training and eating hardcore, like you've been doing. So keep it up."

"I will."

"The bodybuilding lifestyle will take up your life and people around you might bitch about that, but focus on your goal. You'll get size, respect, girls, you name it. You give everything to your gains, and your gains will give everything to you."

I like the sound of that. My summer plans are all about giving everything to my gains.

I bust out my wallet, feel no guilt about taking out five 100-dollar bills. He gives me back a fifty and a twenty. Four hundred thirty dollars is a small price to pay for a body that commands respect. I'm so thrilled I can't stop smiling.

"You wanted to take yourself to another level, bro," Alpha says. "This is it. Now you got ten times the testosterone flowing through you than an average man. You ain't a chump no more. You ain't even a man. You're a *super-man.*"

I like the sound of that.

11

Fifty-five days until school begins

WIDER SHOULDERS! A slight thickness of the arms!

I turn in front of the mirror to see my torso in profile. Yep! A chest that's starting to jut out! I can't believe that body belongs to me!

I go through a few more poses until I'm face-to-face with myself again, busting the double biceps pose—two small bulges swell there.

I catch myself smiling with pride.

This is a straight-up metamorphosis happening. After three weeks of giving everything to my gains, my body has sprouted muscles.

Superman was accurate. I do feel invincible, like I can walk through walls and snap Ricky or anybody else in half. With all this testosterone flowing through me, my energy is through the fucking roof. I could climb a mountain, run a marathon. Both on the same day.

The downside? Only that Dad has been eyeing my growing body with suspicion. Though he hasn't said a word, the way he's been studying me when I enter or leave a room makes me think there's an unasked question rattling in his head.

I keep my gear at Iron Life, where I get my injections in the office from Alpha. Among the weights, as I train, I talk gains with the other gearheads, keep it discreet if less serious lifters are within earshot.

At home it's a totally different story. So I got two separate lives—just like Superman.

"Bring another jug of water!" Dad's faraway voice interrupts my glory.

Oh yeah. I'm in the work bathroom.

"One second!" I shout back.

Dad always ordering me around is getting on my nerves more and more.

I came here to pee and haven't gotten to that yet. Crazy as it sounds, I actually *forgot* to pee.

The thing is, lately I can't pass a mirror or any reflective surface without checking myself out. For just a quick second. That's the plan, anyway, one quick second, but sometimes more time passes than I expect.

What can I say? I'm not used to this physique. Or maybe a better way to put it is that these gains happen too quickly to get used to them.

Done with my self-admiration, I grab for my T-shirt.

Instead of just putting it on I make the mistake of twisting my torso to look at my back.

So. Fucking. Gross. I cringe at the four zits I see behind one shoulder. The reddest one is the size of a dime, white-tipped and shiny, close to bursting. Alpha says not to touch them unless I want scars.

As far as side effects go, a summer with back acne isn't bad. At least the D-bol isn't making me throw up like it does to Tower. I slip on my T-shirt, covering up the twenty or so zits. Problem solved.

I unzip my shorts and pull down my underwear to pee. My dick didn't get smaller. That's a myth. If anything, it looks sort of bigger because my balls have shrunken. It's called *testicular atrophy* if you wanna get fancy.

It's barely a side effect. Two hanging testicles are now a single firm mound hiding behind my dick. Who cares? I don't. Has any girl anywhere ever cared what nuts look like?

Once my cycle is over, my natural testosterone production will kick in and my nuts will fill out to their normal size again.

The switching off and on of my reproductive system doesn't worry me. I'm a responsible user of gear. Let the *abusers* of gear worry about stuff like no more erections or not making babies. The ones who go too long without cycling off, or take too much gear for too long.

I wash my hands and head out.

Gaby is in the back on her little table. She's playing with Legos and singing a song I can't hear too well, one she possibly made up. She loves making up songs.

Dad is standing next to the dispenser near the auto shop entrance, drinking the last of the water from his big cup. His shoulders are crazy wide for someone who's never done lat raises or military presses.

At the shop I swap out the jugs, since he needs to be careful with his back. I bend down and grab a full one with one hand. Like it's nothing. It makes me smile.

I think back to when I used to need all my strength to lift it up. Carried it in both arms like you do with a person.

Dad smiles at me one-arming it. "Ladies and gentlemen," he says in Spanish. "What you're all been waiting for! Here comes the famous Músculos."

Whenever he's in a funny mood now, he calls me Muscles. It's way better than Flaco, a nickname he'll have to retire pretty soon when I'm totally jacked.

I tear off the top of the jug and flip it over without straining one bit. It glugs three times before the water settles.

"Getting stronger every day," Dad says, and wipes his sweaty face with a bandana.

I love getting Dad's approval. This feels better than when I show him straight As. Lately, though, the good feeling is always tinged with the fear of being found out.

He tucks the bandana into his back pocket. "If your

mother could see you now."

If only. She knew me as a crybaby kid, and as a teenager who got sad because of teasing and bullying. Now I'm the guy who doesn't gotta put up with that stuff.

Dad says, "After you help with this transmission, you can go home." After a couple of beats he adds, "Or look for another part-time job."

He's trying to help. Since I'm only going out in public when necessary, he knows I'm only earning what he gives me. Which won't give me enough for a car. My plan was to mow lawns like last summer.

"No, just working here is fine," I tell him.

I come most days, averaging about twelve hours per week.

"Hey, I wish business was busy enough to need you more," he says with a shrug. "*You* were the one so set on buying a car."

Once I'm muscular enough, I'll want everybody to see me. I can have any job, and I'll replace the money I've spent. Plus earn a bunch more.

Besides, leaving work after a couple of hours isn't tragic or anything. Today I'm excited to get home. There are three articles on UndergroundMuscle that I haven't gotten to yet. Plus, two of the bodybuilding channels I subscribe to on YouTube have posted new videos.

"Come on," Dad says. "Let's pull the transmission before it's time for your second lunch."

He laughs at his worn-out joke. Being impressed with my determination and progress isn't going to keep him from poking fun.

He lies down on the creeper, gently, and rolls underneath the Buick. I get under the car myself. The hard concrete presses on my sensitive zits. Ouch.

I take hold of the transmission while Dad loosens the final bolts with a socket wrench. His grease-streaked forearm tenses at every turn. Those thick forearms are impressive. And he got them without doing wrist curls or reverse curls.

My own forearms are still thin. Have they grown at all?

No, they haven't. They're twigs, and the rest of your body hasn't grown much either. You're still a skinny fuck.

Damn. It's the same thoughts that made me take off my shirt in the bathroom to inspect my gains. I keep having to confirm that I really am growing in size, like the logical part of my brain knows. Because the tape measure, the scale, and my heavier lifts are proof.

So I remember that and get all excited, beaming with pride in front of the mirror. But that only lasts so long until I start doubting again. I have this back-and-forth ten, twenty times a day.

Anyway, I'm clearly not as big as Dad yet, so what we have in common for now is that we're both covered in the greasy mess of fixing cars.

That and the sound of metal on metal, amplified under

here, makes me feel extra manly. I almost wanna invite him out for a beer or something.

"You should take your sister to the park," he says in a flat voice.

Says instead of asks—a reminder that I'm a boy and he's the man in charge.

If I don't do it he'll bring it up again, lay this whole guilt trip on me. That's why I joined them last Sunday for movie night, even though I'm sick of watching kid movies.

Yesterday Gaby stayed home and I made time for her, played a game of Jenga and three of Connect Four. Am I really supposed to entertain her every freaking day? It's not my fault Mely and her family got deported.

I mean, I feel bad, but what am I supposed to do?

Take her to the park, I guess. That's what.

It will get Dad off my case. Besides, lately I've only been recognized once, by this one college-aged guy who came to fix a flat last week. His eyes bugged out something serious, then he quickly said something about the hot weather.

While Gaby plays in the park I'll find a shaded park bench and clamp on my headphones to listen to my bodybuilding podcasts.

So I don't blast Dad's eardrums, I turn my face away and shout, "Who wants to go to the park?"

"Me!" Gaby shouts back, with so much joy in her voice. It almost melts my supertough, Superman heart.

"Thank you, Flaco," Dad says.

Dammit.

See? Mirrors lie. You're not bulking up at all. He's being ironic when he calls you Músculos. You're Flaco. You'll always be Flaco.

Not true. It's just a habit he has, using that nickname. What about the arm and shoulder measurements I made this morning? I'm making *incredible* gains.

Sometimes, my reasoning and facts are no match for those annoying thoughts. I have to start carrying my tape measure from now on. I so badly want to confirm, yet again, that I'm as big as I should be.

"I'll give you a few bucks so you can take her to get ice cream afterward," Dad says. "Wait. You're not allowed to eat ice cream. I forgot."

"Dad, for the millionth time, I'm *allowed* to eat whatever, but choose only to eat what's good for building muscles. The right kind of food and the right amounts is how people gain muscle mass. All the websites and even Alpha says so."

"Yeah? Well, I want to meet your friend Alpha," he says.

Dammit. Why did I have to say his name again? I mentioned Alpha once, referred to him as the owner and trainer at the gym. That he's my "friend" is Dad's own invention.

"What friend, Dad? He's a trainer at the gym who knows his stuff."

Dad keeps working the socket wrench that crackles with every counterclockwise turn. The final screw comes off.

"On the count of three," he says.

He counts down and we both pull. The transmission screeches off the car. I help guide it to the floor between us. It's light, which blows my mind. All of a sudden, transmissions are light for me.

All done, I slide out from under the car, feeling every tender zit on my back.

When I get up from the ground, I thunk my head on the side mirror.

"Son of a!" I shout, remembering not to curse around Dad.

An angry heat flashes through me as I rub the spot with one hand. My other hand curls into a fist. The desire to punch the car is so strong that I take a step back, just in case. I take a deep pull of oxygen, like Alpha taught me, hold it for a few seconds. Then slowly let it out.

"You okay?" Dad asks, rolling into view below.

"Yeah, I'm okay."

He rolls back under.

That's not just manly toughness talking. I *am* okay. I'm used to pain caused by clumsiness. For instance, if I get up to pee at night, there's an 80 percent chance that I'll stub my toes against something on my way to the bathroom.

In fact, I've bumped my head about a thousand times

before. So hard that the knot on my skull lasts for days. That side mirror didn't hurt much, I gotta admit. If not for the gear I'm taking, it wouldn't have been a big deal at all.

Okay, so maybe shrunken balls and back acne aren't the only side effects.

Yesterday the rage grabbed ahold of me in the gym, when this fat guy kept hogging the twenty-pound dumbbells. After ten minutes, it nearly made me turn red with fury until I remembered that my hormones were supercharged. Three long, deep breaths brought my heart rate back to normal.

Two days ago I dropped the milk carton on the kitchen floor, spilling most of it. I wanted to kick the fridge or wall so badly. Instead, I took a few calming breaths.

It's all about the focused breathing. Yoga instructors and gearheads know what they're talking about.

Now I catch my reflection in the tinted glass of the Buick—what the fuck? I look really big.

In fact, I look bigger than I did a few minutes ago! I take a step closer to the window and stand straight.

Hell yeah! Check out those broad shoulders! I lift my right arm to flex a bicep, and it stretches long instead of going round.

My enthusiasm sinks.

So *that's* it. The curve of the window is creating a sort of fun-house mirror effect. Making me wider.

It's cool though, this glimpse into the future. This is

what my body might look like when the cycle is done. I check myself out from the side and my chest juts out more. Nice. My round shoulder looks thicker. Who would mess with that guy?

"Is the performance over?" Dad's voice asks behind me.

Gaby laughs.

Great. They've witnessed me posing. Heat rises to my face.

Gaby stands there with her small backpack slung over her shoulder and looks at Dad. "I told you he's becoming a weirdo."

I grab the car keys and take Gaby with me, before Dad starts giving me more grief.

12

Thirty-two days until school begins

I CRUSHED that workout and still have plenty of energy. It's such a high to finish my last set, and to be in the Iron Life office to get injected with more testosterone. As always, the blinds are down and the single fluorescent bulb is way too bright.

I pull down my shorts to reveal my left cheek. Put my hands on the desk to steady myself and rest the top of my left foot on the floor. So I don't tense my leg when I get nervous.

"Here we go," Alpha says.

I feel my face squeeze hard when the needle darts in. Heat spreads in my glute. The burning means the fast-acting steroid is working, that the gains are underway and will continue. I've learned to love the burn.

The office door creaks open. Panic catches in my throat as I turn my head. I see Jake's shiny parted hair and gray camouflage T-shirt with the black Superman S. I don't think he owns a shirt without that S. What is he doing here?

"Hey," he says, and crunches a bite out of an apple he's holding.

Tower follows behind, carrying a blender pitcher—filled with a vanilla protein shake brought from home. "Why's your foot like that?"

"I'm not giving interviews right now, thanks."

What's wrong with these guys? This isn't a show. "Oh, I get it," Tower says. "It's so your leg doesn't tense up, right? That's smart." He takes a long drink from his pitcher.

This may be normal for them, but I'm not 100 percent comfortable with half my ass in full view.

When the needle is out I pull my underwear and shorts up. "What are you guys doing here?"

"We came to see the wild shit you're about to do to Alpha," Tower says.

Jake swallows another bite of apple. "Better you than me, Little Man. I wouldn't be able to do it."

"What are you guys talking about?"

Right then Alpha takes out another syringe from a desk drawer, the cylinder already loaded, and holds it up. "You're going to hook me up with some injections."

"Why me?"

I don't get it. Alpha injects himself, and these guys also self-inject.

"I need a young, steady hand for this," Alpha tells me, handing over the syringe. "This is Synthol."

Alpha explains that Synthol is not steroids. It's a SEO—a site enhancement oil. It temporarily puffs up the muscle to make it look fuller, for days or weeks, depending on how often it's injected.

"The thing is," Alpha says solemnly, "you have to inject the same amount into the exact same spot in the muscles or else I'll look asymmetrical."

"Do you know what that means?" fake Superman asks me.

"Yeah. Not symmetrical."

"Yep," he says, crunching the final bite out of his apple. "Goofy as fuck."

Tower hands his phone to me. It's a bodybuilder, super swole, with deformed arms and shoulders. Blood oozing from a tiny hole in his left tricep.

I'm not the squeamish type but damn. That's hard to look at.

"Gross. I'm not doing that. Forget it."

"You won't fuck this up," Alpha says, and then turns to narrow his eyes at Tower. "Don't show him pictures, bro."

Tower swipes the screen: there's another pic of Synthol gone wrong. A gash in a man's bicep about an inch long, with puss and blood leaking out.

"Fucking hell," I say, before Alpha snatches the phone from my hand.

"Those are idiots injecting too much and too often," Alpha says.

He explains that pro bodybuilders use it only for lagging muscles. In Alpha's case, he needs it for his biceps.

"I want the peaks to be higher for the Mr. Florida competition in a few months. If you mess up a little, my biceps will be back to normal in a few days. We're just practicing."

"Is this legal for competition?"

"Legal and common," Jake says.

So you're not only expected to take steroids, you're also expected to puff some muscles up with oil? Pro bodybuilding is so damn weird.

"But it only works if it looks natural," Tower points out. "Use too much and you get a balloon-look, can't see muscle definition. Judges take away points for that."

"Which is why we have to practice." Alpha takes a seat and spreads his arms in front of him, straight across the desk, palms up. Fear is etched on his face, which scares me more.

"This is some wild shit," Tower says quietly, as if to himself.

"Bro," Alpha says in a stern voice. "Please do me a favor and shut the fuck up." Then to me: "You got this, David."

I *so* don't got this. My stomach is churning. "Why doesn't someone with experience injecting do it?"

The two guys respond at the same time.

Jake: "Shaky hands because of hyperactivity."

Tower: "I don't have my contacts in today."

"It's easy," Alpha tells me. "Just slowly inject half a cc into each head of the biceps."

"And I gotta inject the same spot," I say.

"Right in the middle," Alpha says, demonstrating with a stabbing motion. "And hold the needle in the same angle, straight down."

My stomach churns even more, but fuck being scared. I'm a *man*, dammit. We don't back down from anything. We come through for our friends. It's not just Alpha in this room. I also gotta prove myself to the other two guys.

"Let's do this," I say, resolved to get it over with.

I stand over the desk. Run my fingers over the middle of his left bicep. There it is, the split in the two muscles. I leave my index finger pressed in there.

I take a deep breath and jab the one-inch needle straight into the middle of the inner bicep head. Alpha's face squeezes extra tight. A bird chirp leaks out of his pressed lips.

As I slowly push the plunger to half a cc, I tell myself not to worry if I'm causing Alpha pain or fucking up. He insisted I do this after I said I couldn't.

I inject the other head and then move to the right bicep, each poke causing Alpha to chirp louder. Probably because the needle gets duller with each stab.

After the last half cc is in his arm, I pull out the needle, cap it, and set the syringe on the desk. Then I step back real quick.

If I wasn't accurate and Alpha ends up like those freaks in the photos, it's totally on him. I never claimed to have the hand-eye coordination of a surgeon.

"Fuck yeah!" Alpha shouts.

"I could never do that, bro," Tower tells me. "You got bigger balls than me."

He gives me a fist bump.

"What the hell?" I say. "I thought you couldn't do it because you're not wearing contacts."

"Oh yeah. That was a lie. I got twenty-twenty, baby. I just don't wanna stab nobody in the arms. That's some horrifying shit."

I turn to Jake and just stare, in case he needs to come clean too.

He shrugs. "I don't have a shaky hand, just a queasy stomach."

"You two are pathetic," I say, but the truth is it feels good to be higher on the guy scale for once. I'm manlier than them. For now anyway.

I expected Alpha to be flexing, testing the instant results. Instead he's massaging his left bicep, squeezing and rubbing it.

"So my arms don't get lumpy," Alpha explains.

"Massage them good," Jake says. "You don't wanna look like this guy, am I right?"

He holds out his phone and laughs. It's another shirt-less guy, pale with dark purple upper arms. The doctor is draining one arm, the blood oozing out of the lumpiest part of his bicep.

"Rub those biceps," I tell Alpha. "Rub them good."

Alpha moves on to the other arm, rubbing and squeezing.

Then he walks over to the full-length mirror on the door. Even with the whole gym lined with mirrors, he needs one in here. We gather around. He does the front double biceps pose. Peaks! Beautiful peaks! Symmetrical peaks that look natural!

I don't scream for joy and relief because it's dead silent in here. Jake and Tower have their mouths hung open. I feel a rush of pride followed by worry—what if they want me to start injecting them with that stuff too?

13

Twenty-nine days until school begins

ANYBODY WOULD draw attention in a jacked Jeep Wrangler, fire red with the top down. You put the biggest body-builder in Florida in the driver's seat, and his enormous Rottweiler in the back, you get a spectacle.

So naturally I'm trying to be incognito just like when I ride my bike—cap pulled low and hood blocking most of my face.

Alpha and I just came back from the gym. Iron Life closes at two p.m. on Sunday, but since he did brunch with Mindy he had to get his workout in later. How cool that he can open whenever he wants, and invite me along.

"Are you sure you don't wanna grill something up at my place?" Alpha asks.

"I don't have time."

Dad and Gaby hang out with the Aquino family on Sundays, and will be back in a little over an hour. I used to go there too, to eat pozole and hang out with some kids my age—I always wore a T-shirt in the pool. But if one of them has seen the video—and it's almost certain—they have *all* seen the video.

Alpha says, "Mindy and her friends are still out, Crockett, so it's just me and you."

I check out Crockett in the rearview mirror one more time. He's pushing his head into the wind, the thick tongue out and trembling over Sligh Avenue. His neck and body are a bit leaner. I wasn't 100 percent sure when I first saw him today, but now I'm positive.

"Crockett is smaller."

"Mindy hasn't had time to take him out for runs lately, and he's not getting fed double like before."

So I'd have to keep up with my routine and my diet after the summer, which is not a problem. My plan is to keep getting bigger anyway.

"Disgusting," Alpha says, slowing for a red light. He's looking at the three guys coming outta Chipotle. "I know I'm extreme, as a pro bodybuilder, but that right there?"

"Unacceptable," I say, repeating one of Alpha's favorite words.

These three goofy guys, maybe late twenties, think they're hiding that fat with their tucked-in shirts. The polos and the checkered button-up sort of balloon up from the belt. We're not fooled.

Then I notice their wives or girlfriends, who have

clearly never set foot in a gym either.

Is that mean? Maybe, but I can't help it. I body-watch constantly, zeroing in on the shape and muscle definition. It's automatic, sort of like how I used to be with nice cars.

I barely notice cars anymore.

The weirdest thing is that lately I'm checking out guys *way* more than the girls. Actually, *sizing them up* is a better way to put it. I compare myself to them, satisfied if they're skinny or fat. If they're built, and I'm smaller, I try to calculate how much time until I catch up.

Alpha says, "They probably have some bullshit excuse about not enough time, when even interval training can build muscle in twenty minutes a day." He shakes his head. "Unacceptable."

The man with the superskinny arms and paunch belly could be me in my twenties, if I'd never discovered weight training. Unacceptable.

"You'd think they would have figured stuff out by that age," I say.

"Exactly, bro. Muscles make the man," Alpha says. "A powerful body is what distinguishes us from girls."

I guess that's true. Women can do whatever males can. Play the same sports, be doctors or politicians or whatever. Everything except look like us.

Well, some of those women pro bodybuilders come damn close, but that's because of all the testosterone they take.

Light breaks from the east. Clouds have opened to spill sunlight onto Tampa.

Alpha doesn't notice. He's looking down at his flexed biceps. I injected him once again yesterday and his arms have that fuller look. Now that we're both assured of my technique and skill, we're laying off until he actually needs Synthol injections—just before his competition.

"Check it out," I tell him, pointing.

"Beautiful." He squints up at the sky. Then he takes out his phone and snaps a few pictures for his 176,000 Instagram followers.

He posts mostly bro stuff like show-off poses, big meals, and videos of him going hardcore in the gym. But he also posts stuff like the sky and beautiful trees.

I've created my own new Instagram account, named Big D. But I only follow Natural Nathan and other bodybuilders and YouTubers who give me inspiration. I'm waiting to really become Big D before I post.

We cruise past a hot girl in yoga pants pumping gas at the Shell station. Right away there's a tingling down there. Uh oh.

Did I mention I get hard-ons more often? Just what a horny teen needs more of in his life. Alpha never warned me about that and the forums don't get into it too much.

It's to the point where I'm jacking off up to four, five times a day. It's almost become a chore. Either I jerk it often or sport a boner around the clock.

"Is there any way to avoid sudden boners?" I ask now.

"Ahhhh, yes," Alpha says with mock nostalgia. "The relentless and unpredictable boners of adolescence. Made worse with gear." He laughs. "You getting frequent *broners*?"

I laugh. It's another term to add to my new vocabulary. My *bro*cabulary.

"Is your lovestick getting more excited lately?" he adds, laughing more. "You going full salute often?"

"Forget it," I say, feeling my cheeks get red. "I shouldn't have asked."

"Okay, okay," he says, laying off. He swings a right onto a tree-lined block. "I got an industry secret for you. The best way to stop the boners is to think of something the opposite of sexy."

"I know that trick. *Everybody* knows that trick."

"Well, with extra-hard broners, you have to go extra awful and ugly. I'm talking as horrific as you can. Go deep down into your subconscious for things you've tried to forget. Imagine it even worse."

"Interesting." The stiffness is gone for now, but I'll be testing that theory later.

Mom used to say God puts people in our lives for a reason. I'm not a churchgoer or even religious, but the day I met Alpha does seem too perfectly awesome to dismiss as luck.

Who would've thought that I would walk into the

perfect gym, owned and run by the biggest guy in Florida? Or that I could've scored gear on my first try, from the same bro?

If this happened by luck, I'm the luckiest guy of all time.

Minus, of course, my first seventeen years of scrawny chumpiness. My luck began when I decided to fix my appearance. Ricky might have inspired that, sure, but I'm still going to fuck him up when school starts.

My phone vibrates in my pocket. It's a text from Karina: *where r u?*

"Fuck! I forgot Karina was coming over." I text back that I'm on my way. I'm not too crazy about seeing her. All I wanted was to go home, down my post-workout shake, eat a meal, and relax so my muscles can grow.

"A minute ago you were talking about excess horniness," Alpha says, "and now you got a girl waiting for you at home."

I explain that Karina isn't down with hooking up at my house—she's too worried about my family coming home.

"And at her house it's impossible because her grandma came from Puerto Rico to visit for the summer."

"Karina is Puerto Rican?" Alpha asks. "I thought you were Mexican."

Years ago I accepted that I gotta hear dumb things from white people sometimes, and explain basic race and ethnic stuff to them. It doesn't mean it's not annoying though.

"You thought she was Mexican just because I'm Mexican?"

"No," he says. "I mean, yeah, okay. I assumed she was Mexican because you are."

"Karina could be a white girl from Sweden too, you know. Any girl can be named Karina."

"Okay, you've made your point."

"The law recently changed, and we Mexicans can now date non-Mexicans," I say, my voice thick with sarcasm. "Tell your people to hide their girlfriends and daughters."

He laughs. "Good one."

We're at the four-way stop sign, a few blocks from my house. Salsa music and the scent of grilled meat is coming from a backyard. "Is that Mexican or Puerto Rican music?"

His face shows genuine interest. He's not being funny.

"Salsa music is a bunch of different sounds from a few Latin American countries," I say. "So it's sort of from everywhere, even though it was born in New York City."

He chuckles and glances at me. "You're fucking with me, right?"

I shake my head.

"That's cool," he says. After a pause he asks, "But all Latinos speak Mexican, right?"

"Speak Mexican?" I shoot him a look. "Are you fucking with me?"

"Yeah, take it easy," he says, laughing. Then he adds, "Go, man."

He's talking to the driver to our left, because it's his turn on the four-way stop sign.

Alpha gestures for the driver to go.

"This happens all the time," Alpha says. "Some people are terrified of me and act extra nice."

"What do you mean?"

"Like this morning when I went to pay for gas. The guy coming outta the store held the door open for me even though I was pretty far away. As if he let it close I'd beat him up or eat him or something."

I laugh, but Alpha isn't laughing.

He now drives past the stop sign himself. "They treat me like some kind of monster. Last week when I went to the DMV, the guy behind the desk said, 'Please don't hurt me!' as a joke and put his hands up like he was afraid."

I laugh hard at that.

"Yeah, okay," Alpha says. "Not a bad joke, but it's not funny when it happens all the time. It sucks when people treat you differently because of how you look."

Now *I* feel bad. Because I sort of thought Alpha was goofy-looking before, and I've even made fun of bodybuilders. Not to their face or anything, but still. I guess it's no different than making fun of people for being skinny or fat.

"It's discrimination," I say, realizing this out loud. "Even though you can stop being so muscular if you want to."

"That's right. It's fucked up."

Then, as if he's ashamed for talking about how he feels,

he changes the subject. "So if you aren't hooking up with your girlfriend, why not break it off? Soon you'll have more girls than you'll know what to do with."

There aren't enough hours in the day to explain why Karina is the greatest thing that has ever happened to me.

I remember the constant loneliness, all those crushes that led to nothing. I used to get so sad that I'd lie on my bed wondering if love was something that I wasn't born to have.

Then I met a great girl who proved to be more amazing than I knew. She's handled this whole video crisis so well. She keeps checking up on me, still has my back. Doesn't care that I'm the joke of the school.

I snap out of my daze to say "Karina is a great girl" and realize we're here, parked behind her mom's white Tercel.

I turn to see . . . Karina is not on the porch. And my dad's Pathfinder is in the driveway. Fuck! What's going on? I was supposed to have an hour of chill time, at least, before Dad and Gaby came home.

I know how Dad's mind works. If he sees me with Captain Steroids, I'll be guilty by association. This one time at the supermarket I said hi to Malik from history class. Dad took one look at his nose piercing and asked me, "You actually think a nose piercing is cool?"

I unbuckle my seat belt. "Thanks, Alpha."

He needs to get the hell outta here before Dad spots him.

I hop out and lightly close the Jeep door—not much noise at all.

"Your dad is big for a regular guy," Alpha says.

A chill runs through me. Oh no.

"Does he train?"

I look at the house. There's Dad in the window, his face showing no expression.

No sense in rushing inside now. Which would be suspicious.

"No," I tell Alpha. "He's just naturally big."

"One of those guys," Alpha says, smiling knowingly. "Um . . . your dad is still staring."

Alpha waves. Dad, the weirdo, stares a few more seconds before waving back. Doesn't even smile.

Gaby appears in the window. Her bottom lip drops at what she sees. A moment later Karina joins them and has enough tact to smile and wave.

"Is that Karina?" Alpha asks, waving back.

"Yep."

"Cute girl."

"I'd better go," I say, my heart thumping with fear.

14

SO THAT'S the famous Alpha," Dad says when I walk in.

I mentioned Alpha once, for fuck's sake. Twice, actually, but still. I don't know if my dad is sort of psychic or sort of psycho.

I give Karina a quick kiss. Gaby, who smells like chlorine, puts up a hand to get a high five. She still thinks I'm boring lately, but I guess she's in a good mood after a fun Sunday. Plus her friend Karina is here.

"Yep, that's Alpha," I tell Dad, responding in Spanish.

Gaby stands in front of me, blocking my way to the kitchen. "Why does he look like a superhero? I've never seen muscles that big."

Dad sticks his elbows out, pretending he's super jacked. "I eat much food," he says, walking around all rigid. "I grow big muscles."

His biggest fan, Gaby, cracks up. Karina is about to

until she looks at me and sees I'm not laughing.

The truth is the stiff movements resemble a robot. Not funny. Especially after what Alpha told me about people treating him like either a big threat or a big joke.

And lately with Dad, *everything* about my lifestyle is open to ridicule. My daily trips to the gym and my frequent trips to the kitchen. He nearly busted a gut when he walked in on me—forgetting to knock—and saw me "looking at men in underwear," as he put it. I was actually watching the documentary about pro bodybuilding called *Generation Iron*.

Now he's starting on Alpha. Who's *not* my friend, as far as Dad is concerned. I gotta remember that. Alpha is not my friend. He's just the trainer at the gym.

"Chila made you a plate," he says. "I left it on the stove in case you wanna take a break from your muscle man food."

"Karina brought brownies!" Gaby announces.

Dad puts a finger over his lips and tells her, "More for us if he doesn't eat them."

"I'm going to make my shake," I say, and tell Karina to give me a minute.

She sits on the carpet in front of Gaby to play hand games.

The kitchen smells of chiles rellenos and tortillas. There's the plate, covered in aluminum foil. I don't even wanna look at the brownies, but of course I notice the container.

And there I am in the toaster, my reflection clear in the shiny surface. I take a step toward it. Check out my shoulders from the front and sides.

You're small. Going down in size just like Crockett. All that work you've done is for nothing.

I shake this idea away, and switch on the logical part of my brain. Can I even trust this reflection? It might be slightly curved, giving me the opposite effect of a car window.

The measuring tape is rolled up tight in my pocket. I wanna measure my arms and shoulders to make sure I'm not crazy. But I also need to enter my sets and reps on my latest workout into my data spreadsheet, before I forget. Not to mention I gotta make my post-workout shake and entertain Karina.

I'll start with my shake, as planned. I grab the tub of protein powder from the top of the fridge.

My two favorite girls slap hands and clap, singing.

The sailor went to sea, sea, sea,

To see what he could see, see, see . . .

Time to feed the muscles. I put a heaping scoop of protein into the blender, along with a teaspoon each of glutamine and creatine, with two cups of water.

I press the last button on the ancient blender and

wait, staring at my forearm. I look at both of my forearms. They've gotten thicker, I guess, though more vascularity— veins pushing out the skin—would be nice.

Although my forearms are among the least important parts of my body, I'm forever thinking about them because they're always right there, in my line of vision.

After the shake gets mixed up frothy I shut off the blender. Dad has crept up without me noticing. He picks up the tub of protein, studying the bodybuilder flexing on the label. I'm on guard, ready for whatever he comes at me with.

"Alpha is bigger than this guy."

"I don't think so," I lie.

Alpha *is* bigger than the guy on this cheap-ass protein powder, which is why he'll be on a tub like this soon. He recently got a sponsorship deal with the supplement company BeastMax Nutrition. When he gets his fat check, he plans to fix up the gym.

"We used to laugh at those muscle guys," Dad says. "Remember?"

Why does he gotta be so irritating? Always asking questions he knows the answers to. Yes, I remember. Last year on Clearwater beach we saw a group of bodybuilders with girls, all of them slicked up with lotion, gleaming in the sun.

Sure, I laughed. That was back when I was skinny and stupid and probably jealous. I know better now.

"I remember," I tell Dad, and guzzle the shake straight from the pitcher.

The quicker I can get it down, the better. If it weren't brownish and didn't say *chocolate* on the label, you'd have no idea what the flavor is supposed to be.

"You want to be like this now?" Dad sets down the tub. "You want muscles like that Alpha guy?"

Yeah, sort of, I think to myself. Definitely bigger than I am and bigger than I planned to be when I started on my goal. Fifty pounds of muscle instead of twenty-five would be nice. I was aiming way too low before.

"Muscles make the man," I say. "But no, I'm not trying to be a bodybuilder."

"You think muscles make you a man?"

Even before he shakes his head I know what's next— he's about to launch into a lecture. Here comes bullshit wisdom from a guy who never even finished high school. I feel a stirring of anger inside and tell myself to chill.

"Flaco," he says, "a real man—"

I cut him off. "Is honest, hardworking, and takes care of the people he loves. Does that sum it up?"

I just saved us both about a hundred hours. I swear, Dad should write a book called *How to Be an Average Chump* because his definition of "man" is way off.

Dad nods slowly. "You've been paying attention."

"Women do those same things," I point out, and watch his face fall.

Wow. That shut him up quick.

"What distinguishes us from women are *muscles*," I emphasize. "And as far as being manly, do you think the jerk from next door moved his car that time because you're honest and love your family?" I don't wait for an answer. "*No.* He saw how big you were and didn't wanna mess with you."

"You want to intimidate people? Is that why you go to the gym?"

"I just want respect. And to be left alone."

Like right now, I feel like adding. I'm sick of being treated like a clueless kid. There's a deep surge of heat in my chest and I don't wanna flip out. Alpha says you have to catch the rage before it catches you, and walk away. So it's time to leave.

I'm about to make my move when Dad lays his thick hand on my shoulder. *Ow.* The pain from a sensitive zit shoots all the way to the back of my head for a second.

The singing and clapping in the living room is still loud, but Dad lowers his voice to almost a whisper. "Your friend Alpha takes steroids. You know that, right?"

My heart starts beating in my throat. Dad has mentioned the one word I hoped he never would.

I won't repeat it. Instead, I'll focus on the *friend* part. I need to shut down this conversation for good.

"He's not my *friend*, Dad," I say, as if the idea is absurd. "He's just the trainer at the gym. Remember you told me not to hurt myself? Thanks to him, I know how to work out safely. He makes me use a belt when I squat so I don't hurt my back."

Problem averted, thanks to my quick thinking. I hope.

"Why were you in his car?"

"Because the gym is closed on Sunday evenings but he goes there to work out for an hour and invites anybody else who wants to train. I wanted to, so he picked me up."

I'm on a roll.

Dad squeezes the hell outta my shoulder now. It takes all I have not to wince or cry out in pain. It's actually a light squeeze, but damn do these zits hurt. There must be three dozen dotting the top of my back now.

Dad isn't trying to make me scream out in pain. The hand on the shoulder means a heart-to-heart talk. It means worry.

"I want you to be honest with me," he says in a hushed voice. And with a pointed look I feel all over.

Here comes the dreaded question. Looking away will make him more suspicious. But when I'm looking at him it's hard to lie. The most hardened criminals could fold in Dad's presence. No need for the good cop/bad cop routine. Just send in my soft-spoken Dad with his penetrating eyes.

"I'm always honest with you," I say.

"Are you taking steroids?"

"Of course not," I answer right away.

Too fast? Did I even register shock? I can do that now.

"Wow, Dad," I say, shaking my head. His hand slips off me when I go put the tub back on the fridge. "What kind of crazy question is that?"

With his hand off me, he can't feel me breaking out in a nervous sweat.

The girls in the living room crack up. Gaby says, "One more time!"

Dad has followed me. "People don't wake up one day and decide to do bad things. Sometimes you have a friend who does something and then you think, *Why not me?*"

I know he's making it easier for me to come clean. It's not going to happen. I'm unbreakable.

I force myself to meet Dad's gaze again.

"Alpha is not my friend and I'm not stupid," I say, my voice steady.

"I know you're not stupid, Flaco," he says, "but if you're making a mistake, you need to stop and think about—"

He's going to keep chipping away at me. And I'm going to keep smoldering until I erupt. I'd better get outta here.

I take a step before he says, "Wait," his hand gripping my shoulder from behind. "I'm not done talking to you."

I come to a dead stop. Fuck him for pulling me back like a dog on a leash. Fuck him for getting to decide when a conversation ends. I wanna scream, but instead I try to cool my blood by taking a deep pull of air.

I turn to him because I have to. He's in charge.

"What?" The question comes out harsher than I intended.

Dad moves closer, with a stare so hard it could crack a forty-five-pound plate. "Since when do you talk to me like that?"

I feel so awake right now. Alert to everything. To Dad's hand on my shoulder again, to his eyes, more penetrating than ever. But I'm not afraid. Dad isn't a hitter. When I was little Mom would sometimes bust out the chancla to discipline me. Dad only had his concrete stare. He'd call my name and grab ahold of the side of his belt. That one gesture, together with the hard eyes he's aiming at me now, was enough.

Now his face is inches from mine. The clenched jaw and wild eyes. The physical intimidation after saying size doesn't matter. What a hypocrite.

Not that I'm gonna point that out, which would only make things worse. I gotta get myself outta this situation.

"Sorry." I put all the feeling into that word I can muster.

"That Alpha guy is a bad influence on you." Dad says this with certainty. "From now on, you want to get exercise, you do it here at home or in the park. No more going to that gym."

"What?!"

The. Fuck.

He's *serious*. I watch him walk away, which means the conversation is over.

I'm steaming inside. My fists tighten and my imagination runs wild. How I'd love to punch him right in the back of his stupid head.

Fuck him.

Fuck the idea of some guy bossing me around just because I don't earn enough to go off and live on my own.

Fuck him for trying to control my life.

I'm going to the gym and there's nothing he can do to stop me.

"My dad's such an asshole," I tell Karina when we're in my room.

The door has to stay open—another rule my asshole dad made. Luckily, he's listening to the TV news loud and Gaby is in the shower.

Karina sits on the bed, her face a mask of horror. "Oh my God, David."

She loves my dad—I get it—and I've never said anything even close to that before. I sit on the chair.

"Dad says I'm not allowed to go back to the gym ever again."

"Why?" Karina asks.

"He was bossing me around and I sort of raised my voice, I guess."

I won't give her the details, especially about how he

asked me if I've taken steroids. No need to put ideas in her head.

I sit in my chair and consider how to change Dad's stubborn mind. Can't come up with anything.

"On days Gaby wants to go to work with him, I can slip out to the gym no problem," I say. "But what about the days Gaby stays home?"

I say it out loud just to think this through, not to get an answer. But a half second later I have the answer. Right in front of me. I'm *looking* at the answer.

My idea makes me smile.

"No way," Karina says. "Don't look at *me*."

"You like hanging out with Gaby. Plus whenever you're hanging out with friends or working, it's never in the mornings. It would be only for an hour and a half. Two hours tops."

"You're crazy."

"All you gotta do is pop in a movie for her. You know that Gaby takes cares of herself."

"David, I'm not conspiring with you to deceive your dad. Also, I didn't tell you, but I'm going to visit some family in Miami for two weeks. Not sure when yet, but my job is going to give me some time off."

Dammit. All I needed was for Karina to get on board. I can handle Gaby. We're great at keeping secrets from Dad, and she owes me one. A few weeks ago, she stained the couch cushion with a marker. I got out the stain the best I could, but the ghost of the red marker is still on the gray fabric. We flipped the cushion and kept the accident between us.

For extra-cool points I'll even buy her Sour Patch Kids or purple Nerds, her two favorite candies.

"I'm going to help you out, David, by being real with you." She's sitting stiff as a pole. "*You're* the one who's kind of acting like an asshole."

"Me?"

"Maybe you shouldn't yell at your dad and get grounded."

"Whose side are you on?"

"There are no *sides*. It's just that you've changed since you started going to the gym."

"What do you mean?"

"Well, you're different when I'm around, at least. All spacey and looking at your body. Who knows how you are with your dad."

"Yeah, maybe I'm super into gaining muscle, but it's just for the summer, you know?"

"Sure, fine. I'm trying to be understanding, but I'm just saying. It's like the stronger you get the more different you act. That's all."

Why didn't she say *bigger* instead of *stronger*? She's commented on my bigger size before.

She was being nice. That's why. Didn't want to make you feel bad. Because you're that skinny guy that you saw in the reflection of the toaster. No muscle at all.

So I get up to find out for myself. Look into the mirror, stunned by what I see. This morning I was big and now, even with a post-workout pump, I'm somehow smaller.

Except that makes no sense. Why would I be smaller? I flex as I wait for the logical part of my brain to take over. But I think the same thoughts that bum me out.

I'm about to reach into my pocket for the measuring tape when . . .

"Hello? Why are you staring at yourself?"

. . . I remember Karina is here.

Without realizing it, I've gotten up from the chair and walked three steps to the mirror. And flexed as if I were alone in this room.

I smile. She got me. "I guess my head is still at the gym."

She's standing close to me, her eyes as big as I've ever seen. "Oh my God. You see what I'm talking about? I swear, you've become obsessed with your body."

I take both her hands in mine, determined to change the subject. "Forget the gym, okay? I'm here now. My dad has my brain all jumbled up. I'm sorry. I'm here now."

"Okay," she says, all slow. Like she's giving in but doesn't want to.

"Just give me one minute. Just one. To enter the weight I've lifted today, plus the sets and reps, into my body-tracking chart."

"I understood maybe half of those words." She falls back onto the bed. "Do your weird muscle stuff and tell me when you're done."

I head back to the computer to enter today's numbers on the UndergroundMuscle website.

Her phone does that activated jingle, and I hear the popping sounds of messages received.

The numbers from my last back and bicep day are just as I remembered. Great! I went heavier for all my sets today. And if I'm getting stronger it means I'm getting bigger. That's a fact!

So I lift my arm to flex my bicep, certain that I'll now see it big—wait. I catch myself being weird and let my arm fall back down.

"I saw that slow-motion wing flap," Karina says, laughing. "What was that?"

"Nothing." I swivel in the chair to face her again.

Enough already, I decide. No more thinking about my body. Maybe Karina is right. It might be an obsession, and obsessions aren't good.

I forget my body and consider Karina's. Those black shorts are hiked up because her beautiful legs are crossed.

"You look so damn good, you know that?"

She drops her phone in her bag and smiles. "Thanks."

"If I play a reggaeton song," I joke, "will you shake it like the girls do in the videos?"

"Not going to happen," she says with a laugh.

"Half a song."

She's staring at me while she smiles. At least she's in a better mood.

"Okay, you drive a hard bargain. One quick booty shake and I'll never ask again." I stretch my arm toward her for a handshake. "Deal or no deal?"

She shakes her head slowly and even wags her finger for emphasis.

"Okay, okay," I say, giving up.

I feel myself getting hard. Time to test Alpha's advice.

The half-flattened cat by the side of the road last week.

How that stomach infection in Mexico made me vomit so hard that some ricocheted off the toilet water and onto my face.

The goriness seems to be working.

"Can we finally talk now, David?" she asks, sitting up again.

"About what?"

Her smile disappears and she's giving me an evil stare. What happened? It's like she hates me right now.

She gives her head a slow shake of disappointment.

"You have something important to tell me!" I say, suddenly remembering. "Sorry, my dad has my mind all messed up."

She texted me last night, wanting to talk. It's why she came over today. How could I forget that? I haven't thought about it since.

A boyfriend is supposed to remember planned talks

about serious issues. A boyfriend is supposed to ask her about it just as soon as his girlfriend shows up.

"What do you wanna talk about?" I ask her, all ears.

"Well, I already mentioned that you seem obsessed with your body," she says. "And it reminded me a little of how I was for a while back in middle school."

"What?"

"I was dieting and thinking of my body all the time. Hopping on the scale every day. Sometimes twice a day."

"I didn't know that."

"Luckily, my mom noticed and helped me deal with why I was feeling that way. And you should do the same thing. You have to try to stop being so obsessed about your body. You look fine."

"I'm not obsessed."

"Really?" She tilts her head at me. "I've seen you flexing your forearms and checking them out while I'm talking to you. A few minutes ago you were doing some sort of sleepwalking flexing in front of the mirror."

I laugh at that. Sometimes I laugh when I'm nervous.

"Okay, so I won't be so obsessed," I say. Because denying it won't help. She just witnessed me acting like a freak.

Though I don't see why being obsessed about achieving an important goal is a bad thing.

"You won't be so obsessed? Prove it." Karina reaches into her bag and pulls out a sandwich bag with two brownies.

"With brownies?"

"They're your favorite." She dangles the bag in front of me, like I'm a dog being offered a bone. I have way too much discipline for that.

"You have both," I say. "I'm good. Simple carbs, bad fats, and the lack of protein is not muscle fuel."

"I know that." She takes a square out, the surface glistening, and hands it to me. It's warm on my palm and smells so damn good. "But this is the point. It's not about *feeding the muscles* all the damn time. It's one brownie."

Maybe one small brownie would be fine. How many bad, non-anabolic calories could be in this thing?

Plus it would be rude to turn down something she made for me.

That's two reasons to eat this.

The truth is I'm grateful for any excuse to enjoy something delicious for a change. Brownies are the best.

I take a bite. Karina takes a bite of hers.

Wow. It's deliciously soft and chewy. Most importantly, it's actually chocolaty, unlike the sludge I drank in the kitchen.

"Mmm," Karina says, closing her eyes. "Doesn't this taste better than what you've been eating the last few weeks?"

"For sure," I say.

Yet I'm feeling bad about this. Like I'm destroying my gains by swallowing that bite.

My body is in an extra-high anabolic state post-workout,

and I'm feeding it mostly sugar?

But there's nothing to do now, with Karina watching and judging me. I try to enjoy it as best I can.

After we're done she leans over for a kiss. I meet her halfway and, even though I'm kind of worried Dad or Gaby might walk by, it's a long kiss I feel all over. Yes, especially down there.

I break away from the kiss and my brain searches for horrific images.

The Mexican earthquake on the news, the rubble covering those dead bodies.

The shiny, white-tipped zits on my back.

Her eyes narrow at the sight of something on my face. "Are those hairs?"

I go to the mirror on the wall, and move in really close.

Yep. Those are three thick hairs on my cheek.

Wow. The androgen effects of steroids. Or else they're the natural changes that were already underway. The ones that began with my growth spurt months ago.

I run a finger over the short bristles. "Yep. Three little hairs."

I turn to her and make my voice deep. Try to sound like Morgan Freeman with a cold. "Guess I gotta start shaving. I'm becoming a man."

"Mmm-hm." She looks me up and down. "You were always sort of cute, in a baby bird sort of way," she says, and laughs. "Now you're sort of hot, you know that?"

I laugh but she's serious. No smile at all.

I turn to check myself out again. I've always had a small waist. Now I have broader shoulders that give me that V-shape girls like.

Karina is right. I'm sort of becoming hot.

Sort of though, and nowhere near big enough. I can't wait to hit the gym tomorrow, for my next workout and injection.

15

Twenty-four days until school begins

AFTER A THIRD SET of dumbbell lat raises I got an intense pump going, my shoulders swelling with warmth. I guzzle water and notice I'm good on time. It's forty-two minutes into my workout and I'm more than halfway done.

With Gaby at home by herself I need to keep the gym visits to ninety minutes, max. I have a no-chatting rule to cut down on how long I spend here. It's easy to follow today since none of the gearheads are here and Alpha has gone home for something he forgot.

Just like the other two times I've left Gaby alone, I popped in a DVD before heading out the door. Told her I'd be back before the movie ended.

She's safe behind the locked front door. I don't worry about her using the stove or playing with knives or anything stupid. So why can't I stop thinking about her? There's some guilt for sure, the lie that we reestablish every day, the bribe I come home with in the form of candy, so I'm greeted with a big smile that makes most of my guilt disappear until the next time.

I watch the red second hand go around on the gym clock, buzzing with anticipation when my minute break has completed. Since Rassle took off, all I'm left with is two chumps working out. If you can call it working out.

One is around fifty and the other half that, both on different machines. Pathetic. Machines don't give you the full range of motion, don't build muscle like free weights and compound lifts. I mean, the guys are lean and all—at least they aren't fat—but it's obvious why they don't have impressive physiques. They don't exert themselves like me and the serious lifters.

The machines are here to attract those kinds of members. A gym for those driven to greatness wouldn't keep this business afloat. That's what Alpha says, so soon there will be even more useless equipment in here. Just as soon as the BeastMax sponsorship check comes and Alpha does the renovations.

More chump members are fine with me as long as they stay outta my way.

I bend down to grab the weight and stand up straight. *That which does not kill me makes me stronger.* The dumbbells touch just under my navel. I bring them up straight-armed to my sides, like a bird flapping its wings. Go through the whole set, rep by rep, squeezing at the top, really feeling my deltoids contract.

Your arms are small. Pencil thin.

I watch my reflection and wonder if that's true. Or maybe my shoulder pump is making my arms look small by contrast. Just as soon as I knock out the last rep I'm going to the bathroom to measure the circumference of my upper arms.

I groan with the final, eleventh rep, and let the weight drop to the rubber mats with a thud.

In the bathroom, I wrap the measuring tape around my arm. I confirm, yet again, that my arms are not shriveling.

Then my phone jingles with a received message. It's from Alpha: *Come over NOW.*

"What the hell happened?" I ask, looking around.

My first thought, looking at the half-empty house, is that somebody robbed this place. But then why are the TV and Blu-ray still there? They're sitting on the floor with the cords in a tangle. But the entertainment center has disappeared, along with the matching coffee table. A huge rectangle of lighter beige carpet highlights where the couch should be. The cushy brown recliner is still there. Same with the dining room table with all four chairs.

Nothing on the walls except for the large framed photo of Mindy and Alpha. She flashes perfect teeth, while square-jawed Alpha has that gap in his smile.

Alpha's in the kitchen, flipping five chicken breasts in a large pan.

"Can you believe it? Mindy left me while I was at work, bro." He shakes his head like he can't believe it himself. "She's probably heading to Tallahassee to stay with her parents or sister, and I gotta go after her. You're the only one I could call. The other guys are busy."

He sets down the spatula and hurries into the garage.

I pet Crockett, who's the chillest dog ever since the gear has worn off. He's even smaller than last time I saw him. He looks like the Rottweiler that nature intended, only sad.

"Your mom left, huh, buddy?"

It's clear now Mindy was dead serious about her ultimatum. Alpha didn't give up steroids so she gave up on him.

A thought occurs to me, so dark that I feel a pang of guilt. Sure, I feel bad for Alpha. I really do. Poor guy just got hit with a serious blow. That sucks. But I can't help thinking about how this might mess up my gains.

He'll make it to Tallahassee this evening, no question. But what if he doesn't come back by tomorrow? I'll miss an injection, and that can't happen. If he can't bring Mindy back right away, I'll miss *even more* injections.

That. Can't. Happen.

I hear Alpha moving and banging around in the garage.

A man chasing after the woman he loves would be

super romantic if only he left right away. Instead, Alpha is searching for something first.

And cooking. He doesn't trust restaurants. Says they claim to use olive oil when it's refined, unhealthy vegetable oil. That they also sneak in other ingredients so you can't know the actual macros of a meal.

Alpha comes back with a cooler large enough for a family. Or for one professional bodybuilder.

"She doesn't even want a baby any time soon," he says, setting it next to the fridge. "My sperm will be working fine by the time we're ready."

He moves toward the cupboards before deciding to open the fridge first. Alpha is a hot mess right now, unable to think, talk, and do at the same time.

"I've been all about bodybuilding since *before* I met her." He reaches in for the large tub of cottage cheese and drops it into the cooler. "What does she care that I'll be on gear for just one more year?" He drops two heads of broccoli in too, and a bag of carrots.

Alpha told his girlfriend "one more year" twice before, according to him, but I won't point out the obvious. That would be a total dick move.

I already feel like a dick, thinking more about my gains than about my friend's life collapsing.

Alpha walks over to the cooking pan and picks up the spatula. Then, as if remembering it needs a while longer, he goes back to the fridge. Takes the spatula with him.

I take it from him. "I'll keep an eye on the chicken."

"How could she do this to me?" he asks, going through the shelves. "I love her."

It's on me to be consoling, to say something that will cheer him up. All I can come up with are versions of *there are other fish in the sea*. Lame. Not helpful at all.

"That sucks, bro," I tell him.

Okay, so maybe I'm not the ideal friend during this kind of crisis. But I doubt the super-jacked squad from the gym could do any better.

"I'll get her to come back," he says, his voice too low to be convincing. He drops a bag of washed spinach into the cooler. "Hopefully soon. I don't wanna be away too long."

Yeah, I don't want that either. My gains! How will I get my injections?

I lift a chicken breast to check. Nope, still pale.

Alpha tosses me a set of keys. "Give those to Tower for me, because he'll be handling everything at the gym. I need your help for something else. Can you come by to walk Crockett at least once a day and feed him?" He shows me where the leash and dog food is. "I ask because you live close by and have more time than the others."

"I got you, bro," I say.

I turn off the burner and set the sizzling pan aside.

Alpha looks directly at me for the first time since I

walked in. "That only leaves one thing." He's grinning now, which is weird.

"What's that?"

"I gotta teach you how to self-inject."

Part of me is like, *Great! My progress will continue!* Another part is like, *Nooooo!*

I've injected Alpha's biceps with Synthol on three occasions. But just because I can handle a syringe doesn't mean I'm down with stabbing myself with an inch-and-a-half needle.

We go to Alpha's bedroom, where there's a full-length mirror. It looks burglarized in here too. The open closet doors reveal mostly empty space. Mindy must have taken the dresser. Alpha's folded clothes sit stacked on the bed. I see the tapered T-shirts he special orders from a bodybuilding website so the shoulders are 4XL but the waist is small.

He hands me the rubber-stopped bottle and syringe. "Load it up, bro. This is what distinguishes you from average chumps. You can do this."

I fill it, flick it, and press on the plunger so that only one drop leaks out. These injections are what make me feel more like a man than anything else, so why am I shaking like a little boy? I take in a huge breath, as if the extra oxygen contains the courage I need.

"So how do I hold it?" I ask Alpha.

He moves my arm behind me like I'm getting arrested. The needle points at the glute. "Your thumb on the plunger like that. See?"

I tug my shorts and underwear down to reveal my right ass cheek. The syringe is pretty much horizontal.

I'm holding it *behind* me and have to stab *forward*. This is going to require some serious hand-eye coordination. Step one is getting my hand to stop trembling.

Alpha snickers. "Chill out, bro. Don't mess up and shove it up your ass."

He sits on the bed for a front-seat view of my anxiety. The only way he could enjoy this more is if he were munching on popcorn.

"I'm glad this is entertaining for you," I tell him. "Glad to cheer you up."

"It's a rite of passage. You had to learn eventually."

I side-look into the mirror, syringe ready. *Your arm is so skinny.*

Now is not the time. I focus and take a deep breath and tell myself it's just like all the other times I've gotten injected. The easy part is popping in the needle. Just pop it in, dammit. *Do* it. You're a man.

My hand trembles less.

"Aim toward the middle of the cheek," Alpha reminds me with a chuckle. "Do you need me to draw a target?"

I give him the finger with my free hand, which makes him laugh more.

I take another deep breath and, so as not to overthink it, jab the needle in.

"Ohmygod, ohmygod, ohmygod." I wanna pull the needle out so badly. No. I have to inject. This is crazy! What the fuck! Ow!

It's hurting bad for some reason. Even though I'm not pushing in the liquid yet.

"You have the syringe at a slant, dumbass!"

When I straighten it the pain subsides. Then I push the plunger down. As fast as I can to get this over with.

"Slowly!" Alpha says, and laughs so hard he leans back, knocking over a stack of T-shirts.

As my right glute burns extra hot, I pull out the needle and press a tissue against the dot of red forming. Why did they used to call steroids *juice*? More like acid.

I pull up my shorts and try to walk off the pain.

After that mishap with the angle, the burn I've gotten used to doesn't feel too great.

I catch my arms in the mirror again. Where are the gains I've made? How is that skinny fuck in the mirror ever going to get respect from the world or revenge on Ricky?

Maybe Karina is right. I'm obsessed with my body. Maybe that obsession is driving me crazy.

Alpha starts packing. He grabs a random stack of T-shirts and shoves them inside a duffel bag. Everything this guy does looks like he's flexing. Those slabs of muscles contract and shift and elongate with every move. His arms, stretching out his short sleeves, look bigger than my legs.

How cool it would be to look like that. If I did, I wouldn't worry about looking too small. That idea would never cross my mind.

"This is going to sound crazy," I say, "but sometimes I see myself as small. Like *really* small. Smaller than a week ago or even smaller than before I started training."

He stops packing socks to look at me. I warned him it was going to sound crazy. Now he's going to think I'm a madman and ask for his keys back. Won't trust me with his house or Crockett anymore.

"Crazy?" he asks. "That's normal for true champs, bro."

"Normal? For real?"

"Sometimes I think that way too. If you're satisfied with how you look, you stop trying to get bigger."

He zips the bag and takes it out to the living room. I consider those words. He's basically saying that never being satisfied helps you achieve your goals.

Do rich people become richer by being dissatisfied with the money they have? Maybe. But I doubt they feel *poor*. What about athletes? Do they gotta believe they suck at a sport in order to improve?

Something about Alpha's words don't make sense.

I head out to the living room, where he calls Crockett's name and bends over. "Who's my boy?" he says, using his baby-talking voice. "Who's my best boy in the entire world?"

Crockett's tail wags.

Alpha gets down on both knees to receive licks on his face. "I'm going to miss my best boy."

I'm witnessing, yet again, one of the greatest things about being huge. Something Alpha and the other guys never mention. If you're jacked, you can be yourself all the time without the risk that people see you as less than a man. No need to constantly prove yourself to be a man by doing scary or stupid stuff.

I think of the great lengths I've gone through to prove myself over the years. The tree I climbed, despite my fear of heights, when I was twelve. The snail I stomped on when I was ten. God, how I hate that memory, the gooey insides of that creature splatted on the sidewalk. All so the neighborhood boys wouldn't call me a girl.

This constant manly act is why I wouldn't tell any-body, not even Miguel, about how many hours I used to spend with my mom in the kitchen. It's why I won't take an umbrella to school on a rainy day, even though we have two at home.

Alpha can baby-talk a dog or take pictures of sunsets and post them on Instagram. He could probably suck on a lollipop while skipping down the street—if he were allowed to eat sweets.

Crazy how being unnaturally big lets you be natural in other ways.

16

Twenty-one days until school begins

WHAT ARE YOU UP TO? Karina's text reads.

She's been texting from Miami as much as she did when she was here. I text her back that I'm at the gym, that I'll text her later.

It's a lonely feeling for me, I gotta admit, to only share the bare facts of my life, where I am and what I'm doing. I used to tell her everything and now I have to hide what's become the most important part of my life—everything related to gear and what it's doing to me.

I put the phone away and strap on the weight belt for legs day, still feeling soreness in my chest and arms as I buckle it tight. I love the pain in my muscles, how every workout lingers for days.

Tower also puts on his weight belt. He's wearing pants, as usual, to cover up his nonexistent calves. They're strong as hell from doing calf raises with a ton of weight, but he's got that common curse. Some calves don't grow no matter how much you train them.

He has an appointment for implant surgery though, and will be wearing shorts by the end of the summer.

Gaby is with Dad today so I don't gotta worry about getting home in a big hurry. Don't have to worry or feel guilty at all for lying to Dad, who actually trusts me. He believes I'm doing push-ups and other calisthenics in the living room.

After Tower finishes his warm-up set, I do my twenty warm-up squats.

"Let's do this," Tower says.

We load up the bar for his first real turn. Slide three big plates on either side.

"Where's the vomit bucket?" I ask him. "Or do you plan on throwing up right here on the floor?"

I love being able to tease a guy as big as him without getting snapped in half.

"I finished my cycle, Little Man." He slides a plate on his side. "Not that vomit would make this place much dirtier than it already is," he adds with a laugh.

The floors do need a good sweeping and mopping. Alpha has been too bummed to do any cleaning around here. He got back the day after he left. Without Mindy.

Tower motions to reception with his bandana-wrapped head. "The guy's a wreck."

Alpha is at his laptop but not looking at it. His head is tilted up at the ceiling. He's spaced out all the time now. Even when he's walking around, giving somebody a spot or chatting people up, he's not all there.

I never imagined that Mindy not coming back would mess up a tough guy like Alpha so bad. I'll hang back after my workout to get this place in order. Help Alpha out.

I tell Tower, "He'll be getting that forty-five thousand bucks from BeastMax Nutrition soon."

"Money will cheer him up. Getting this place looking nice should cheer him up even more." He enters the squat rack, back in lifting mode. "It's go time."

He gets under the barbell, all energy. We're not going to let a sad friend keep us from going hard as fuck in our workouts.

"How many reps last time?" I ask.

"Ten."

Since he's working with the same weight, today he needs to do more reps.

At least thirteen or fourteen.

His legs tremble with the seventh rep and he lets out a tiny groan. What the hell?

Maybe he didn't sleep or eat well yesterday. I move in closer. Just in case.

He groans and winces with number eight.

"That weight ain't shit!" I shout. "You got this!"

Except he doesn't got this. On the eighth rep he stalls halfway, knees bent.

"Aaargh," he lets out as his whole body trembles.

I hug him tight from behind and squat with him. Up we go. Then I move him forward and help him rack the weight.

He does the post-squat pacing to get his heart rate back to normal, hands on his hips. The largest muscle groups on the body are the glutes, hams, and quads, and you work all three with squats.

"What happened?" I ask him.

"Happens every time," he says when he's somewhat recovered. He takes a plate off his side. "It's that fucking off-cycle loss."

I hold the plate on my side. "What loss?"

"I told you, bro. I'm cycling off for a month," he says, taking off another plate. "It's your go. How many reps are you going for?"

There's a jerk in my chest, but I try not to panic. "So you're losing strength?"

He notices the uneven bar, how I haven't moved an inch, and steps away to get a better look at me.

"Wait." His eyebrows are up so high they're touching the bottom of his tight green bandana. "Do you think your steroid gains are maintainable?"

A paralyzing fear takes over me while my own heart is racing like I've knocked out a set of squats. I turn to look at

Alpha, who's still slumped in the corner. Did he trick me or something?

I lock eyes with Tower again. "You telling me I don't keep my gains?"

"You keep *some*, sure. You drop maybe ten pounds of muscle during those weeks off gear."

"What?"

"But when you get back on, you recover your size, and gain much more."

"I'm not getting back on. It's just this one cycle."

Tower steps closer and speaks with a lower voice. "Are you serious? If you don't go on another gear cycle, you'll lose everything."

"Everything?" I repeat, trying to keep it down.

I don't care that Alpha's heartbroken. And a million times bigger than me. I so wanna punch him right now.

"Well, not *everything*," Tower clarifies. "You keep the muscle you would've gained naturally."

Which isn't big enough to be the new me. It wouldn't even make me big enough to kick Ricky's ass.

I look across the gym to Alpha again, and catch Rogelio in my periphery. He's doing crunches on a floor mat. I remember how he warned me, my first day here, to stay away from gear.

"Alpha!" I shout, and wave him over.

His eyes brighten. He hops up from the reception chair and makes his way here.

I'm about to get some answers. Either Tower is fucking with me, or he's full of shit, or . . . I don't wanna think of the other possibility.

"Wassup?" Alpha says.

Tower looks at the floor like a kid in trouble, while I tell Alpha everything I've heard.

Alpha speaks with calm. "Some of the weight loss is water weight."

That's his fucking response?

"True," Tower throws in, excited to be positive about something.

"The *point*," I say, "is that I'll lose my gains if I stop doing gear cycles. Yes or no?"

Alpha looks away and does this weird shrug, palms facing up. "Why do you only wanna do one cycle though?"

How I wish I could body slam Alpha right here. Or lift one of those benches and hurl it at least, to release all this pent-up anger. How I wish these average chumps weren't here so I could at least scream.

There's all this red-hot energy in me trying to get out and I gotta be chill, concerned with not making a scene.

I mean, how the fuck can I go back to being Bitchslap when my cycle is over?

"You know I wanted to do only one cycle. It makes no sense to do a cycle if the gains aren't permanent."

I say this with a tight jaw, careful not to raise my voice.

"Besides," I add, "I'm not rolling in money."

More importantly, I'm not so stupid that I'd take steroids again and again. But I'd be an idiot to call the two biggest guys I know *idiots*.

"Friends get a hookup," Alpha says, giving me two thumbs-up. "You'll get your next gear cycle at cost. That's a promise."

I close my eyes and take a deep breath so I don't kill him. Then another, deeper breath.

I open my eyes. Nope. I still wanna kill him. That he's still holding his thumbs up makes me wanna do it all slow, with torture devices so he suffers as much as possible.

"I need to clear my head," I say, walking past him.

I head out the door and into the sunny day. When the door closes behind me, I let out a scream so loud my own dad might hear it three miles away.

I felt dumb as a brick when I found out Van Nelson's gains weren't natural. Now I'm that same clueless kid all over again. I dig into my pocket for my phone, wondering what the actor looks like now. Narrow my search to the last month.

In one picture Van Nelson is smiling and flashing a peace sign for TMZ. No longer jacked under that sharp gray suit.

In another picture, from the Ellen show, he sits at a slant just like the hostess he's talking to. You can see he's lost the heft in his arms, the short sleeves of his shirt loose around them.

Unfuckingbelievable.

After playing the most badass action hero of all time, he's back to looking like an average chump.

How could I be so stupid to believe I'd keep my steroid gains? You stop downing beers and eventually you're no longer drunk. You stop hitting the weed and hours later you're no longer high.

I pace, angry with myself. Angry at Alpha too. I had to hurry outta the gym so I didn't shout at him, *Why the fuck didn't you tell me the truth before?*

Now I gotta put a question to myself: Would it have mattered?

Since the beginning I vowed to do whatever it takes. *This*, apparently, is what it takes. First, a gear cycle to get big enough for the start of school. Then, after five weeks of cycling off, another cycle to recover the lost pounds.

So I don't shrink before school ends I'll have to do, let's see . . . three more cycles. Maybe two and a half.

I don't like the idea of showing up to college all scrawny. So maybe another tiny cycle? The point is I'll eventually wean off the gear. I'm not doing it forever.

What's a year or two on gear? Alpha, Tower, and the others have been on it for way longer and they're fine.

The alternative is going back to being Bitchslap David, which is unacceptable.

I push through the door into the gym and head to the squat rack to do my first real set. I get under the barbell and push up, the weight heavy across my upper back.

Then I lower it, going deep, my ass nearly touching the back of my heels as Tower begins to count.

Last time I did eight so it's twelve reps today—no fucking excuses. I'm still gaining strength instead of losing.

17

Nineteen days until school begins

IT'S PAST SEVEN when I'm driving on my way home from the supermarket. I'd better get used to the puttering sound of this Pathfinder, and to asking Dad to borrow it every time I wanna go out. Any money I make is going into the next-cycle fund.

The moment Dad got home today he gave me the car keys, some money, and the shopping list. Said he wasn't feeling well.

I guessed right that the supermarket would be packed. The rush hour crowd filled several checkouts, each line at least three carts deep. I kept my hood down. Nobody showed a shock of recognition.

I may retire the hoodie soon. The gym guys all say I'm unrecognizable now. Not just because of my bigger size, how I've grown into my oversized head. It's because of my new scraggly beard, which I keep trimmed neatly.

Dad, Gaby, Karina, and the guys at the gym have all commented on the change.

That puts some confidence in my walk. Other times I see myself as not big enough, nowhere near as big as I could be, and it brings me down. That champ mentality is still at work.

When I pull up to the driveway, I call Karina to tell her the bad news that we can't hang out tonight. We haven't been hanging out anyway, since I've been busy with my muscle gains and she's been busy with her friends and volunteering.

"Listen, Karina," I say. "My dad is feeling sick so I can't hang out. I'm going to hold things down at home, okay?"

"That sucks. I was looking forward to seeing you."

She tells me to take good care of him, and mentions Universal Studios. "We've decided to go the weekend before school starts."

Miguel is still excited about Universal Studios too. He mentioned it when he emailed me and sent pics of historic Santo Domingo.

"Sounds good to me," I say, but I don't wanna spend money on that anymore.

In fact, it seems so childish to me now, visiting a theme park. Just like the video games I haven't played. Maybe I've grown more than just muscles and a beard.

I come through the front door with six shopping bags. "Hey, Gaby."

Three bags in each hand when this would've taken me at least two trips at the start of summer. I'm so baller.

Gaby doesn't raise her eyes from her My Little Pony coloring book or say a word.

It's quiet in here, the TV black and silent, which is weird for the evening. If Dad isn't watching the news he must be resting in bed.

"We'll hang out just as soon as I put these groceries away," I say, heading to the kitchen. "Whatever you want."

I start with the refrigerated items.

"Jenga?" I ask her. "Memory? Pickup sticks?"

Not a word from her. She doesn't look up either. The crayon in her fist just wiggles faster. What crawled up her butt? We were cool before I left.

I close the fridge door and grab the two big cans of sardines. Dad likes to eat them with hot sauce and those flavorless Goya crackers. When I walk over to the cupboards I notice a square of light spread against the hallway wall—that can only be coming from my room.

A cold panic hits me when I think of my stash. But Dad can't suspect anything. Besides, the gear is well hidden in the pocket of a jacket hanging in the back, the thick one I only wear two weeks out of the year, if at all.

No parent, nobody at all, would ever think to search the pockets of clothes.

Dad must be on WebMD since I have the only computer in the house. Anytime his stomach feels funny or he starts coughing he wants to get on that site. A terrible idea. That site will get you thinking you have pancreatic cancer or tuberculosis when it's just indigestion or bronchitis.

I put away my big bag of oatmeal and two bags of brown rice.

Dad won't come across *my* favorite websites. I browse in private mode. Still it's annoying to have him in there without me knowing. I mean, sure, get on WebMD if you want, pop into my room to use the computer, but what about respecting my privacy? He should've asked is all I'm saying.

Wait a sec. How long does it take to check symptoms on WebMD? A couple of minutes?

I leave the groceries and walk to the living room. "Gaby? How long has Dad been in my room?"

She shrugs without looking up.

I walk to where she's sitting, and stand over her. "Has Dad been asking you questions?"

She drops her head so low I can't see her eyes. She has stopped coloring to grab a pink crayon. Then she drops it to grab a yellow one instead.

If it takes two minutes to get a diagnosis from the website, what else has he been doing in my room?

"Gaby? What's going on?"

"He kept asking me," she says, in that creaky voice that means tears will soon follow.

Since she refuses to look up, I lower myself to the floor

so that we're almost eye level. "What did he ask you?"

"Doña Carmen told him." It comes out high-pitched, and a teardrop streaks down to her chin. "He kept asking me, David. I didn't—it's not my fault, okay? He kept asking me."

My hearts pounds so hard I feel it in my ears.

Why doesn't Doña Carmen from across the street mind her own fucking business? She used to take care of us back in the day, but nobody needs her anymore.

I'm grounded for life. Whether or not Dad has found the gear, leaving Gaby alone is a million times worse than anything I've ever done. And what if he *did* find my stash? He'll take it from me and won't give it back and it's good-bye gains and hello Bitchslap. I'll lose everything I've been working for.

I take a deep breath and head into my bedroom.

It's chaos. Dresser and nightstand drawers yanked open. Clothes spilled out or on the floor. The closet doors are also wide open but the clothes inside are still hanging. I tell myself that's good.

There he is, sitting on my chair and looking at my monitor like he belongs here.

My worry turns to simmering anger.

"Why did you go through my stuff?" It comes out more sharply than I intended. And in English. I tell myself to get a grip. Talk to Dad in a calm voice and in Spanish.

He turns his gaze from the computer screen—some Google results there—and locks wild eyes with me. He rises from the chair. Slowly as usual because of his bad back. He walks over.

"*My* stuff," he says in Spanish. Taps his chest twice with a finger. "My bedroom, my computer, my house, my *everything.*"

He tells me to close the door so I do.

"You've been leaving your little sister all alone at the house. Doña Carmen told me, so don't even try to say—"

"To go to the gym," I say, cutting him off. "And I'm going to keep going. I'm going to the gym no matter what you say!"

These words just rip outta me.

His eyes get rounder than I've ever seen, anger flashing in them. "You want to yell at your father now? Yeah, I know all about it. I've been reading about how the drugs make you angry."

"Drugs?" I ask, and move toward the computer screen.

He steps in my way but I can see symptoms listed on the screen. Symptoms of steroid use.

I start sweating like when I bike to the gym.

"What are you talking about?" I say as calmly as I can.

He points to the bed. "Shut up, sit your ass down, and listen to me!"

The cursing is a first. It shocks sense into me. I do what he says. Getting angry won't help me one bit.

"I wouldn't take drugs," I say, maintaining my calm. "Why do you—"

"I told you to SHUT UP!"

It's the loudest he's ever yelled at me. What he does next is even more shocking. It leaves me dumb and breathless.

He picks up my stash from the desk, which I didn't see because the stack of DVDs on the end was blocking it. The small plastic bag with the Suspension, D-bol, and three syringes. I jump up and grab for it. He swings it away.

"You're taking drugs," he says, dropping his voice on the last word. "Bringing this garbage into the house."

"They aren't *drugs*," I say, standing right here. I'm getting that bag. Just as soon as I have a chance I'm snatching it. "Steroids are just hormones our bodies already produce."

He leaves the bag next to the keyboard and takes a step toward me, closing the space between us. It blocks my view of the entire desk.

"I knew something wasn't right," he says, containing his anger. "That gym and that new friend? You wanted space and privacy, and look at what happened. A bunch of gringo bullshit."

"Dad, you don't understand. Just listen to me," I plead. "Hear me out and you'll get it."

I struggle to form some kind of explanation in my head, but all I can think about is that small bag behind him. Which is mine. Not his. Which he has no fucking right to keep from me. He doesn't even have my permission to be in this room, for fuck's sake.

The fury and desperation is so big it's not even inside me. It's all around me, in this room. I'm stewing in it. It takes effort to focus on Dad and what he's saying.

He puts a hand on my shoulder. "You'll be okay, mijo," he says with determination. "We're going to get rid of the drugs and get you some help for your drug addiction."

The words *get rid of* hit me hard, and the last ones, *drug addiction*, hit me harder. There's no way he'll hear me out and no way he's getting rid of what's mine. The rage swoops me up.

I shove him aside as hard as I can to clear a path for the bag. I take my first step toward it, already stretching out a hand to grab it.

His arm blocks me. Somehow he's back. He snatches the bag from the desk and shoves me with one hand. I fly backward onto the bed like a doll.

"You crazy drug addict!" he says. "Putting your hands on your own father!"

My heart still racing, I push myself up into a sitting position.

His wide and thick body, those arms that can shove the whole weight of me away. I don't care. I vowed to never let anybody fuck with me again. That goes especially for somebody who has what's mine.

I don't know if the room shrinks or if it's the fury growing. It's too much though, completely overtaking me. In a flash I'm up again. I rush at him, gripping his shirtfront with my fists, and keep rushing. I slam him against the wall. He lets out a pained groan and slides down the wall.

I bend down to pick up the bag. As Dad groans, I check the bottle of Suspension—it didn't crack. The tablets of D-bol are still there too.

I turn to Dad, who's writhing on the floor. My relief turns to fear. What have I done?

The door opens. Gaby's face is wet with tears. She must've heard everything and now she sees what it's come down to.

She sobs and hurries to him. "Dad, what's wrong?"

The toughest man I know is wincing and groaning with pain because I've hurt him. It's the most terrifying noise I've ever heard.

As Gaby huddles with him, pleading with him to get up, I remember the stash in my hand. I gotta keep it safe. What if the cops are on their way? If our fighting was loud enough for nosy Doña Carmen to hear, that bitch might have called 911.

With no time to grab anything else, I hurry out to the backyard and roll my bike over to the gate. Swing it open and pedal outta there as fast as I can, down the street and toward Alpha's house, my brain heavy with what I've done and my heart pumping so fast it just might explode.

18

Eight days until school begins

SOMETIMES SOMETHING HORRIBLE happens that ends up leading to something pretty great.

Like half my life ago when Dad booted me out one extra-hot summer day and I ended up meeting Miguel.

Like how a slap across the face became a metaphorical kick in the ass, the push onto the path to greatness I needed.

Like leaving my dad's house and moving into a place that I can truly call home.

At Alpha's, there's nobody nagging or supervising or asking annoying questions. I don't gotta put up with teasing or snide remarks when I cook or heat up my muscle food. I don't gotta hide my stash or who I am.

I guess you don't realize how trapped you really were until you have freedom.

As I'm organizing my bedroom for my special visitor,

it's cool to know the room is mine. My desk. My bed. My everything.

The morning after I left Dad's house Alpha drove me by the auto shop to make sure Dad made it to work. He did. I felt ashamed about what I'd done, but it was a relief to know Dad wasn't in the hospital. And wasn't at home either. I went there to pick up all my stuff and the computer.

Dad reached out two days after the incident to ask if I was fine, if I needed anything. I responded with no, just that one word. I was still angry. Now I'm less angry and more guilty, feeling like I should apologize but not ready to do it just yet. My thoughts keep landing on how he tried to take what was mine and boss me around.

Gaby is caught up in the middle of this, which sucks. If nothing else, I have to make things right with Dad so I can see her.

Anyway, although my new life is without rules, I make my bed today and tuck in the corners all nice, to impress Karina, who's coming over for the first time.

I gather up the cup and plate from last night. That's something I could've never done at my dad's house, leave dishes unwashed overnight. I take them out to the kitchen.

"Karina should be here in about half an hour," I say. "She got back from Miami last night."

Alpha's on the recliner watching Netflix. Even though

it's late morning on a beautiful Sunday. Even though it's his birthday.

Day after day Alpha is either out here watching TV or heating up a meal, the only sounds being the drama coming from the TV and his fork scratching the plate.

Without moving his eyes from the big screen, he gives me a thumbs-up. "Cool."

And it is cool with him. That's freedom. I told him someone's coming, didn't ask for permission.

The house looks both better and worse since Mindy took off for good. On one hand, Alpha replaced the furniture. He bought it secondhand—and mismatched—when I went shopping for a bed in order to turn the office into my bedroom.

On the other hand, the place is a mess, which is all Alpha. There's a T-shirt of his on a dining room chair and another rumpled beside the recliner since who knows when.

"I was going to get that," Alpha says, barely moving his eyes from the screen.

It's not the first time I've cleaned up for him. I figure it's the least I can do since he's not charging me rent. He said I can stay as long as I like, that it's nice having me here.

I'm practically the only person he talks to all day. Besides going to the gym for a workout and to check on how the renovations are coming along, he doesn't leave the house. One of three newly hired trainers is covering what used to be his own shift during the day.

I work there evenings, as I'll continue to do when school starts again. I'm not giving advice or anything—just making sure people use proper form and don't get hurt. The money is consistent, unlike at the auto shop.

The coffee table is cluttered with dishes from two, three days ago. I gather them up—plates with crumbs and shriveled avocado skins. The bowls with bits of oatmeal hardened on the bottom.

I put them in the sink to soak. Then I cover Alpha's box of gear, put it on the fridge, and push it way back against the wall. Karina knows Alpha takes steroids—how could she not?—but I don't need her seeing them.

I gotta admit it's the first time in a while that I'm actually happy she's coming over. Not that it was a drag before. It's just that since the summer started, I haven't been excited to see her. It's like my goal takes up all my time, and my gains give me so much satisfaction, I don't need her like I used to.

Alpha has a point when he says the gym is enough. On most days it's enough. Even so he needs to get out and have fun. He's not hiding from the public like me, and moping around because he's heartsick over Mindy isn't doing him any good.

That's why Karina and I are gonna take him out to his favorite place, Patio Grill. I'm excited because I'm finally big enough to be a little bit in public, like a restaurant.

First though, Karina and I will be kicking it in my bedroom. I haven't seen her since I left Dad's house, and we haven't had sex since early May.

Okay, so that's probably the main reason I'm excited. That's easily the best thing about my newfound freedom.

A while later, with the house in order, there's a knock at the door followed by Crockett's excited barks.

Alpha surprises me by opening the door and introducing himself. "You must be Karina," he says, inviting her in.

"You must be the birthday boy," she says. "Happy birthday, Alpha."

"Thanks."

"Is that what you always go by or . . ."

"Yeah," he says. "Just Alpha."

I forget that his real name is Alfonso. Nobody ever calls him that.

"Let me give you the tour," I tell Karina.

I lead her to the kitchen, where the counters are cleared away, the sink empty and shining. I open the back door to show her the small yard, the big red Snoopy-like doghouse where Crockett sleeps unless it's a rainy night.

Then I lead her down the hall.

"And this is my bedroom," I say.

How strange to call it *my bedroom*. It still makes me think of Dad's house, which I try not to do. Though I'm glad I left, I'm not proud of what I did. I know I gotta make things right. I just don't wanna think about it for a while, and keep forcing it outta my head when the memory of that evening pops in there.

"Nice," Karina says, looking around.

The bright blue curtains were chosen by Mindy for what was the office, along with the wide desk, which still looks new. They're super nice and make the bed and dresser I bought look shabbier than it did at the garage sale.

My *Nightchaser* poster is up, next to the extra-large mirror I bought.

My action figures are on a shelf. I could give a damn about kid stuff like comics and superheroes anymore. I just like the bodies on those figures. Like the Van Nelson poster, they serve as a sort of inspiration.

Done looking around, Karina says, "It's sort of dark in here."

Yep, to get a mood going. I'll be closing the blinds completely and also shutting the curtains before we have sex. She can't see what non-awesome things the steroids have done to my body. My balls are still hiding and my back acne is still bubbling up.

She tells me about the Greyhound bus trip yesterday, and how much she's missed me. I tell her I've missed her too, even though the truth is I've been too busy to feel anything like that.

"So are we taking Alpha to lunch?" she asks, still standing, though she has the bed and a chair to choose from.

"We have time before lunch," I say, hoping she gets the hint.

"What do you want to do?" she asks, her face blank.

"Well, let's see," I say, pretending to think about it. I scratch my chin. "We could play Ping-Pong or we can have passionate sex in various positions."

Her eyes widen. "You have a Ping-Pong table?"

"Nope." I shrug. "Oh well. Sex it is."

She laughs. "Not with Alpha out there."

"Why?"

"He's going to know we had sex. Even if we just hang out in here alone for a while, he's going to *think* we had sex."

"What's the big deal?"

"So when we go to lunch, the whole time he's going to be thinking, 'Those two just had sex.'"

Karina crosses her arms, done with her explanation.

"You're crazy," I say. "You know that?"

As if to emphasize how serious she is, she pulls the cord of the blinds. "Much better."

The harsh light makes me squint. "You're completely outta your mind," I tell her.

I wanted to get Alpha out of the house for his own good. Now I'll need to get him out of the house for my own good.

Karina takes a seat on my chair. "So this is really where you live now? Like, for good?"

"Yep." I've already explained it to her, how I can't live with my dad's stupid rules.

"All because your dad won't let you go to the gym?"

"It's about me having my own life, Karina. My dad wanted to control it." It's the truth, though not the whole truth. She can't know what actually went down. "Besides, I was gonna be outta his house and living on my own in less than a year. My plans got moved up is all."

To change the subject I mention Universal Studios. "Did you figure out what time we're leaving on Saturday morning?"

Okay, so now I'm just flat-out bullshitting. Because I'm not going. That's money I can spend in better ways. I'll just invent a stomach virus or something the night before to get out of going.

The five of them can go without me and I'll see them all at school next Monday.

"Janelle says seven in the morning, on the dot, but you know how she is," Karina says. "We'll meet at her house, gas up, and then go."

I pat the bed and make a motion with my head for her to come over.

She does and I pull her in for a kiss. We start making out. Man, I want her so bad. For the first time since summer began, there's something more important than consuming five hundred calories every two and a half hours.

I hold her tighter. Just as it seems this might go

somewhere she breaks away from me.

"Let's go have lunch." Karina is on her feet, smiling.

I think of horribly graphic stuff in order to calm the stiffening down there. Maybe she'll change her mind when we get back from lunch.

We head out to the living room. I may never get used to Alpha's big size, those thick slabs of arms and how he fills up that large recliner.

That's what you should look like. Your body is nowhere near as impressive as that.

I shake that thought out of my head and focus on our goal at hand. Karina and I are getting Alpha out of that recliner and into the world. It will make him feel so much better.

Crockett is in his favorite spot, on the middle cushion of the couch. I sit on one side of him and Karina sits on the other.

Alpha pauses his show and hands me the remote. "You guys wanna watch something? I was just about to heat up some lunch."

"About that," I say. "We're taking you out to Patio Grill."

It's one of the few places he trusts. You see them grilling without adding oils or butter to your food.

"For your birthday," Karina adds.

"You can't say no," I say quickly, before he can protest.

I'm getting this guy outta this house. It's my duty as his friend.

At that moment the front door swings open.

Rassle comes in, orangey-red from the sun as usual, carrying a supermarket bag. His stringy tank top shows just how much bigger he's gotten with his cycle. There's the alligator tooth, still lodged on the side of his right bicep.

"Check it out, bitches!" He brings up each arm to kiss each bicep. "Twenty-two-inch arms!"

With how big those arms are, he barely raises them a few inches to plant his lips on them.

"Hell yeah!" Alpha shouts, getting up to greet him.

I feel a tingling of nervousness. Alpha likes to monitor all the guys he hooks up with gear, takes pride from their gains like he does with me. *He* won't mention steroids— the first and only rule of Gear Club is his, after all—but Rassle might let something slip.

They meet in the middle of the living room to hug like they just won a championship.

"Thanks to you, bro," Rassle says. "And be careful with the tooth, bitch." He heads into the kitchen.

"So that's a tooth in his arm?" Karina whispers to me.

What a relief that she's only curious about the second comment. "I'll explain later."

Jake comes in with a case of Bud Light in each hand. The gel in his parted hair is extra shiny this afternoon. His Superman T-shirt of the day is the original one—blue with the red-and-yellow *S* logo. "Happy birthday, bro."

"You too, man?" Alpha says, grinning from ear to ear. "Hell yeah!"

Since Jake's hands are busy he gives Alpha a hardcore chest bump. "Hey," he says to Karina and me with a nod on his way to the kitchen. "I'm going to keep these cold."

Karina leans over to say, "I don't remember Superman having a receding hairline."

Great, I think. The two guys who have come over to surprise Alpha are the biggest freaks we know. Why did Tower have to get his implants surgery last week and have to be at home resting? He's relatively normal, a family man who would've made a good impression on Karina.

Alpha makes a move to close the door when his eyes go round again. "Launchpad!"

Uh oh.

Mateo, better known as Launchpad, has no filter. Alpha has to remind the guy not to talk about gear at the gym or to keep his booming voice down, at least. At 6'1" and close to four hundred pounds, he's equal parts fat and muscular. Powerlifters like him are all about being strong as possible, not looking good.

He usually comes to the gym much later in the day, so I've only seen him a few times. "Happy birthday, Alpha," he says, as calm as he'd say hello to a store clerk.

Launch hugs Alpha, lifting him up in the air like nothing.

Please don't mention gear. Please don't mention gear.

Tower appears in the doorway, walking in slow motion. "Happy birthday, brother," he says.

He's in shorts for the first time and his new calves look amazing. All round and natural. At least from the side they do. He heads straight to the couch, wincing with pain. I move outta the way so he can collapse into it. The doctor said he'd need two weeks to fully recover and he's barely passed one week.

Alpha says, "You're supposed to be resting."

"I wouldn't miss your birthday for the world," he says.

He gives me a fist bump and says hi to Karina.

Alpha peeks outside before closing the door. I guess that's it. Four more people for Karina to meet instead of just Alpha. More possibility someone might let my secret loose.

Rassle comes back from the kitchen to offer Karina a handshake and introduces himself. "I meant to call the two guys bitches, not you," he clarifies in his southern accent.

"That's okay. I'm Karina." She glances at his right bicep before letting go of his hand. "What's that on your arm?"

"Aw this?" He looks at it. "A gator tooth."

He describes how the alligator got loose at this wrestling show in GatorWorld. How it slipped underwater for a second before coming back up to clamp the tip of its jaws on Rassle. The guy never tires of telling the story.

"Is that your pretty lady, Little Man?" Launch gives

me a fist bump before shaking Karina's hand too. "Nice to meet you, Karina. I'm Launchpad, or just plain Launch."

"Something tells me that's not what it says on your birth certificate."

He cracks a smile, showing a tiny gap between the top front teeth, and I know what's coming. An explanation. Why can't everybody leave their oddball stuff to themselves today? I'm trying to convince Karina that I'm fine, that my living arrangements are fine. That my gym and bodybuilding lifestyle is fine.

These guys are messing me up.

Launch tells that he got the nickname when he first worked as a bouncer in an Ybor nightclub.

"I used to literally throw out guys when they fought or were about to."

"What do you mean?" Karina asks, her face sort of scrunched. It's like she's unable to process all the weirdness. She was getting to know one monster gains guy, and three more showed up.

"I worked with him," Alpha announces, a big smile on his face. "He'd toss them into the air, usually by the back of their belts, so that they'd land in the middle of Seventh Avenue."

Launch laughs and pops open a beer. "Your gains are *sick*, David. Are you at the end of your cycle now?"

I ignore the pang of fear so I can play this off somehow, but what the fuck is wrong with Alpha and Rassle looking at each other and then looking away? They should act cool. "Cycle" can mean anything. Like what, for instance? I think fast.

"Yep, I'm almost done with my workout cycle," I say. "Next week I start a new routine. All new exercises."

Launch blinks and looks at Rassle and Alpha.

"I'm firing up the grill!" Rassle announces, saving us all.

"Come, Launch," Alpha says. "You're the best at getting the charcoal burning."

All three of them leave. I look at Karina, who's unfazed. My quick thinking worked.

Jake cracks open his own beer.

Karina says, "I'm guessing your nickname is Clark."

"Me, Clark?" he asks, not getting the reference. "I'm Jake."

For the first time I realize he isn't a fan of the Superman comic, the TV shows, or the movies. He just sees himself as a super man, and wants others to see him in the same way.

"Aaahh!" Tower groans in pain.

It makes Karina and me jump.

He's getting up to join Jake and the others in the backyard.

"These calf implants hurt like hell."

He takes his time walking over there and you can see the blue stitches in a long line, running the length of his calves. They look great. Thick and natural.

Karina studies his calves as he leaves, her face blank. I wonder what she's thinking, but glad she's not saying her thoughts out loud.

Then she gets up. "I should get going."

"What do you mean?" I ask, relieved. I don't like the idea of her hanging out with the guys.

"This is a guys' party." She turns to me to add in a lower voice, "You stay and celebrate with your friends, and I'll see you tomorrow."

She flashes the sweetest smile and gives me a quick kiss before I know what to say.

"Um, yeah, sure—if you're sure."

But something about the way she walks out, the smile already gone from her face, tells me she might not be okay with this.

By the time I head to the backyard, where the grill is already burning, and the guys are laughing and having fun, I realize today's mission has been accomplished already. The point of today was to cheer Alpha up, and I haven't seen him this happy in weeks.

19

Seven days until school begins

I'M ROLLING a coat of white paint on the back wall of Iron Life, which makes the other three walls and columns look even dirtier. Two professionals are doing the harder work—fixing up the outside of the building. They've already hidden away the exposed wiring and replaced bare light bulbs with rectangles of fluorescent light.

I wanted the extra money so Alpha is letting me do the work that doesn't require a professional. After painting the wall, I'll re-vinyl the older equipment to match the red-and-black new equipment, which includes the cardio area in the corner.

I could've lived in this gym, before the renovations, so I'll be falling in love more with every change that's made. There's nothing better than hanging in the place that's responsible for my great physique. I can't think of a better place to work; in fact, nothing I'd like to do more than be a licensed personal trainer. That's my career plan now, to transform guys from chumps to champs. I'd be working for myself and eventually I could even open my own gym.

I've forgotten about college, which I know most seniors will be obsessing over once school starts. What to major in, where to go, not to mention all those hours studying for the SATs.

I dip the roller in the paint and keep going, thrilled to be a part of the renovations. With a fresh new look Iron Life will attract more members, even girls.

"So this is where the magic happens."

I didn't mean it would attract girls right this moment. I didn't mean Karina.

"What are you doing here?"

"I thought I'd surprise you," she says, her voice all joy. "I have my mom's car today."

My hands are smeared with paint so I just stand there. She grabs my face to plant a kiss on me. I figured we'd hang out today, since we didn't get a chance to yesterday, but I was thinking in the evening. It's just past four.

"Alpha told me you can finish painting later," Karina says. "And you owe me because we didn't hang out yesterday."

He's talking to one of the renovators outside.

"Yeah, sure," I say. "Can I choose the place?"

On our way to the movies, Karina sings along with a few lines of a song I haven't heard before. The only music I've heard this summer is my hip-hop workout playlists or the high-energy songs coming from the two gym speakers.

I'm glad Karina was down with my idea to go to the movies. Nobody goes on Mondays, so Karina and I will sit among empty seats in the dark. Later we'll get something to eat, as we were going to do yesterday, where there's sure to be more people.

Next week I'll be officially out in the world. But until then, I wanna take it slow, take baby steps to being out in public with kids my age again.

These normal clothes have me feeling weird. My jeans, usually a bit loose, hug my ass and thighs. This size medium T-shirt that used to hang on my skinny frame now fits snug on my shoulders and chest. It's the first time this summer that I've worn them or anything else that isn't grease-stained or for working out.

Weirdest of all is that Karina is driving. We usually take my dad's car. I don't know what it is about being in the passenger seat that makes me feel less than a man. It's stupid, I know, but I can't help it.

Of course you're less than a man. You saw how small you were in the mirror when you were changing.

I did feel small. Now I remind myself that I can't be. The way these clothes fit me now are the proof.

Karina turns down the stereo. "Is it okay for me to say I'm worried about you?"

"Why would you be worried about me?"

"Because I met all your friends yesterday, and let me tell you . . ."

But she doesn't say anything else. Just shakes her head in disbelief.

"They're more like Alpha's friends. I know they're weird, but they're okay."

"They're all on steroids, David, and I think you are too." She keeps her eyes on the road while saying this.

"Why do you think that?" I ask, all innocent.

"That's what *cycle* means. I've been looking into it, because, I don't know . . ."

"What are you talking about?"

"*Zillions* of guys take nutritional supplements and don't get so big so quickly. So I looked into it, did some research. You've been so desperate to completely transform yourself, as you say. Also, your friends all take them."

"They're *not* my friends, Karina. Just some guys from the gym. Besides, why would I take them just because they do?"

"'Dime con quien andas,' my mom says, 'y te diré quien eres.'"

My mom used to say the same thing, always reminding me that we become the people we hang out with. Is that true though? In my case I wanted to get big *before* I met Alpha.

Can't Karina just accept my new body without worrying how I got it? The problem is that she remembers the skinny twerp. I wish I could be who I am without also carrying the history of who I was.

If only those guys hadn't shown up yesterday . . . If only Launch could keep his stupid mouth shut.

"Can we forget this and have fun?" I ask.

She sighs. "Yeah . . . sure."

But the way she says it, hesitant and with a pause between those two words, tells me she's only willing to let it go for now.

Sirena Movie Theater comes into view. Over half the spaces are full. Like it's the weekend instead of a Monday.

"What's going on here?" I ask.

"Mondays are two for one this summer."

Half off tickets means I save ten bucks—that's almost one injection of Winstrol, which I'll be running for my next cycle. So that's good, but still.

"You knew about this?"

A smile sneaks onto her face. "Hey, *you're* the one who wanted to go to the movies."

When we're lined up outside to buy tickets, I check out the people waiting. Nobody from Culler High. It's a young crowd though, kids from nearby Rivera High, maybe the college too, with one couple probably over thirty. *All* the guys are average chumps, which makes me swell with pride. I stand tall, confident that I look great.

Done sizing up the guys, I now look at the girls who are

all in shorts, and other skimpy clothes that make me happy to live in Florida.

A tall one seems like she might be hotter than Karina. On second thought, I decide it's pretty much a tie.

The winding ticket line moves up and the tall girl now faces me from the opposite end. She stops chewing her gum when she sees me. Does a slow double take before looking away for good.

Can't blame her. The guy she's with is extra chumpy—a pretty boy, but with the bony physique of a tall ten-year-old.

"Not the horror movie," Karina says, snapping me back into the moment.

All summer I've been thinking about my body, and I've only taken a break from that to think about other people's bodies. For two hours I wanna think about something else. All of a sudden I'm glad we're at the movies.

Karina checks out the listings on the display. "I assume *Forest Killer* is a horror movie."

"Okay," I say, and notice another movie to veto. "And no to *Forever Together*. That's a cheeseball romance for sure."

"Actually, if 'forever' is literal, it could be about vampires."

"Good point," I say, laughing. "It might be the opposite of a romance. Maybe it's about a gang of vampires who prey on people in love."

But an image of the movie slides onto the screen: a smiling bride and groom looking into each other's eyes.

We consider the four other movies showing.

Some couples take turns choosing the movie. They sit together in the theater, one person enjoying it while the other one suffers, looking forward to the next time. But that's not how Karina and I roll.

We decide on a comedy about high school.

As skinny pretty boy pays for two tickets, his hot girlfriend comes into view again. Her gaze wanders before falling on me. Yep, she's definitely a fan of the new David. And yep, she's hotter than Karina.

Alpha has been saying, "More girls than you'll know what to do with, bro," and maybe he's right.

I watch her walk toward the entrance, those legs so firm and tan under that skirt.

"You're going to drool all over your shoes." Karina is holding her cupped hands under my chin.

I act dumb. "What are you talking about?"

She inches up the aisle without a word. When I join her and lean in for a kiss, she turns her face away.

"A kiss won't save you," she says. "Why were you gawking at that girl?"

Because at the moment I have supercharged horniness because of all the extra testosterone in my body. But because of the first and only rule of Gear Club, all I say is "Sorry."

After hiding from the world for so long, maybe I've forgotten the rules. You steal glances rather than look directly.
You only do that once or twice. Gawking is *not* okay.

We step inside with our tickets. The video games by
the entrance ding and zap, playing soundtracks of cheesy
music. Past them is the Candy Mix station, about twenty
bins full of colorful sugared treats. A few people are filling
up tiny bags.

We're walking by the snack bar when Karina comes
to a stop. The warm buttery smell of popcorn is a strong
temptation, but I'm stronger.

"No popcorn for me," I say, "but I'll get you some."

"We *always* get popcorn," she says, like I'm breaking a
rule.

It's true that we've always gotten popcorn. A large popcorn with two drinks. She loves popcorn and so do I. So
much that I shove it into my mouth in fistfuls. But I can't
have it.

"It's not muscle fuel," I remind Karina.

"Popcorn, just this once, won't make your muscles
shrink."

Something has ahold of my pant leg. I look down and
see a tiny fist belonging to a four-year-old boy with a bowl
haircut. What the hell?

I scan the room and spot Rogelio from the gym about
fifteen feet away. He's in line with a woman and a little
girl. A second later he notices me and hurries over, smiling,

to get this kid, who must be his son.

The boy sees his dad, lets go of my jeans, glances up at me, and starts bawling.

How could I ever believe that Rogelio had a perfect physique? He's not skinny or anything, but he's nowhere near big enough.

He scoops the boy up to hug him. "Everything is okay," he says, bouncing the boy in his arms. Laughs as if to show just how fine everything is.

I'm wearing dark blue jeans, just like Rogelio's. The kid mixed us up.

It's sort of awkward seeing Rogelio in the real world. I remember the day we met, my first visit to the gym, how we both knew which guys were on steroids. Now he sees me lifting and hanging with them. It's a little uncomfortable is all I'm saying.

We make the introductions all around as I steal glances at his shoulders, chest, and arms. He's gained some size since we first met, yep, but he's still not big enough.

"Let me ask you something, Rogelio," Karina says. "Will you be eating any of the snacks your wife is buying?"

I look over at the counter, where a large popcorn and a box of Milk Duds sits as the cashier fills drinks.

"Sure," he says, not understanding. The boy is finally calm in his arms.

Karina flashes me a satisfied smile. "Yet he also goes to the gym and seems to be in great shape."

Great? That's a stretch. He's been working out since forever, and I just started this summer, so I'm not impressed.
But Karina is being nice—and trying to make a point.

Rogelio laughs. "Too many fitness people see food as
good or bad. They're happy with themselves when they eat
healthy and feel guilty when they don't. You end up devel-
oping an unhealthy relationship with food."

"Exactly!" Karina says, unable to contain her excitement. "That's *exactly* how it is."

It's the whole brownie conversation we had. And yes, I
did feel guilty. But that's the champion mentality at work.
Guys like Alpha and I go further, are willing to do whatever it takes. If it were easy to achieve greatness, everybody
would. Clearly, Rogelio doesn't have the discipline it takes.

Time for him to go before he and Karina become best
friends.

"Your wife just waved to you," I say. A total lie.

"You two enjoy your day," Rogelio tells us, and carries
his son over to join the rest of the family.

As they walk away, I do more than just glance. I take in
his whole body one final time. I really can't believe I used
to think he had a great physique.

A few minutes later, as I wait for Karina to come back from
the bathroom, I look everywhere but at the tray in my
hands. The buttery smell is absolute torture. I see Laurie
from my social science class last year. She's taking tickets,

ripping them, and directing people left or right down the hall with a pointed finger. Hasn't recognized me although I'm in her line of vision, four steps away.

To take my mind off the popcorn, I take a sip of my no-calorie drink, an unsweetened iced tea. Okay, so maybe one little kernel of popcorn won't hurt me. I crook my neck and lift the wide tray up to my mouth. My lips touch on the saltiness and seconds later the tiny fluff of deliciousness dissolves in my mouth.

"Nice technique," Laurie says.

It's just her and me now, nobody else around. She still doesn't recognize me.

"Thanks."

I'm about to say more when Karina walks up and takes out the tickets. "Hey, Laurie! You work here now?"

Laurie smiles at her and then tilts her head to study me. "Um, hey, Karina." She takes the tickets, rips them, and hands two halves back. "Yeah, just for the summer."

She looks at me again. "Hey, David. I didn't recognize you at first."

To be unrecognizable is the point, so I should be happy that I've accomplished my mission. But something about this interaction makes me uncomfortable. I'm still thinking about it as Karina and I enter the half-full theater.

"Row seven," Karina says, heading down to our favorite seats.

In the middle of the seventh row you're far enough

to see the whole screen without shifting your head, yet close enough so you don't see the walls in your periphery. I taught her that.

I don't recognize anybody in the theater. And if anybody recognized me, it would only be because Karina is right here.

I realize now that's what bothered me about Laurie. She probably saw me as this cool guy, and then once Karina walked up she realized who I *really* was. That sucks. I wanna be me without my whole history attached.

I take a sip of my iced tea and, fuck it, three pieces of popcorn. I'm only human. It makes Karina smile. This tastes better than anything I've ever eaten. Corn must be in my Mexican blood. I won't feel bad about eating a few pieces.

The room darkens. We settle in to watch the movie.

It's funny from the very start, though annoying to see that the high school kids are played by people in their twenties. That's the only reason some of those physiques on the screen are better than mine.

By the time I'm their age, I'll be much more built and with just as much definition as those guys.

In fact the blond lead actor, Jeremy Evans, is not very built at all. He's ripped—I'll give him that—but dude needs to hit those compound exercises to gain some size. I could out-lift him.

The theater fills with laughter. Totally missed the big joke.

On second thought, I'm not so sure he's smaller than me. Dammit. Why can't I tell?

I lean in close enough to smell Karina's flower-scented hair. "Is Jeremy Evans bigger than me?"

"No," she whispers back, eyes still on the screen. "What does that matter? Watch the movie."

I feel a smile grow on my face. I'm bigger than Jeremy Evans. What kind of heartthrob is that?

My attention shifts from the guys to the hot girls they're with—perfect tens, totally outta that guy's league.

That's how it always is, on the screen and sometimes in real life. The girl is too hot for the guy. That's how it is with Karina and me. I mean, that's how it *was*. Things have changed. Am I out of *her* league now, looking as good as I do?

No way. How stupid of me. I even close my eyes for a second—the shame hurts that bad. As if our relationship has ever been based on looks.

I take two pieces from the tub of popcorn Karina is holding—that's six total now—and realize that toward the end of this movie it will have been 2.5 hours since my last meal. Good thing I brought along a frozen protein shake, blended with peanut butter and oats. I'll chug that replacement meal just as soon as we're outta here. No time to wait for dinner with Karina.

Now that the beach scene is over, all the bodies covered up, the movie and all the jokes are easy to follow.

Karina laughs so hard at the restaurant scene that a piece of popcorn shoots outta her mouth, landing on the empty seat in front of us. Which makes us both laugh even more.

I wonder if things between us will go back to the way they were before the summer. Although we haven't hung out much, a bunch of stuff has changed. Does she fit in my new life?

It's horrible, I know, but I can't help it. She's the same Karina, while I'm a totally different person, inside and out.

I think about all I've been through this summer and who I've become. Turn it all over in my head until the credits start rolling and the theater lights snap on.

As we head toward the lobby Karina grabs my hand. It feels different. Warm and dry as usual, but different.

"The ending was disappointing," she says. "Don't you think?"

"Yeah," I respond, though I didn't actually catch it.

More people swarm the video games and snack bars than before. I'm thinking of that meal replacement shake in the car. The movie lasted longer than I thought it would. It's been almost twenty minutes since the 2.5 hour mark, and I need calories. I know some YouTubers call it "bro-science," the idea you might lose gains or even go catabolic for not feeding your muscles on schedule, but I'd rather be safe than sorry.

"Did you even hear me?" Karina asks.

"Yeah. The ending was disappointing."

"No." Karina lets go of my hand and stops at the edge of the game area, next to a large cardboard ad for a new Pixar movie. "I said something after that."

"Sorry. I got stuff on my mind."

"Girls?"

"Food," I confess, so she doesn't get the wrong idea. I mention the 2.5 hours and how it's been twenty minutes since I needed more calories. When she narrows her eyes at me I realize it sounds sort of crazy. I get it. If you're not into bodybuilding it could sound crazy.

"Constantly thinking about food," Karina said. "That's something I read about too. You think about your body and food constantly."

"Gimme a break," I tell her, because I don't love being analyzed like this. Scary is what it is. It makes me feel like running away and hiding.

"For real, David. I read about this. I love you and I want to help you. It's not normal to be obsessed in this way because . . ."

Why the hell is this happening here and now? Is she some kind of expert because she read something on the internet? Is she suddenly a therapist?

Besides, anything she wants to say could wait until we get to the car. That's where the shake is. I'm not hungry and it damn sure won't taste good, but my body needs those macros, especially the protein.

"So I just want you to be aware of that, okay?" Karina asks.

I just spaced out and missed what came before that. "Okay," I say, which is obviously the answer she wants.

"I miss the fun, laid-back David you used to be."

I wonder about that for a second. "You're saying I'm not fun anymore?"

"You are, but it's like your obsession has taken over a bit."

"Obsession?" I repeat, because I don't know what else to say. That word really burns me up inside. I'm so ready to go.

"Yeah, obsession. I really think you need some help and I want to help you find some."

"Enough already, Karina," I say. "Jesus. Give it a rest."

Her eyes go round. "Don't talk to me that way. What's wrong with you?"

She said that way too loud. Even before I look around to confirm it, I feel everybody eyeballing us. Great. Karina has turned us into a spectacle. I feel heat rise to my face and my jaw tenses.

"Keep it down, Karina."

"Don't tell me what to do!"

What's wrong with her? She's just as loud as before. A rage takes hold of me and my arms tense up. I take a deep breath and pause to consider something. Did I talk to her all bossy? Maybe that was my bad.

"Okay, fine," I say. "Let's just go."

"I'm not going anywhere with you right now. You're acting like an asshole and raising your voice."

Me? Raise *my* voice? *She's* the one who . . . But I gotta deal with this so we can get outta here. Talk privately in the car. Where I can have my shake. My muscles are begging for fuel.

"Is everything okay here?" a man asks.

Another flash of heat, and I turn to him. He's wearing the same orange-and-beige uniforms as the other employees. A manager, according to his nametag, who's gripping a walkie-talkie like he's ready to use it. So I won't tell him to fuck off.

"We're fine," I say.

I turn back to Karina.

She looks at him. "We're fine," she echoes.

Then she heads to the door. I follow. When we're out in the early evening air, she stops. It's only about a dozen people out here compared to the big crowd inside. It's an improvement. I feel calmer already.

"If you're not on steroids," she says. "What was that rage in there?"

Maybe I was louder than I realize. But rage? No way . . . I had it under control.

"That wasn't roid rage, Karina. I don't know what you're talking about."

She crosses her arms. "Is that what happened with your dad? Is that why you got kicked out?"

An angry heat is coursing through me. I exhale a long breath so it can escape. Why is she bringing that up? It has nothing to do with anything.

"I didn't get kicked out," I say, keeping my cool. "I *wanted* to leave. Are you calling me a liar? I told you what happened. He was on my back all the time and I didn't want to deal with his bullshit anymore."

For some reason she glances down real quick and her eyes go extra wide. Then she takes a step back.

"Is everything okay?" a lady's voice asks.

I turn. She's calling out from way over at the ticket line. Everybody there is frowning our way. They've somehow heard me.

Shit. I guess I've been shouting. I lower my head and see what Karina has already seen: my fists clenched to my sides. I see myself the way she does and become aware of my heart racing superfast.

I lift my head to meet Karina's eyes. Her face isn't showing shock. It's fear. Karina is scared of me. I open my mouth to speak. It's an impulse, nothing more, because I have nothing to say.

She turns and takes off in a hurry. Walks out to the parking lot and keeps moving.

If I go after her, one of these people in line may call the

cops. So I'll let her leave.

Then I have another thought. Maybe it's best that I don't try to fix what just happened between us. Today or ever.

Karina knows I'm on steroids and won't accept it. Not now, and definitely not when I do my next cycles. And if she's read up on it as she said she has, she'll know about all the side effects. I won't be able to hide anything from her.

If our relationship is going to end, maybe this is the best way to do it. No awkward conversations or text messages. Just a clean break without tears.

I see the white Tercel pull back from the parking spot and then start to drive away. My damn shake is in there.

Anyway, even putting the whole gear issue aside, there's something else to consider. Something that puts a sort of positive spin on what just happened: although Karina has been a great girlfriend, and though it's not nice to say out loud, the simple fact is that the new David can do better.

20

Zero days until school begins

I'VE NEVER been more excited to get outta bed! Not even as a little kid when it was my birthday, or on Christmas when I still believed in Santa Claus.

I throw the blanket off me and hop up, ready to check out my full transformation. The *before* video I shot at the start of summer has been chilling in my hard drive, unwatched.

I find the file I saved three months ago and click *play*.

No. Fucking. Way. Was I really *that* skinny? It makes me cringe, seeing that stick kid flexing in his dad's house. The only definition he has is the top of his rib cage—two protrusions on each side, underlining his bird chest.

He busts the double biceps pose—it's nothing but two straight lines from elbows to shoulders.

Pathetic.

Now I step in front of the mirror to do the same poses,

feeling a glow of pride. Damn! Look at those two bulges staring back at me! Who wants tickets to the gun show? I got you right here!

And check out the thickness of my chest! I let my eyes fall just below to the square, hard muscles of my abs. Anybody order a six-pack?

The gym scale yesterday showed me 25.7 pounds heavier than when I started this journey, but here's the visual proof.

A second later I remember I'll be dropping weight soon. Yesterday I gave myself the final injection of this cycle. Popped the last D-bol tabs.

But why worry about that today?

For now, I need my nuts to produce testosterone again. I grab the box of Nolvadex on my desk. It's anti-estrogen medication normally prescribed to treat breast cancer. I pop four 10-milligram tabs for my post-cycle therapy.

When you up your testosterone with gear, your body ups your estrogen to compensate. When the testosterone suddenly drops, and the estrogen stays high, you get gynecomastia—a.k.a. bitch tits. Actual breasts that might lactate and everything.

So yeah. Totally worth the hundred and fifty bucks.

I remember the next gear cycle coming up in four weeks, wondering how I'll come up with the money to—

No! There's no need to think about that either, dammit. Why do I have so much negativity clogging up my brain space on a happy day like this?

After a trim of the beard and a quick shower, I pick out some new jeans with a new T-shirt.

I know—more money disappearing from my tiny roll of cash. But the new body requires a new look and I got the brand names on sale.

Now that my hair has grown back, I rub a dab of clay into it and make it messy but stylish. Sort of like Natural Nathan does his hair.

In front of the mirror I take in the final result. I'm not just big but cool, looking so good even Karina might be surprised.

Outta all the stuff trying to invade my brain on this special morning, please let it not be Karina. I've been thinking about her since last Monday when she walked away from me and outta my life. I left it at that, deciding that's best—didn't text or call and she didn't either. But damn if I don't regret it sometimes.

Alpha says all I need is another girl. True. These last three months I've been without sex and I'm aching for some release. I'll have another girl soon. Several, maybe. I'm gonna wow the girls at Culler High.

In the kitchen I'm making an eight egg-white omelet and thinking of Gaby. By this time, she'd be eating the breakfast I served her and wearing the hairstyle I've given her. I hope she's okay.

I think about Dad too, how he's getting ready for work and all. I feel guilt every time I think of him. It's always the same memory of me going Incredible Hulk in that bedroom and hurting him. I know I have to talk to Dad and make things right. It's been over two weeks. But all I've been thinking about is the start of school. Maybe next weekend I'll pay him a visit.

So much to push outta my mind. At least no negative thoughts about my body are creeping into my head this morning. Because they can't. I look great. It's undeniable.

Apha drags himself into the kitchen, yawning big and loud like a wild animal. He's showered and wearing a Iron Life shirt with my favorite quote: *That which does not kill me makes me stronger.*

He smiles big and says, "First day of senior year. Lucky bastard."

I bump the fist he puts out for me.

He's been as excited about my first day as I have.

"You're going to leave Ricky alone, right?"

"Hell no."

He returns my confused look with a shrug. "You haven't mentioned him lately, so I figured that you let it go."

"I'm not trying to step to him at school, but I'm catching him afterward, somewhere and somehow. I got to even the score."

"You got your revenge already," Alpha says. "This physique here is your revenge. Ain't you ever heard of that saying? The best revenge is a well-lived life."

"Sounds like that was invented by a person fearing pay-back."

Alpha laughs. "Fear is right. You'll strike terror in Ricky when he sees you. *That's* what I'm saying. That fear is better than anything."

"I don't know," I say, though it does make some sense.

What's the downside to kicking Ricky's ass though? Suspension, I guess, if the school finds out about it. A blemish on my record. Big deal. I don't need to be overly into school anymore. As long as I get my diploma I'm good. It's not like I'll lose out on a scholarship or anything. They don't give them out to study personal training.

21

I ACCEPTED Alpha's offer to drop me off at school. I got out a block away, so nobody would see me and him together and immediately suspect steroids. It's what has caused all the trouble with Dad and Karina. One look at Alpha and I was guilty by association.

A line of cars inch in front of the entrance, doors opening to let teenagers loose. I can't believe I used to be afraid of them. They're just boys and girls.

Here we go, I say to myself, walking through the entrance with a confident stride. No more nervous stickboy hunching through the school.

The wide hall is noisy with first-day excitement, all those teenage voices going at once, sounding like a steady roar. I pass them slowly, notice how some heads turn to me, the new kid, their eyes full of admiration.

Billy Robeson is slinking my way, shoulders slouched, neck curved so he could just as easily be looking on the floor or straight ahead. I used to shrink myself in the same way to be unnoticed. His eyes raise to find mine, and I veer right as he veers left to avoid a clash.

Why did I do that? Bad habit, I guess. As the more muscular guy, I don't have to make that chump move ever again.

Up ahead and to the left, Heather Aquilar is eyeing me as she talks to three friends. A girl I had a crush on in sixth grade suddenly has me on her radar—and it looks like I'm on her friend's too. Her eyes linger on me as I pass.

A new joy overtakes me, unlike any I've ever felt. Alpha was right. If you give everything to your gains, they give everything to you. That includes attention from girls.

Up ahead I spot Miguel at his locker with Enzo. Same guys with the same body shape. I'm excited to see them, but really more excited for them to see me. Rob is there too, gripping a fat novel with a bookmark in the middle of it. He's a drifter between two groups of friends. Either with us during lunch or at the table of comics and anime fans.

I feel a smile grow on my face. I've missed my friends. Rob I haven't seen since last semester, and the other two not since they stopped by the auto shop. Although I did talk to Miguel last week to catch up with him.

"Hey, guys," I say. "What's going on?"

The three turn to me. All six eyes pop. I keep my cool and slap five with them.

"No way," Miguel says a little too loudly.

"It's no big deal," I say with a shrug. "I told you I was going to hit the weights all summer."

Rob looks me up and down. "No fucking way." He squeezes my shoulder and pokes me in the chest.

"I'm not a melon."

I can't believe how frail Rob looks—like a hard wind could knock him right over. I can't believe I used to be skinnier.

"My mind is officially blown," Miguel says, not lowering his voice.

"Keep it down. It's no big deal."

"Keep it down," Enzo repeats. "Or David will snap you in half and eat you."

Which gets everybody laughing, even me.

It feels good to be laughing again, but it also feels sort of weird being around these guys. For a moment I wish I could just slip into the conversation they were having, without them noticing any different about me.

I don't like all this attention. Maybe by lunchtime they'll have had time to get used to their friend's new look and treat me normal.

"See you guys later," I tell them, and keep moving.

As I head to my locker, eyeballs keep noticing me. They

belong to admiring girls and envious guys. Then I see Ricky up ahead and feel the briefest squeeze of my heart before it starts beating fast.

Residual fear, I guess. Because the guy's body is unchanged since I saw him last and I'm bigger. I could destroy him. Could do the same to the two friends flanking him.

My thoughts turn red as I wonder which sidekick recorded the slap. As the heat rises in me, I remind myself the gear is still in my system and that maybe I won't do anything to Ricky. His fear might be enough.

Here they come, closer every second. I'm not gonna budge one inch left or right. I'm walking slowly down the hall in a straight line. Ricky sees me staring him down and looks away—a small victory.

With him a few steps away I amp up my pace and determination.

He and the chump to his right break apart at the last moment to let me through. My shoulder knocks into Ricky's. The adrenaline is really flowing now, my neck and face hot as I wonder what's coming next.

I stop and whip around.

This is how fights happen, but Ricky doesn't want that.

I hope he doesn't want that.

He stops and turns to glance at me. Also at his friends, to consider the situation. When Ricky turns back he keeps going, like nothing has happened, his bitchass sidekicks joining him.

Alpha was right. This body right here is the absolute best revenge.

I feel so alive!

I tell myself to knock off the smiling and be cool. This is my new life. Getting respect is normal.

I pass the drinking fountain that doesn't work and see something off in the row of lockers coming up. Something dark on one of the blue metal doors. I can't be sure it's even my locker with the people talking in front of it, blocking my view.

But then I see it *is* my locker. *BITCHSLAP* is scrawled in big black letters. Probably Ricky, I think, as my blood goes hot again. I calm myself down with other thoughts. That the janitor is quick about removing graffiti. That nobody will ever tag my locker again once they know who I am now.

I put my midmorning shake and oat bar in my locker, along with my muscle meal for lunch.

Yeah, a janitor will soon remove that graffiti. I walk away from the locker, leaving the nickname behind for good.

22

HERE THEY ARE, the same faces in homeroom since freshman year, the same cute girl, Julieta, thumbing at her
phone. Some kids eye me like *Is that a new student?* as I
make my way to my usual seat. They pause with curiosity,
probably wondering if I'm new or lost.

I go down the first row by the windows.

I drop my backpack next to my alphabetically assigned
spot, right behind Julieta. Slide into the seat, which feels
smaller than I remember.

Soon the classroom gets quieter as people lean close
to each other to talk. About me, if their eyes drifting over
here are any indication.

The ringing bell brings Ms. Chou. She sets down her
oversized mug and bag. I've never looked in that mug but
my guess is that it's filled with extra-strength Red Bull
instead of coffee.

"How's everybody doing?" she asks, all energy. "Did you have fun during vacation?"

There are a few yeses and some chatter.

I wonder if I had any fun. All summer it was work and more work, and I don't mean the hours in the auto shop or renovating the gym. Making gains was a full-time job.

I'm thrilled with my results, but was it fun? No, I wouldn't call it that.

"It's so great to see all of you again." She scans the room. Her eyes hold me for a beat longer and widen. "And there's a new face."

A few giggles rise up among the uncomfortable silence.

I fight the urge to slump in my seat to make myself small. "It's me, David," I say.

Laughter all around.

"David!" she says with high-pitched relief. Like she's found me after a long search. "I didn't recognize you with your facial hair. It looks nice."

More laughter.

As Ms. Chou takes attendance I wonder how long before people here accept the new me.

Steve, who sits next to me, has been goth for two years. Nobody thinks about the kid he was as a freshman, the parted hair and colorful clothes and unblack lips. Did that take days to accept? Weeks? I can't remember.

It should be quicker for me. My new identity isn't just

some clothes I slipped on.

Julieta turns around so her face is in front of mine. She does this all the time, to talk to Kat who sits behind me.

"It's not just the beard that's different," she says.

It takes a second for me to realize she's actually talking to me. For the first time in the hundreds of homeroom periods I've sat through, I don't gotta make myself small and sort of lean away when she talks to Kat.

I smile, pretty sure she's making a joke. "Yeah, I guess not."

"Ms. Chou is funny," Kat says. "Like she didn't notice your whole body looks different."

I twist in my seat to tell her, "Yeah, I spent some time in the gym."

I try to say this casually, but the attention almost makes me blush.

"That's what it is!" Julieta says with a laugh. God, she's cute. Then she adds, "Good for you, David."

This is crazy. I've gone from being an obstacle to practically spinning nonstop so I can talk to both of them at once.

"Yeah, man," Kat says. "Maybe you can give my boyfriend some weight training tips."

We keep talking, which is hard for me, turning back and forth like an oscillating fan.

I could get used to this.

* * *

Finally it's time for lunch! I get my container of food from my locker. The paint over the graffiti was still wet after first period, but now it's dry. "Bitchslap" is forever gone.

I step inside the bustling lunchroom. Though some people have claimed their regular tables, more are in line or heading out of the cafeteria, trays in hands, the nervous freshmen trying to figure out where they should sit.

I head to my table by the vending machines, where Miguel and Rob are already seated.

And yes, there's my ex-girlfriend's table two away from them. Only Janelle is sitting there now. She catches me looking and narrows her eyes at me.

It's awkward, what with half the people at this table, Miguel and Enzo, dating two of the girls who sit at that table. Between second and third period, Miguel told me nobody ended up going to Universal Studios. The girls opted out when Karina decided she didn't wanna go.

When I approach the table, Rob says, "Take my lunch money, just don't hurt me," and puts his hands up, pretending to cower.

Miguel laughs harder than I do. It's sort of funny, I have to admit, but I remember it's similar to what people do to Alpha all the time.

I take a seat with them, at our end of the long table. "Come on, guys. Treat me like you always do, okay?"

"That will be hard," Rob says. He pops a fry into his

mouth. "You're so different. Everybody is talking about it."

"No kidding," Miguel says. "They keep asking me questions like I'm your publicist or something."

"Yeah," I say, not surprised. "I've been getting questions too."

Are you really David?

What kind of exercises have you been doing?

Those are the two most common ones, and the others also get on my nerves. The constant calling attention to how different I am means they're still focused on who I used to be. I'm done with surprising people. For real. I'm totally over it. I just want to be who I am now.

I wonder if that will even be possible at Culler High. A school where every single student has seen the video.

"Man, you should've invited me to the gym this summer," Miguel says. "So I can become sexier."

Rob pretends to choke from laughing too suddenly.

I consider Miguel, a round mess of a guy. I'm not being mean or anything. I'm just calling it like it is.

Last year he tried to get in shape. Cut out all sugar, swapped white bread for whole wheat. That, together with the running and sit-ups worked well—for two weeks. He couldn't stick with it after that.

No motivation. That's something I could give him. How cool would it be to have another friend at the gym? Someone closer to my age. Because the truth is something new has to link us, and if it's not weightlifting I don't know what it could be. I'm off that kid stuff like video games, anime, and superhero movies.

Also, if he leans up, he won't have to go out with fat Liliana anymore.

"You could join my gym," I say. "I could get you a discount."

A boost would be *super* motivating for him. I can put Miguel on some Anavar or Clen, the gear for losing fat. It's what Alpha and others use to get shredded before a competition. I've met Ray, Alpha's dealer, who likes me and will probably hook me up. So I can hook people up like Alpha does. It's not like I'll be stepping on anybody's toes.

"Yeah, maybe," he says, wiping ketchup off his lips. "Liliana might get mad though. All those hot girls swarming me all the time."

Still joking, but he might come around anyway.

"You brought your own lunch?" Enzo asks me, setting down his tray. "You could just take somebody else's."

"We're not making a big deal about David's new muscles," Rob informs him.

"Right. Okay."

Without meaning to, I glance over at the table where Karina will be sitting by now. Yep, she's there, facing the other way. The back of her black hair is wavy and shiny.

There are more girls than I know what to do with, I remind myself. Literally hundreds in this room alone.

I turn my attention back to the container of chicken,

yams, and broccoli. I try the chicken, which I've gotten so bored with it wouldn't taste better warmed up. I take a bite of a yam, boiled and unsalted, and remember what the cafeteria fries tasted like. All three of the guys have fries with ketchup drizzled on top. They were never anything to get excited about, Culler High fries, but compared to this they'd be so delicious.

"So is it true that you live on your own now?" Enzo asks.

I tell them what I told Miguel last week. That I'm living with a friend I met at the gym. They don't need to know he's a pro bodybuilder. Just the gym owner who's letting me stay rent free.

"I got sick of my dad always up in my business," I say. "He used to walk into my room without knocking."

"I know all about that," Miguel says. "My bedroom door doesn't even lock. When I get horny I gotta yank it in the only bathroom at home. Which means I gotta finish in about ten seconds and without candles or music to make it romantic."

That gets us laughing.

"Parents invading your space?" Enzo asks. "I couldn't deal with that."

"I do what I want in my room now," I say. "Though I do it without first creating an ambience."

"Lucky bastards," Miguel says, shaking his head.

"So you can throw parties and everything!" Rob says.

The thought occurred to me, when I first moved in with Alpha. But now I can't imagine having anybody but these guys over my house—without their girlfriends, of course, who hate my guts. Why would I want a bunch of other people from school? People who remember Bitchslap David?

It's sort of sad, but I'm also having a hard time imagining a friend get-together at my house. What would we do? What would we talk about? They're the same guys I've known, but they don't know me. Not anymore.

"Well," I say. "My roommate is a fitness guy who goes to bed really early and needs quiet. That's the only thing."

I'm really getting bummed out all of a sudden. Are these guys just my school crew so I don't sit alone? No way. That's not right. We have to remain real friends.

"We can have a barbecue sometime," I say, and remember the Mr. Florida competition Alpha has coming up. He'll be in Miami all weekend. "We can do a movie night and a sleepover too."

My dad never allowed me to have sleepovers, or to sleep over someone's house. He used to say, *You have a house and bed. Puras tonterías.*

Besides bodybuilding documentaries, I haven't *really* seen a movie in *months*. When I went with Karina to the movies last week, I barely paid attention.

"We always choose movies based on a director's work," I say. "How about we watch those old movies based on

Philip K. Dick's books? You know, *Blade Runner, Total Recall*—the original one, of course—and what's that one with Tom Cruise?"

I'm snapping my fingers to remember it, the title on the tip of my tongue, when all of a sudden my heart stops.

It's Ricky in my line of vision. My stomach rumbles.

A stupid smile is on his stupid face and looking my way. He and his two smug sidekicks are seated at the table in the corner. The one closest to the garbage can where we put the empty trays.

"*Minority Report*," Miguel says. "I love that one."

"What's wrong, David?" Rob asks me.

I feel a sharp heat in my chest when I realize Ricky is *staring* at me and that it's not just a smile. He's grinning.

What the fuck is so funny? My jaw clenches so tight my teeth might crack. I hear a snap. The plastic fork has split in two inside my tight fist.

"It's Ricky," Miguel tells Rob.

I breathe deeply, eyes steady on the guy who slapped me. What Alpha said doesn't apply. Since Ricky isn't afraid, he'll have to learn a lesson.

Miguel asks, "Why's he smiling?"

"Because he's a fucking idiot," I say. "Because he wants to get his ass kicked."

"Don't do it here," Enzo warns. "After school is better."

"For sure," Rob says.

My brain agrees. It's my body that's amped and itching

to hop up this second, go over there, and stomp him.

"Not now, and not after school," Miguel says. "Come on, forget Ricky."

Forget him is what we used to say whenever one of us got pushed around or dissed. So we wouldn't feel bad about not standing up for ourselves.

When Miguel got knocked into a puddle last year, and stood up dripping, I said, "Forget Pedro."

When I got slammed against the lockers, Miguel said, "Forget Josh."

But things are different now. For me, anyway. I'm not the dorky, defenseless kid anymore.

I turn to Miguel to make that clear. "I don't let people fuck with me."

I take another glance at Ricky. He's still staring, and somehow smiling as he chews his food. He seems to know something.

"What have people been talking about?" I ask.

Rob shrugs first, then Miguel. Enzo sort of looks away.

I look at my best friend, a straightshooter. "Miguel? You said they kept asking you questions. What about?"

"People ask stupid questions." He shoves a bunch of fries into his mouth. More than usual.

"Such as . . . ," I say, losing my patience.

"They wanna know if you're taking steroids," Rob says.

My stomach sinks. So all that leaning in I've seen and all that whispering wasn't about admiration or envy.

I sneak out my phone because they aren't allowed to be out, even during lunch, and open the TrashTalk app I should've deleted a long time ago.

"I told them no," Miguel says as the Culler High page pops up automatically. "I know you wouldn't take steroids."

I enter the username that keeps me anonymous: *popcornboy.*

Rob says, "I told them I haven't seen you all summer."

My heart thumps faster as the app loads, the blue TT logo doing a spin.

Then it's me on the screen. A picture of me walking down the hall today. What the fuck?

My eyes fix on the words below: *Bitchslap David is on steroids.*

538 likes.

"Don't look at that app," Enzo says.

I scroll through the comments, one by one, as rage in me rises and overflows so much that it fills up the room. All day people have been smiling in my face while talking trash behind my back. I imagine them laughing, saying out loud what they've written here.

What an idiot

fake ass muscles

I have a look around the lunchroom, disoriented for a second. Then everything feels familiar. Too familiar. This is the place I've always known. Full of assholes since I was a freshman. All these years I've been below them, which they've reminded me of every day with the teasing and taunting. With their kicks and shoves.

And now that I'm above them they want to drag me down to their level? Or even worse, shove me below them all over again? Fuck these anonymous cowards.

How I'd love to know which one wrote each particular comment.

Yep, obviously on steroids

i'm assuming bitchslap had a micro penis so i guess it disappeared now

There's no doubt among Culler High students that I'm on steroids.

The few comments on how great I look don't make me feel better. I'm in full panic mode right now.

"That app is trash," Rob says. "That's why it has that word in the name."

I hold the phone in both hands, unable to stop reading. If I let go of it I swear I'll end up flipping this fucking table over. I wanted to leave Bitchslap David behind me, but is Steroid David any better?

Nobody is stupid enough to call me that to my face, but that's not the respect I've always wanted. That's just fear.

A long comment catches my eye. It has 438 likes so far.

u can get bigger muscles with steroids but nothing u do will delete the video or unbitchslap ur stupid face. ur 4ever bitchslap david

The username is *rikky2002*.

"I'll kill him," I say, looking over at his table. He's gone. His two friends are eating by themselves.

"Hey, Bitchslap," I hear him call out.

Ricky is in front of the vending machine two tables away.

The rage closing in on me makes me want to get up. But a hand presses down on my shoulder.

"You'll get suspended," Miguel says. "Mr. Trevors is by the exit. Plus the security cameras."

A silence has fallen around me and I can feel people watching.

"Do you have a dollar I can borrow?" Ricky asks, all fake polite and smiling.

"Not for you," I say as calm as I can.

My fists are clenching but I got this. I can control my rage. Save it for a few more hours, until school lets out. The roids have made me lose my cool twice before, so I'll listen to friends, the voices of reason.

"No dollar?" Ricky asks. "Must have spent it all on your fake muscles. Too bad that taking steroids doesn't make you less of a bitch."

I'm up now, a fireball of rage heading his way. My hips bump against people's backs and chairs.

Ricky stays put as I come up on him. I zero in on his face and cock my fist back. Then let it go as hard as I can.

Glass shatters into the vending machine. The few shards clinging to the top, swinging, fall and crumble onto the floor.

Hundreds of chairs scratch against the floor as kids get on their feet, the whole lunchroom buzzing with excitement. I turn to my left, where Ricky squares up, fists framing his face. Like a boxing bell just rang.

I let out a fast hard left. Straight through the air because Ricky is gone. I turn to my left again. There he is. I swing a right. He ducks under it like a pro and pops up again.

This guy knows what he's doing. Like I care. I've got power and strength, so fuck the boxing.

I can take a punch or two as I charge at him. Once I get him on the ground I'll pound him with my fists as hard as I can.

I rush forward and heave myself on Ricky, my arms wide open. As I bring my arms together to grab him my face gets smashed. With the second smash my face jerks to the side. My body twists and my vision blurs.

With another punch everything goes dark around me and the floor disappears.

Among the steady roar of excitement in the lunchroom, distinct voices swirl above me.

Ricky: "I didn't do nothing!"

Miguel: "Dude, wake up! Come on!"

Mr. Trevors: "Everybody get back!"

I open my eyes to see the faces of my friends and some curious onlookers. I sit up.

Three teachers have closed in on Ricky, about ten

feet away. I push myself up with Miguel's help and check myself for blood. Nothing from my nose. I wipe my mouth with the back of my hand and there's a smudge of dark red.

"Your lip is busted," Miguel says.

"To the nurse's office, young man," Mr. Trevors says, holding me by the back of the elbow.

"I'm fine." I jerk my arm away to get his hand off me.

The whole lunchroom is watching, their laughter swarming. Though no phones are allowed, I'm pretty sure at least one person snuck theirs out to capture some of what just went down.

Even if the whole world doesn't see this one, I've been humiliated again. Part of me wishes I were still out on the floor, unaware of what's going on.

"Let's go," Mr. Trevors says, the soft worry gone from his voice. "To the nurse and then to the principal's office."

It's so ridiculous, this chump trying to tell me what to do. I don't wanna be here. Not just now but in general. Who needs Culler High? Who needs this bullshit?

"Let's go to the nurse," Mr. Trevors repeats more forcefully, and makes a move toward me.

"Get your fucking hands off me," I tell him.

I walk the other way, down the aisle toward the rear exit. People call out to me. Only a few of their words reach me clearly.

"You got knocked the fuck out."

"Hey, Bitchslap, what happened?"

My mistake was coming back to this place. I'm so done with high school. I walk out the back, Mr. Trevors following a few steps behind.

"You're not going anywhere," he says.

I cross the parking lot, glancing back only once to make sure nobody's following. Faces are in the lunchroom window and two teachers stand in the doorway, watching me make my escape.

Find somebody else to entertain you from now on, assholes. This is the last you'll ever see of me.

23

TWO WEEKS LATER I'm sitting in a rickety desk in history class, jotting down today's homework—the pages to read, the questions to answer. Though we have shorter classes at Franklin Adult School, and get out earlier—at noon—we gotta make up for that with more homework.

It's the same amount of work, when I think about it, the same number of hours per day spent on school. So why is this so fucking depressing? Sure, I have no friends here, but do I need some from seven a.m. to noon?

No way. It's enough that everybody leaves me alone.

Not that they recognize me. There's no video of the punch that laid me out on the lunchroom floor. Even if there were, it would be a typical knockout video—not an epically hilarious one like the first video.

I wanted to quit high school completely, but Alpha put his foot down and said I'm finishing. That the personal trainer degree I want requires a diploma. He even called up Launch and asked him to help me register. At forty-two, Launch can pass for my dad. The school administrator called him by his name, Mateo, and I called him "Dad," feeling weirder about it every time I did. Not just because bigmouthed and crazy Launch would make a terrible dad. It was because I hadn't heard myself say that word for a while.

I remember what it meant. I remembered my own dad and how I love him and miss him and really should make things right.

Just as soon as I'm back to my regular size. I can't let anybody who knew me bigger see me smaller, especially my dad, who will feel like he was right and I was wrong about using steroids. So I've been trying not to think about Dad and Gaby.

Anyway, with thoughts about Culler High outta the way, I am more focused on my goal of becoming a You-Tuber. Natural Nathan will be turning twenty soon—no longer a teen bodybuilder, so I plan to guide the new generation.

By next summer I'll have done three more gear cycles. That and my continued dedication will give me the best teen physique on YouTube. A year after that I'll be a certified trainer and pulling in hundreds of thousands of subscribers. No longer focused on teens but everybody in the fitness world.

To think I was focused on wowing Culler High. I've taken on a bigger dream now—to wow the entire world.

"Read all of unit four," the teacher says with the same monotone as always. "Answer all the exercises at the end, and use complete sentences. Are there any questions?"

I don't have any, and probably wouldn't ask them if I did. He's harsh, Mr. Alexander, like all the teachers here. I guess because they don't have to put up with anything. There's no getting sent to the principal's office for messing around. They'll just kick you out of the school.

And you can walk right out that door whenever you want to.

"It's too much homework, Mr. Alexander," the blond pregnant girl in the front row says. "I gotta do homework for other classes too."

"This is *adult* school," he reminds us. "In the real world you can't tell your boss it's too much work. You just do it."

There are a few girls at the school, about half of which are moms or soon-to-be moms. You notice them arriving late to the first class, studying harder than the others, and leaving in a hurry, as if they have something way more important to do.

When the bell rings we get up, all thirty or so of us, without the excited chatter of regular high school. I head out quickly—in order to reach the 53 bus two blocks away by 12:10. Miss that and I have to wait another hour.

The halls are full of guys who got kicked outta

traditional high schools. Guys suspended one too many times or fresh outta juvie. Guys with a quiet desperation who either don't make eye contact or stare at you for too long.

"Where you going, baby?" a guy asks the girl hugging textbooks against her chest. "Where you going so fast?"

"To get away from you."

"Fuck you, then, bitch."

The guy with knuckle tattoos is at his spot outside, leaning against the side wall of the entrance, lighting a cigarette. He blows the smoke straight ahead, onto anybody going down the wide steps. He checks out the girls, sure, but he seems to be mostly staring down the guys, hoping somebody meets that stare.

I feel like he stares me down harder, maybe because he has something to prove and I'm the biggest guy here. I never look back. Me trying to get big was all about avoiding fights.

Besides, being bigger than someone doesn't mean I can take them in a fight. I've learned that lesson.

I get off the bus on my stop and see the new Iron Life sign, light gray with black letters, that's brought in so many new members. It mentions we're right behind the Laundromat.

My mood doesn't improve when I step inside. Even though this is my favorite place. Even though it's chest and tris day, my favorite workout. Lately, workouts do the opposite of giving me an ego boost like they used to. I'm lifting less weight all the time and have barely enough energy to survive them, even with the help of my pre-workout energy drink.

Without that extra testosterone, my energy is down in general. All damn day.

I wave to Keith, the part-time trainer who's chatting up a cute girl working with green dumbbells. As usual, there are less than a half dozen people here between noon and one.

In the locker room I take off my regular clothes and make the mistake of looking into a mirror.

You're so small. Four stick limbs stuck onto a stick torso. Unacceptable. Pathetic.

My mind isn't playing tricks on me anymore. I've lost three pounds already.

I change into gym clothes and head out. Alpha comes out of his office.

"Time to grind, bro," he says. "What's with that face?"

"I don't have much energy, and I already know I'm not going to lift as much as last time."

I miss the excitement I felt all summer just before hitting the weights, the intense desire to get to it and beat my previous lifts. I miss the small victory after every set.

"Are you sure that depression isn't a side effect of going off gear?" I ask him.

"You aren't gaining lots of mass as before, and you'll be

losing some soon," he says. "That's the reason you're all sad. It's all in your head. Ride out the off-cycle for a few weeks and focus on the upcoming cycle," he says.

"And the lower testosterone? I mean, how do I know if I'm already producing my natural testosterone again?"

"If your balls have filled out again, they are probably—"

"Probably?" My balls do look normal, but it's not like I can be sure. I should've taken a before pic of them too. "What do you mean probably?"

"Patience, bro. Waiting out the off-cycle isn't easy for anybody."

After warming up on the bench press I set up the same weight as last week. You got this, I tell myself, but I don't believe it. I doubt I will even do the same amount as last time—ten reps.

I start pushing out the reps and counting. At the sixth rep, my body knows I can't do another. I rack the weight and feel more depressed than ever.

By two o'clock I'm at the reception desk. Nobody but Jake hitting the weights and Susan, a new member, walking at a moderate pace on the treadmill.

My mood is a little better only because I'll be making some money in the next hour, when James comes by to pick up the gear I have for him.

Evenings are busy with lots of members working out and some people trickling in to ask about memberships, which I sell them. So I ask my gear clients to come by in the early afternoons.

Done with the reading and questions of history class, I get busy with my advanced algebra homework. The automatic discipline I used to have for homework is gone. I gotta push myself to open the book and get to it. Once I'm doing it, like now, I tell myself to focus.

Maybe I do have depression. Just because Alpha and the others guys say they don't get the side effect doesn't mean I can't.

The bell on the door jingles and here comes the USF student James, skinny as a rail and carrying a shopping bag—he follows instructions well.

"I didn't even know this place was here," he says, setting the bag on the reception desk.

"We're here, bro," I say, trying to summon some excitement. Whether I'm helping out on the floor or receiving people at reception, I gotta be upbeat. "We got all the equipment you need and are less expensive than Snap Fitness."

I've done the same with my three other clients. When they come to pick up their gear, I take the opportunity to sell them a membership. More money for me. They've said they might sign up just as soon as their membership at their current gym runs out.

I take James's shopping bag. I open it to discover an empty bottle of Gatorade and weightlifting gloves. This nonsense he took to Snap Fitness is only one reason I knew he was a potential client.

What I did to start selling was, I got a free three-day pass at Snap Fitness, and a free five-day pass at CrossTrain Gym.

Alpha told me what two types of guys to look out for.

First, there are people like me. Guys who go hardcore, have that determination and power in every rep. Between sets they're checking themselves out in the mirror, oblivious to everything in the world except for that image in front of them.

Devon, a senior at Rivera High, and Mark, a thirty-one-year-old manager at Panera by the mall, are both in this category.

The second kind of potential users are like James. Guys who think bullshit like Gatorade and gloves matter. Guys who drift into the gym as if lost, no plan of action or workout in mind. They wander from one easy-to-use machine to another—never getting the full range of motion in exercises. Between sets they look at their phones or at the TV.

"These are both orals," I tell James, dropping D-bol and Trenbolone into the shopping bag. This chump is scared of needles. The bag is for discretion. I hand it back to him. He takes it just like he gave it to me—completely chill.

The other guys didn't follow instructions too well. They strolled in all cool, but once I handed over the bag they got twitchy and paranoid, looked from side to side. Like I just handed them crack in front of a police station.

"Don't forget to train hard and eat big like I told you," I say. "You give everything to your gains, and they'll give everything to you."

About an hour later, I'm done with homework and reading about ways to boost testosterone naturally. I have to do whatever I can to get out of this depressive slump.

Get plenty of sleep.

Not a problem for me. I'm sleeping more hours than usual. Sometimes I even take a nap during the day.

Get more vitamin D, preferably through sunlight.

Okay, I could do that. Lay out in the backyard.

Reduce stress with exercise.

The only stress I have is that I'm not producing enough testosterone. And when I exercise, and lift less than I did the time before, it stresses me out even more.

And here comes more stress. Rogelio is crossing the parking lot. I haven't seen him since the movie theater. I remember he used to work out in the late morning, and that's when I'm at school. I'm feeling nervous, wondering if he'll be all chatty. All I remember is that he warned me against taking steroids.

"David! What are you doing here?"

Chatty, see? When he can just scan his card like the others and walk right on past with a simple hello.

Besides, I should be asking *him* what he's doing here. This isn't his usual schedule.

"Working," I tell him. "I hold things down here in the afternoons."

"Why aren't you in school?" he asks.

Why don't you mind your own business? I wanna shoot back.

But I won't, because angry thoughts are easier to keep to myself lately. A good thing about being off gear.

"I'm going to adult school," I say. "We get out early."

He nods and stands there. Doesn't move toward the locker room or gym floor.

"Have a good workout," I tell him, pressing him to go.

As if he didn't hear me he says, "That quote on your shirt is one of my favorites."

That which does not kill me makes me stronger, my T-shirt says.

"It's the only Iron Life quote I really like," I say.

"I mean that it's one of my favorites of all time," Rogelio says. "Nietzsche has some great quotes."

Neecha? I've never heard of that bodybuilder. Never bothered to look him up.

"He was a German philosopher," Rogelio says.

Okay, so he was a philosopher. Why is Rogelio telling me this?

I imagine Neecha as an old man with white hair and a

beard. Something like Santa Claus or how they draw God in cartoons. The truth is I've never read any philosophy.

"You really got into fitness," he says. "Good for you. Looking good."

He's making fun of you. You're smaller than he is.

A sort of "hmph" sound comes out of my nose.

"What's that?" Rogelio asks.

All of a sudden the logical part of me understands that I do look better than when Rogelio first met me. So he's probably being sincere. "Nothing. Never mind."

"You don't like how you look?"

I open my mouth to speak, but then all I do is shrug.

"Do you want to talk about that, David? When I was your age, I struggled with muscle dysmorphia, and it's something anyone who's into fitness needs to watch out for."

"Muscle what?" Now I'm really interested. It sounds like some disease you catch at the gym.

"Muscle dysmorphia. Basically it's this idea some people, mostly guys, get in their heads that they don't look good enough. You obsess about your looks and over food."

"That's not me," I say right away. "Have a good workout." I don't want to hear more.

"Um, okay. Thanks. Take care of yourself."

I watch him walk away. See him slide some 25s on the bar to warm up with the behind-the-neck press.

He's a lot stronger and bigger than you.

Sure, but he's been working out forever.

Excuses, excuses. He's warming up with weight you can barely lift. It's true, which makes me feel worse than ever. Just when I feel like my mood can't drop further, it does, going lower and lower. If I could only gain some size, take a little tiny bit of gear even though I'm supposed to cycling off.

But no. That's dangerous. Then I think of that other thing I can do to gain some size fast. Instant size. I text Ray to ask him for Synthol. Tell him to add it to the order Alpha and I already sent him for our customers.

24

WHAT I LOVE most about riding in Alpha's Jeep is how connected I feel to everything we pass. With the top down, the world out there feels within reach. Everything's so vivid. It fills me with a joy I haven't felt in a while.

Or maybe I'm just happy because I'm on my way to pick up my Synthol. If can't do gear for another two weeks, at least I can puff up my muscles a bit.

An expected expense, one hundred seventy dollars. No big deal. It's not like I'm spending on other stuff, like dates with Karina or other girls. I'm waiting until I get my size back—my confidence back—in order to start going out.

"Hot girls," Alpha says, nodding toward the Starbucks.

They're coming out, drinks in hands, one in tight jeans and the other in shorts. Yep, totally hot.

Maybe that's another reason I've been so depressed. No action at all. Alpha needs some action too. It's been over a month since Mindy left him.

"You need to get on Tinder and get laid, bro," I say. "They got all kinds of girls on there, you know?"

He drains the last of his protein shake from his bottle shaker. That's his silhouette on the bottle, him flexing one arm. He gets so much free protein powder from the endorsement, he can afford to give me some. It tastes the same as the one I used to drink.

He keeps his eyes on the road and says, "Tinder ain't for me. I'm old school. Prefer to meet girls in real life."

"Next month in Miami seems far away," I tell him, meaning the Mr. Florida competition.

Alpha and the gearheads were telling me how it is at those meets. Though most girls don't like guys as big as Alpha, the ones who do tend to show up. Even the guys who place fourth or fifth might have groupies.

During competitions, pro bodybuilders know what it's like to be rock stars.

"You'll meet girls in Miami, but what about now? You only leave the house to go to the gym."

Alpha says nothing. Just stares straight ahead, his face unreadable.

I worry about the guy. Sure, he's right that all his sleep and all that chilling on the recliner watching Netflix is good for his gains. He needs people though.

I mean, lately I'm bummed all the time, but that's

because of the way I look. Alpha is always huge. Even if he lost half his muscles he'd be big. Once I get my gains back I'll have the confidence to talk to Dad and Gaby finally. I have to make the first move because Dad hasn't tried contacting me once, even though I'm sure Culler High called him after my fight. It's not like people call you up to ask for an apology. They probably don't care that I'm smaller, but it's hard to look at anybody when I can't look at myself in the mirror, literally. I'm just too bummed for anything.

Alpha though? It makes no sense that he's so sad and mopey.

Alpha pulls into the long, curved driveway to park behind Ray's Ford Expedition inside his open garage. There's a classic Harley Fat Boy right beside it, midnight blue and black.

Ray is an AT&T executive who does well even without selling gear. The last time we came here we chilled a bit inside his smart home. I got a kick outta opening the blinds and pouring water into my glass from the fridge with voice commands. He's a tech junkie who didn't get a chance to show me even half his gadgets.

"Stay in the car," Alpha says when I unbuckle my seat belt. "This is going to be quick."

He opens his hand for money.

"Why quick?" I ask, and stuff my wad of cash into it.

Fourteen hundred and fifty dollars. Two cycles for new

customers and the Synthol for me.

"He's really busy today. Told me to come by myself."

He gets out and goes to knock on the door.

This sucks. Even if Ray doesn't have time to chill or show me more of his house, I would've liked to say hi at least.

I flip down the visor to look at myself in the mirror.

You skinny fuck. Pencil thin and pathetic.

No way to argue against that. It's not like I can shut my brain up like I did during the summer, by hopping on a scale or measuring my gains or lifting heavier weights. Though I do hope I'll feel better after the Synthol injections.

All of a sudden, I remember the other reason I wanted to see Ray. So I could ask him about taking a tiny bit of gear during an off-cycle. This morning when I walked into the kitchen, Alpha was popping Tren and washing it down with water. Claimed it was only one tab, not four, and it's every other day, not daily—therefore totally fine.

It goes against everything I've read and heard, even from Alpha himself, so I wanted to double-check with Ray.

Now I get it. That's *precisely* why I'm out here in the humidity like a jackass. Alpha didn't want me to dig deeper.

Alpha never seems to get smaller because he doesn't get smaller. Just keeps taking and taking.

Like some drug addict or something.

Rogelio said something about obsession. Dismal muscles? Morphic muscles? I pushed it out of my head because, well, whatever.

I bust out my phone now to look it up and Google corrects me: muscle dysmorphia.

Muscle dysmorphia is a fixation, often to the point of delusion, in which a person believes that they are not muscular enough, too slender, or too little. However, the individual often presents with a normal build or can also present as brawny and large.

My heart wiggles. That sounds like me and Alpha, I have to admit. No wonder I wanted to shut Rogelio up so bad.

The website explains that it's a mental disorder. A second website says the same.

The following website, written by a bodybuilder in recovery, says the condition usually goes undiagnosed because people don't realize it's a problem. Because going to the gym and eating right is seen as positive.

The websites sort of make sense, but even supposing they're right—what am I supposed to do? Give up the gear and gym? I'm small as fuck now and I'm supposed to be okay with getting smaller? Not going to happen.

Besides, Alpha and I have a drive for greatness. What do psychologists know about greatness and sacrifice? What do they know about going that extra distance in order to be your best self?

Nothing. They just probably want everybody to be average.

Fuck average.

Back at home, Alpha is loading the syringe with Synthol while I'm trying to forget the look on his face when I injected him with it in the summer. We're in the bathroom where the light is the strongest.

"Don't worry," Alpha says. "Oil doesn't burn going in."

"So why did you make those pained sounds and sometimes twist your face when I injected you?"

"Because the needle sort of hurts going in."

The oil reaches four cc's in the cylinder. I'm getting half a cc of Synthol in all three heads of both shoulders, and one in each pec. I have measured out the location and marked the right spot with a black marker. One inch above each nipple and three spaced out on the side of each shoulder.

I can't wait for the instant size that should hold up just before my next cycle starts. I just wanna look into the mirror without feeling disgust.

Alpha flicks the cylinder to remove the tiny air bubbles. Pushes on the plunger enough so that one drop clings to the tip of the needle before falling.

"Ready?" he asks.

"This is crazy," I say.

"No shit. I'll be doing it for the competition, because

my peaks need it. But you don't need this."

"Come on," I say. "Let's get this over with."

I close my eyes like with my first gear injection. The needle penetrates my left pec. I told myself to hold on to the pain but it hurts like hell.

I'm surprised by the loud sound that comes from me, with my lips pressed so tight.

"Relax," Alpha says.

Damn that needle goes deep. The oil oozes in like a warm tingle. He was right. It doesn't burn. It's only the poke that hurts.

Alpha slides the needle out—that doesn't feel too great either.

Alpha stabs my right pec, taking his time with the injection.

"Aaaaargg," I say when it goes into my right shoulder.

It hurts more with every jab, like the needle keeps getting thicker, until he finishes with the left shoulder too.

"All done," he says, setting the syringe on the counter.

Drops of blood leak out of my chest. Even more drops from my shoulders. Alpha pulls some toilet paper from the roll to wipe it up. I rub several alcohol-soaked cotton balls on all the perforations in my body. The aim was perfect. I just hope the angle and the amount was precise.

Alpha leaves me alone in the bathroom.

But totally worth it. You'll be less pathetic than you are.

Which is true, but then another thought creeps in. *It's not about your body though. It's about your mind. You'll never be big enough, to your mind.*

I rub and squeeze my chest, like I'm fondling myself. After a minute I move onto my shoulders. I work on them with my arms crossed, looking like a steroid genie about to grant some wishes. I switch back to my pecs, and then one more time to my shoulders.

Done with that, I look into the mirror again. No lumps—great—but where is the extra size?

Why did it work when I injected Alpha but it didn't work for me? Did Ray sell me some bullshit?

I head out to talk to Alpha about it. "Hey, bro."

"Let's see what you got," he says, his back to me.

He takes his plate of food outta the microwave and turns to me. "Nice!"

"Don't bullshit me, Alpha."

The smile becomes a frown. "You see lumps? You see something asymmetrical?"

"Where's the increased size?" I ask.

"I'm *looking* at it, bro." He's back to smiling. "I'll go get the tape measure."

Alpha comes back and wraps the tape measure around me, getting the middle of my shoulders and the top of my chest. "See? An almost three-inch increase." He laughs. "That's champion mentality. You wanna get even bigger, and you will. Just wait until you're back on a cycle."

Champion mentality? Or a sickness?

"Have you ever heard of muscle dysmorphia?" I ask Alpha.

He tilts his head at me. Then picks up his steaming plate again.

I say, "It's when you think you're—"

"I know what that bullshit is," he says, heading outta the kitchen.

I follow him. "Why is it bullshit?"

"Because there's nothing wrong with wanting to get bigger, right?" He takes a seat on the recliner, plate in his lap. Pulls on the lever just enough so his feet rise yet his body stays upright. "Just look at what your gains have given you."

"I'm not saying there's anything wrong with gaining muscle. I'm talking about what the term *means*."

Alpha looks at me with narrowed eyes. Then he sighs and takes his first bite of green beans.

What's up with his attitude? I'm not trying to be annoying.

"We're driven to be our best selves," Alpha says, a bit of green mush in his mouth. "That's not a mental disorder. It's called *motivation*. Do we feel small? Sure. That's what keeps us motivated."

"But tons of people are motivated to do things and you

don't hear about it becoming some mental disorder."

"But, but, but," he practically shouts.

A chill runs through me. I've never seen him angry like this.

"Forget it," I say, and start to walk away.

"Listen to me," he says, and I take a step back. "Nobody is perfect, okay? We got an obesity epidemic in this country because people eat junk. We got people drinking alcohol every day from the moment they get home until they go to sleep. Just because that stuff is socially acceptable doesn't mean it's good. Agreed?"

"Definitely."

"Okay. Well, we take gear in order to be our best selves."

What does that mean? How is being as muscular as possible your "best self"?

Alpha grabs his fork and spears a bite of chicken.

I ask, "Why is having a great body better than anything else?"

"Fucking hell." He lets his fork drop on the plate in anger. Some quinoa falls off the side and onto his shorts.

"Sorry, I'm just curious."

He pinches the tiny fluffs of seeds and tries to drop it back on the plate. It turns to mush in his fingertips.

He breathes deeply, in through his mouth and out through his mouth. Just like he taught me. But it's not calming him one little bit. I can tell.

He looks up at me now. "Are you just going to stand

266

there asking me questions or are you going to let me eat in peace?"

I walk to my bedroom and close the door. I don't want to be anywhere near him when he's angry like that.

25

I'M BACK! With more energy than ever, more confidence and quicker recovery times after each workout. Most importantly, after two weeks on my cycle, stacking three types of gear, I have my gains back. Real size, not the Synthol puffiness.

I got nine more weeks of growth left on the cycle. Every day closer to my goal of becoming a YouTube teen sensation. I've even started jotting down episode ideas, topics the other guys have never even touched on.

There are fewer thoughts popping into my head of me being too small or too obsessed or anything else that totally bums me out.

Best of all, with my confidence back I was able to post pictures on Instagram earlier this week, and even got a date because of it. A girl named Isabel commented *u look great* on one of my shirtless pics, so I commented on some of hers before deciding to DM her.

A gorgeous girl, no doubt the hottest one in her high school one town over. Which means she doesn't know that I used to be Bitchslap David.

I hop into the steaming shower and start with the soap, loving the curves of muscle on my body. My balls have shrunk again to a tiny hard mound.

Done with the regular soap, I bust out the orange acne soap Tower recommended. Pour some on the back scrubber and attack the newly arrived zits for a good two minutes. I'm trying to stay hopeful.

After I dry off and change, I head out to the living room, where Alpha is practicing his choreographed posing for Mr. Florida next week. I'm grateful for the music playing—he chose some upbeat electronic song. It's a heads-up to expect my roommate in skimpy red underwear.

There he is, holding a side biceps pose in front of the mirror angled against the wall. He's looking more shredded than before. Judges want to see the definition of every muscle, so Alpha has slathered dark oil on from the neck down to help with that.

For days he's been practicing his choreography to put on a show, make the most of his two and a half minutes of stage time.

He spots me in the reflection and shouts, "There he is!" Presses *pause* in the middle of the song.

He's smiling big, clearly thrilled with how he's looking.

Since he started practicing, he's been in a better mood. Spends more time at the gym after his workouts. Takes Crockett out for longer walks too.

"Sorry, I didn't mean to interrupt," I say. "I'm just heading out."

He comes up to me all normal, as if he has regular clothes on. "Ready to go?" he asks, looking me up and down.

I'm just not comfortable around male nudity. It's the same at the gym when I go to the bathroom and guys are changing or naked, going to the showers or heading back from them.

"My boy's got a date!" Alpha grins like he did on my first day of school. "I'm so happy for you."

Since he's letting me borrow his Jeep, he starts to explain how to use the alarm system on it. I'm super excited about cruising around in that sweet ride, but it's hard to pay attention to him when he's mostly naked and looking like his face and body are two different ethnicities.

"Do you mind being less naked or something?"

"Sure." He puts on a T-shirt, and actually looks weirder. It's not just his size. Maybe only girls can pull off the just shirt and underwear look.

He says, "Stay out as long as you want, bring the girl back here, whatever. I'm cool, you got me?"

I laugh. "I'll try."

"There ain't no trying, bro!" he shouts like he's spotting me. "There's only *doing*!"

I love seeing him in a goofy mood like this. It's been forever since he's been fun. He keeps it up, telling me my teenage years are running out and not to waste any time. He could be my cheerleader, if cheerleaders were 270 pounds of muscular beast.

"So will you be trying or doing?" he barks at me once again.

"Doing!" I shout.

"Damn right!"

Then he stands closer to me, shoulders curved back, which can only mean one thing: chest bump.

"Do we have to?" I ask.

"It's safe. This T-shirt is covering up the grease."

The chest bump feels like running into a wall. I stumble back a few feet.

He tosses me the keys. "If you crash my Jeep I'll kill you."

I text Isabel to tell her where I'm seated as soon as I arrive. This coffee shop downtown is fancier than I expected. Pale wood tables and chairs that shimmer. Contemporary paintings hanging on the side wall. The wall where we're seated, on the second floor, is nothing but glass. I look down on the darkening evening. The streetlamps already on and the cars easing down the street, some with the headlights on. I can see the crowd of people gathering at the park, over by the Tampa Museum of Art.

It's a free music concert Isabel heard about, featuring a few local bands. A fitness girl who's into free stuff. Lucky me.

I try out different sitting positions while I wait. I sit up straight, then a little slouched, before deciding that the coolest position is one in which I look relaxed. So I lean back, my legs sort of spread. Like I'm the most confident guy in the world when it's the exact opposite. I can't believe how nervous I am. I guess because it's my first time on a date-date, completely winging it with someone I've seen for the first time in real life. It feels like an audition.

After about fifteen minutes waiting, I message her again, but she doesn't respond to that text either.

Thirty-three minutes later, bored with Instagram and feeling like a total loser sitting alone while the rest of the tables have filled up, I decide to call Isabel. We haven't actually talked yet, and I know it's a weird first conversation to have, but how else can I find out what the hell is going on if she won't text me back.

The call goes to voice mail at the second ring. I tell myself not to get angry, but it doesn't completely work. I leave the coffee shop, jaws clenched and brain turning over all the reasons why she might be avoiding me. I can't help but think she found out about my previous identity, and had no interest in meeting Bitchslap David.

When I put a few blocks of distance between me and the coffee shop I get a text from Isabel.

I won't be able to make it. Sorry. I got busy. Maybe some other time?

Maybe? It doesn't sound like she's sorry at all. Though it's annoying, I tell myself there are other girls. Tons of girls who want to get with the new me. I see two check me out as I pocket my phone and decide I'm not ready to go home so early. It's barely after eight.

The music coming from the concert is some guy strumming an acoustic guitar, far from an exciting opener. So I decide to walk the downtown streets.

People don't walk in Tampa. It's what my uncle, when he visited from Mexico, thought was most bizarre about this city. From the airport where we picked him up and all the way to our house we didn't see a single pedestrian. *Lots of cars*, he pointed out, *but where are all the people?*

Downtown is an exception. There are actual people walking down the actual sidewalks. I go down Morgan Street, the neon signs of the bars and restaurants throwing colorful light onto the passersby. The tall modern buildings tower over me like protection, and then it's the open greenness of Courthouse Square.

I walk and let my mind wander all over the place but somehow my thoughts keep landing on my family. I pass a woman pushing a stroller and think of Gaby. Remember how I used to hold on to Gaby's stroller when walking with Mom through the stores.

Another woman, close to forty, has her blond hair in a braid. I think about braiding Gaby's hair in a few styles that I learned from YouTube tutorials.

It's crazy the connections I make in my head, how anything can bring back a memory of my family.

I pass the Subway, all those pictures of sub sandwiches in the window, and think of the tamales Dad and I made last Christmas—we tried and failed to replicate Mom's recipe. It's crazy that subs have me thinking about tamales. They *do* sort of have a similar shape, but still.

I miss my family. More than ever. Maybe because Gaby's birthday is in two weeks, which is weighing heavy on my mind lately. I have to be there for her party. Which means I have to apologize.

I pass a smoothie shop that's closed for the night and remember the meal replacement shake I left in the Jeep. It's time to feed my muscles.

I go back and drink the thick liquid.

Then I make my way to the concert, the rock music getting louder with every block. Curtis Hixon Waterfront Park is really packed now, more couples everywhere.

I study them. Their bodies, sure, but mostly how close they walk together. Guys with girls, two guys together holding hands. Tons of people paired up and out tonight, just like I would be with Karina, if we were still together.

No, I won't think of Karina. I just need to meet another girl, I tell myself.

I lean back on the concrete barrier of the Hillsborough River to watch the crowd and listen to the fast-paced rock music from here.

After a few minutes I see Karina. With a guy. A fucking chump who wouldn't know a barbell if one landed at his feet.

They're walking past, about twenty yards in front of me, too busy in conversation to turn their heads, much less notice me. Why would Karina go out with a loser like that? What's wrong with her?

But after I watch them for a few seconds, a different feeling settles in me and I'm no longer clenching my teeth. There's a deep stab of sadness in my gut and regret for how badly I fucked things up with her.

I gotta admit that I'm not angry at her or the guy she's with. I'm mad at myself.

I watch them go, keep going, until they get lost inside the crowd.

As I drive north on I-275, the roar of wind rushing down on me, I wish there was somewhere else to go, something

I could do to cheer myself up. Because Alpha will already be in bed. I'm not eager to return to a dark house, and then into the total silence of my bedroom.

I consider calling up Miguel, who I've messaged with a few times since the first day of school. He keeps saying we should hang out, and maybe we should. But not spontaneously at 10:24 on a Friday. Besides, he's probably out with his girlfriend, who hates me.

Oh well. Nothing to do but go home. I pull up to the house to find the lights on in the living room. Alpha must have forgotten to hit the switch before going to bed.

Inside is the aftermath of a party. Opened cans of beer and a tequila bottle clutter the coffee table. Nobody's around. Looks like the guys invaded the house to drink before taking the party elsewhere.

The toilet flushes. The one from the bathroom I use. Seconds later Alpha comes out, glassy-eyed and stumbling. He puts his hand on the wall to steady himself.

"What are you doing back?" he slurs.

Holy shit. Alpha is *drunk*. Wobbling even, with a hand against the wall.

I can't believe it, the guy with a superclean diet. The guy with a qualifying contest in Miami next week.

Alcohol is kryptonite to gains—the worst thing to consume when you're looking to get shredded. His body will be metabolizing the alcohol instead of calories until it's all burned up.

"It's pretty early," he says, disappointment showing on his face. "What happened to your date?"

I don't wanna get into it, so I say what the guys at the gym say whenever girls disappear from their lives.

"She's crazy."

He walks over to the couch as I collect the empty beer cans.

"You weren't supposed to see me like this, bro." He says this in a tired, barely intelligible voice. "Can't believe I'm actually drinking. I hadn't had a sip since . . ." He hiccups. ". . . in years."

He sinks back into the middle of the couch. Good idea. He could have busted his ass trying that with the recliner.

I hug the six empties, carry them to the bin, and dump them.

"Friday nights are for partying," I say, trying to lighten the mood. "So was it just you or did the guys come over?"

"Just me." He tips his head back so that it rests on the top of the cushion, his eyes cast up at the speckled ceiling. "I fucked up, David. I fucked up real bad."

He sure did. If he doesn't win Mr. Florida next Saturday, he can't compete at the World Muscleman Championship.

"One night won't ruin you," I say, trying to be optimistic. "Just go to bed and hit the gym hard as always tomorrow."

He leans forward from the couch to reach for the tequila bottle. Misses. On the third try he manages to grab it and moves it toward his mouth. I snatch the bottle from his hand.

"It won't ruin you as long as you *stop drinking*," I add.

I go into his bedroom for a pillow and the bedcover, which is rumpled on the floor like most of his clothes. What a disaster. No wonder he always keeps the door closed.

The door of his bathroom is wide open. A syringe rests on top of the toilet lid. I go inside and find ampoules of Sustanon in the wastebasket. Plus syringes and the plastic wrappers they come in.

What the hell is he thinking? Taking a few tabs of Tren occasionally, as he claimed, was bad enough. This is a full cycle he's on.

But I won't get any answers from him now.

Back in the living room, I set the pillow and bedcover next to him on the couch. "Here, buddy. Get some rest, okay?"

Tears well in his eyes. While it sort of surprises me— you don't expect such a big guy to cry—I know why he's sad. I know why he decided to drink tonight. It's the same reason he can't leave the house or try to meet other girls.

This is all about Mindy.

"You'll be okay, Alpha. You'll see."

"I miss Mindy." He lifts the collar of his T-shirt to wipe the wetness under his eyes.

"You'll find somebody else," I tell him. "You just gotta

get on some dating apps, leave the house. Next Saturday in Miami you'll hook up for sure. Now you need to lie down and get some sleep."

Crockett has walked over to set his chin on Alpha's knee. I'm glad to get some help here. Love is what my friend needs.

"We had the perfect woman, Crockett," Alpha slurs. "I fucked it up."

"There are tons of girls out there," I say, full of hope. "You'll meet a few for sure next Saturday in Miami."

He breathes in deeply and lets out a big sigh. "I can't have them." He tips his head back again and closes his eyes.

"Your gains give you everything," I remind him. "Even girls."

His eyelids tremble and a drop oozes out the bottom of each one.

"No, I mean I *can't*. I can't get it up." He says this with a hushed defeat, as if I've been pleading to get this confession from him for hours.

Even if that means what I think it means, he's drunk. People say crazy stuff when they're drunk.

"What are you talking about?" I ask him, just in case.

"I pretty much haven't cycled off gear in three years and it finally caught up with me."

I open my mouth to speak and then close it. What the hell is wrong with him? He told me to ride out the loss and he can't even do it? It's like he's trying to ruin his health as quickly as possible. I think of what steroids are doing to me, but this is only my second cycle and there won't be many more. I think. I hope I have enough self-control to eventually stop.

In any case, I'm not going to panic or call him crazy right now. Not when he's in this condition.

"I got checked out by the doctor back in January. Then I went to the men's clinic in St. Pete. I even saw a specialist in Orlando two months ago."

He opens his eyes, which are wet and unreadable. I need to say something. Twenty-four years old without erections? That's . . .

Is that the reason Mindy left? I don't know what to say.

"With another cycle," I offer. "Or maybe if you cycle off for a really long time you'll be fine."

Which he can't do because of the upcoming competitions.

"After you win the WMC title," I say, correcting myself. "You can get off gear forever and then you'll—"

"No!" Alpha says.

He pushes himself up from the couch. I walk over to make sure he doesn't fall. To steady himself, he grips my shoulders with both of his hands. I ignore the pain of my zits.

"I've tried everything," he says, his breath reeking of alcohol. "I even cycled off for a whole two months, in the spring. I've tried different medications."

You can hear the hopelessness in his voice and see it all over his face.

He sinks back into the couch, which exhales loudly from the pressure of all that weight.

I feel so useless. What can I tell him?

I take the bedcover in one hand and pat his pillow with the other.

He nods and allows himself to drop his head on it, lifting his legs onto the couch with some effort.

Then I cover him and shut off the living room light.

By the time I pass through the dark to go to my room, I hear a drowsy murmur, then a nasal rasp as he falls asleep.

26

ON SATURDAYS, the morning trainer opens the gym at seven, which is Alpha's favorite time to work out. I figured he'd be treating his hangover for most of the day so I'm shocked to see his Jeep gone when I wake up a little past eight.

I head to the gym to work out, and also to tell Alpha what I couldn't last night.

"Where's Alpha?" I ask Rassle, who's doing bicep curls.

"In the bathroom. I don't think he's feeling well."

I find Alpha bent over the sink, rinsing his face. Then he sucks up water to swish and spit it back out. Nobody else is here.

"You had a lot to drink," I say, "and you probably shouldn't be—"

"Listen, about that." He dries his face with a paper towel and tosses it into the trash. "Thanks for taking that bottle of tequila and listening to me. But let's forget it ever happened, okay?"

"Sure, no problem. So are you cycling off, then?"

"Let's *forget it*," he says forcefully.

"I know you want to win the WMC, but why ruin your health forever over it?"

He stares me down. I know he has more experience controlling his roid rage than I do, but it's still scary to have his fierce eyes on me like this.

"All this hasn't been for nothing, David. Getting sponsored by a supplement company and winning a few competitions wasn't my goal. *Nobody* ever remembers the guy who got fourth in the World Muscleman Champion-ship."

"How about *nobody* cares about the WMC," I tell him. "Ninety-nine percent of people can't even name last year's winner."

"*I* care," he says, all offended.

"Yeah, well, maybe you should care more about other stuff, like your health."

And your relationships, like with Mindy. But mention-ing that might be mean.

Alpha's nostrils flare and then he nods, calming him-self down. "It's nice that you're worried about me, but I'll be fine. All I need is to win the championship and then I'll give up the gear forever. And to do that, I have to qualify in Miami, which is in a week. So excuse me."

He heads outta the bathroom to finish his workout while I think about his words.

Will he really give up the gear if he wins? I wonder about that and wonder about me. I try to imagine a time when either of us, when any of the gearheads, will be fine with lifting less weight, having less mass.

But I just can't picture it.

27

THE BACKYARD is ready for the celebration. No need for streamers, balloons, or cake. With the gearheads all you need is the large foldout table and chairs, which I have set up, some meat, which is on the way, and a hot grill, which I'm taking care of right now.

I've stacked the charcoal pyramid-style, like Dad taught me. Now I squeeze just a swirl of lighter fluid onto the briquettes. When I drop a lit match onto it, I step back.

The pyramid flames with a flash before settling into a steady burn.

Alpha won Mr. Florida this afternoon. He might have the most impressive physique in the *world*, so beating out every guy in the state was a cinch. Even with that one drunken night.

After a four-hour drive back from Miami, he and

Rassle stopped by the supermarket for this celebration. They left Tampa yesterday morning. I stayed here to hold things down—watched over the gym and the house.

When Crockett starts barking crazier than normal, I know they've pulled up to the driveway.

"Here's the champ!" Rassle announces. He's carrying three full supermarket bags with one hand and opens the gate with the other.

Alpha walks through, lifting the trophy high enough so leaping Crockett doesn't knock it outta his hands.

The trophy, marble and gold-colored, gleams even in the fading evening light.

"Congratulations," I say, and try for something like a hug.

It's not easy getting your arms around Alpha. He gets his free arm around me just fine though. Damn near crushes me.

He lets go. "There was no close second place, bro. I absolutely destroyed the competition."

Rassle gives me a fist bump and says, "This guy wanted to leave right after the damn show and interview. Can you believe that?"

The grin slides off Alpha's face.

Rassle is referring to them not staying all weekend to hook up with girls. I gotta steer away from this awkward topic, keep the moment fun and happy.

"He wanted to come back and celebrate with his friends," I say.

"That's right," Alpha says, setting the trophy down in the middle of the table.

"David, there were some girls there like you wouldn't believe," Rassle says, handing me the heavy bag of meat. "If I had girls half that hot waiting for me after I got finished wrestling a gator, I wouldn't be in a rush to come home."

"Let me throw some of these steaks on the grill," I say.

"I love my friends," Rassle says. "But y'all would've had to wait a little bit longer to celebrate. I mean, it makes no sense to—"

"Hey," Alpha cuts in. "I'm going to hit the shower real quick before the others show up. I still feel greasy from the posing oil."

After lots of hovering over the sizzling meats, the guys worried about the steaks being overcooked, and me telling everybody to back off, we're all grubbing at the table.

The night air is nice. It's full of hazy light from the porch, and the smell of meat and onions.

The grill oozes smoke from round two, which is bar-becued ribs.

It's eight of us, everybody but Alpha and me eating and drinking whatever the hell they want. The table is full of pretzels, Doritos, and other chips. Plus all the fixings to heap on the baked potatoes: butter, cream, bacon bits, and shredded cheddar. We don't cheat, Alpha and I. We stay looking lean and good.

As usual, nobody says much while feasting. I look around at all of them. The wide shoulders I want so badly. The roundness of the biceps when their arms are bent, the forks about to go in their mouths.

That's what real men look like.

I take a drink of water and try to think of something else.

You've gotten your gains back, and even some few extra pounds, but you're still a skinny nothing of a boy.

Sometimes these guys serve as inspiration, and other times they just make me feel like crap for being half their size. Not even half. All of a sudden, Jake asks about Mitch Bayer.

"Mr. California is next week," Alpha says.

"It was *today*," Jake declares with certainty. "Mr. *New Jersey* is next week."

Avaristo Mendoza from New Jersey won number two in the World Muscleman Championship last year.

Launch asks, "Who's Mitch Bayer?"

Powerlifters are all about how much you can lift, not how good your physique is, so I explain that Bayer won the WMC last year. "He's Alpha's main concern."

"Yep!" Rassle is looking at his phone. "It was today. Bayer won Mr. California alright, but the guy ain't at your level, Alpha."

I lean over to have a look. Bayer looks amazing—I can't

deny that—but Alpha is bigger with more definition. His biceps' peaks, which were lagging, are now more impressive than Bayer's. Partly because I'm so damn talented with the needle.

"It's true!" I agree.

While everybody else looks for it on their own devices, Tower hands his phone across to Alpha, who takes it with curiosity.

His expression doesn't change as he studies today's picture, zooming in to look at different body parts.

I know what's happening. He can't see the truth. He needs other people to confirm it.

"It's a wrap for Bayer," Ray declares. "The championship is all yours, Alpha."

Devon says, "Keep going hardcore, brother, and that motherfucker doesn't stand a chance."

After everybody agrees, Alpha's back to smiling.

Now Devon stands up, lifts his fourth beer of the night, and waits.

"You going to stand there looking like a bloated Statue of Liberty?" Jake asks.

"I'm waiting for you guys to quiet down so I can propose a toast."

"I'd like to propose you buy a Weedwacker to deal with some of that armpit hair," Rassle drawls.

Devon takes a sip of his beer as he waits for the laughter

to die down. This time he lifts it up as high as his chin. "Is this better?"

"Better," everybody agrees.

"To Alpha," Devon says, "who has the biggest, leanest, most amazing symmetrical physique in Florida."

"On the planet!" I say, feeling proud.

Alpha lifts both of his fists. "That's right!"

"That's what I meant!"

"So why don't you try again?" Tower suggests.

"Why don't you all shut the fuck up?" Devon fires back. After clearing his throat he tries again: "To Alpha, who has the best physique the world has ever known!"

Shouts of "Damn right!" and other affirmations rise up in the night.

"To a man we all admire and love!" Tower throws in.

To a man who can't get it up, I think to myself. It pops into my head and I force it out right away.

"To Alpha," I say, "who will be the next World Muscleman Champion!"

The guys get even louder because of my last comment. They're hollering and banging the table. The backyard is so loud a neighbor might call the cops. Even Crockett starts barking.

Alpha is suddenly shy from all the love, but just look at that face. Beaming like when he walked in with the trophy. I admire his dedication and his hard work, the sacrifices he's been willing to make.

Who am I to worry about Alpha or judge him? I'm going to be happy for him tonight. I'm going to be happy for him for the next few months, until he returns to Tampa with the WMC title.

28

THE JEEP'S car alarm jolts me awake. Crockett's bark from the backyard is even louder.

"My Jeep!" Alpha shouts. "Thief!"

I hop off the bed, slip my bare feet into sneakers, and dash outta my room. I'm running through the living room, through the open doorway, past the honking Jeep with its flashing lights.

There's Alpha, bare-chested and barefoot, tearing down the street, arms and legs pumping like mad.

He's fast but I'm faster. I gain speed on him as I try to make out who we're chasing. Towering streetlights send down yellow splotches of light. A block and a half away, a lean guy in a hoodie enters the glow for a moment.

He's not getting away. I'm Nightchaser running through downtown streets, after the group of guys who framed me.

My heart beats pure adrenaline and my fists tighten

from the excitement. I can already feel my fists slamming against the thief's face. All that rage I've had to keep at bay is bubbling up and for once I can let it loose.

This thief fucked with the wrong guy.

"Get him!" Alpha shouts when I bolt past him.

The alarm and Crockett's barking start to fade as my sneakers steadily scratch against the asphalt. My eyes, now fully adjusted to the dark, fix on the silhouette of the thief less than a block away.

He enters the light on the corner and cuts left. I'm going full speed toward that corner when I hear a pained howl behind me.

"EEEEEyaah!"

I look over my shoulder—Alpha's arms are flailing as he slows down.

I stop. "Alpha?"

I'm torn between checking on him or continuing the chase.

When Alpha presses a hand against the middle of his chest, I run through the dark toward him.

"Alpha! What's wrong?"

There's no answer and his hand stays pressed to his chest. His face contorts in the harsh yellow light as he struggles to breathe.

"Call 911!" I shout into the night. "Somebody call 911!"

This will be okay. This will be okay.

But I think of his heart. Of the plaque buildup and how

the heart is just another muscle that grows on gear.

I grip the sides of Alpha's shoulders, hold him as best as I can as he wheezes.

"Breathe, Alpha. In through the nose and out through the mouth."

It's the technique he taught me for controlling rage. I'm not sure it will work for whatever's happening to him.

Lights in houses have switched on. Windows cast soft glows onto the lawns.

An old man in pajamas hobbles out from the house in front of us, cordless phone pressed to his ear.

"They're on their way!" he shouts at us. In a lower voice he says, "Yes, that's the address."

"Alpha," I say to my friend's twisted face. "What's going on?"

As an answer, he slips from my grasp. Drops on both knees and topples sideways. His face changes from tensed to relaxed.

"Alpha!"

I shout that as loud as I can, as if he's only in a deep sleep from which I can wake him up.

I put my two fingers to the side of his throat.

"They're on their way," the old man repeats, finally reaching us.

"I don't feel a pulse!" I let out in a panic, my own heart thumping wildly.

Maybe I'm not doing it right. It's not like I know first aid or anything.

The old man goes down on one knee with much effort, to check for himself.

An ambulance siren sounds out, somewhere west, faint but getting louder as neighbors appear on their porches.

I watch the man's face. Study the deep lines on his forehead and around his mouth for a sign. I wanna see a calm expression, better yet a smile. Anything but that look of horror he's showing now.

"What's wrong?" I ask in desperation. "What's going on?"

The man lowers his hand and says, "He's dead."

29

I **LIKE** to have the TV on. Louder than normal so I can hear it from any room. It gives me the feeling that I might step out to the living room and see Alpha there, watching Netflix or sports, maybe in a good mood like he was sometimes, ready with a quick joke.

With the TV off, the crushing silence of the house is unbearable.

There's some congestion on I-275, due to a car accident. Commuters are advised to take the Lynn Street exit . . .

For weeks after Mom died, I would play the kitchen radio in the evenings, just like she would while she made dinner.

In my room, I button up my new white shirt. The one I wore to Emily's party, way back in May, no longer fits. I'll put on the black tie on my way to the funeral. Tower should be here in about twenty minutes, and I'm running late.

. . . and lawmakers expect the bill to pass without any pushback.

Out in the living room, Crockett rests on the recliner, curled in a half circle. Just like when Alpha went to Tallahassee for Mindy, or to Miami to compete, Crockett got sad by the second day without Alpha. He has moved from his favorite spot, the middle cushion of the couch, to Alpha's favorite spot.

Mindy told me she'd pick him up after the funeral. She showed up at Tampa General a few hours after Alpha died, an absolute wreck.

In the kitchen, I put a heaping scoop of kibble into Crockett's dish.

. . . which will remain closed until the health department does a thorough inspection.

Alpha's parents have the Jeep and will be figuring out what to do about the gym. I really hope it will stay, and I can keep working there.

As far as living here, Mindy was nice enough to give me six weeks to figure out what to do. I'll find a cheap room to rent, which shouldn't be too hard. I can't go back to Dad's house.

I know I'll make things right with Dad though, as soon as I can. For the sake of Gaby anyway, because Dad won't stop seeing me as a drug addict, won't accept me for who I am.

I don't know what to do, what to say to him. Don't

wanna think about it either. For now I just need to make it through today's funeral.

The woman's body was dumped near I-275 in Lutz . . .

I pull out the big box of thirty-six eggs to start on my breakfast. An eight egg-white omelet, with a cup of oatmeal and banana. I should've eaten around seven a.m., to get my workout in by now. But I didn't sleep well last night and got up late. I'll have to hit the gym later.

When I place my hand on the fridge door to shut it, I notice the growth hormone on the top shelf of the door—a tiny clear bottle you gotta refrigerate. The other steroids I collected from the whole house, put in this one box, and shoved it deep under my bed before Alpha's parents came over.

I haven't taken a single injection or popped a single pill since Alpha died. I got as far as loading the syringe, but in the end couldn't go through with it. I'll get through today, and tomorrow I'll start again. As long as I keep eating big I should be fine.

But when I break the first egg, I imagine the taste and texture, the slimy egg whites in my mouth and sliding down my throat. No way.

So I'll make a meal replacement shake.

. . . although above capacity, will receive forty abused puppies . . .

I put a scoop of whey protein into the blender, followed

by a half cup of oats, and a whole banana. Fill it halfway with water.

A push of the button emits a sound like a speeding motorcycle. The ingredients mix until they blend into a smooth light brown goop.

I turn off the blender and drink. It goes down my throat like wet sand.

. . . right here from our very own Tampa. Alfonso Rich-ardson, known as "Alpha" in the bodybuilding community, is another life lost to anabolic steroid abuse.

I walk out to the living room, pitcher in hand, to get a better look at the TV. It shows him doing his posing routine at the last WMC. The flashing from cameras lighting up his darkened and oily skin.

He had won Mr. Florida three times, including this year, and last year he placed fourth in the World Muscleman Championship, the most important bodybuilding competition in the world.

Then it cuts to a special report.

Studies show that steroid abuse has increased a staggering four hundred percent in the last year. . . .

So that's it for Alpha. A brief mention of two competitions and then they drop numbers. Treat him like a statistic.

There's no mention that he was a successful businessman, the owner of Iron Life Gym for three years. No mention that he was the face of BeastMax Nutrition.

What *really* gets on my nerves is there's no mention of his actual life, the day-to-day details of who he really was. I guess you gotta get kidnapped or murdered for reporters to wanna find out about the real you.

If they'd asked me, I would've told them Alpha was a great friend, always there for me and supportive. Whether I needed advice or a place to stay or was just depressed and doubting myself.

In fact, the youngest death from a steroid-related heart attack this year has been a seventeen-year-old boy.

My heart feels like it stops and I fix my eyes on the boy on the screen. He's bigger than me, with sculpted arms and six-pack abs—looks absolutely great. I mean, he *looked* great. Now he's dead.

What if that happens to me? I try to think of myself dead, but it's a hard thing to imagine, you not existing. I can't do it. Maybe it can't be done. All I can think about is Dad and Gaby and how sad they'd be.

I try to push it outta my mind as I hear the reporter say stuff like *impressionable youth* and *teenagers* and *ignorant of risks.*

The sludge in my stomach turns and turns.

Experts say tens of thousands of young men are at an increased risk of dying early from complications brought on by steroid abuse.

There's a quick cut to man with a graying beard wearing

a white coat in a doctor's office, the words *Jonathon Weber PhD* on the bottom corner of the screen. That's the expert whose articles I read—and then ignored.

There are various factors contributing to this increase in anabolic steroid abuse. Girls and women have long felt the pressure to be attractive, as we all know. Being constantly confronted by images of impossibly thin models, many young women try to achieve that look. They go to great lengths and develop bulimia or anorexia as a result.

Boys and men are increasingly subjected to images of overly muscular men with visible abdominal muscles, and are feeling the pressure to drastically alter their bodies.

Dr. Jonathon Weber mentions the images we get bombarded with. The video games and movies. I've played those games and have watched those movies. Hell, I have a poster of Nightchaser hanging in my room.

He mentions how the action figures have grown in size.

What kind of message does it send to boys when everything they are told to admire is unattainable without drugs? When their role models are bulking up with the help of illegal drugs?

The irony is that steroid abusers are often health oriented, but they are using drugs that do irreparable damage to their organs, to their livers and hearts in particular.

I grab the remote on the coffee table and turn off the TV.

If I hear one more mention of heart attacks caused by what I've been taking, I'll lose my mind. I swear I will.

I mean, I get it. Steroids killed Alpha, and the damage I've already done is irreparable.

When will I ever give it up? When will I ever be okay with looking smaller than I am now?

"Give everything to your gains," Alpha used to say, "and they'll give everything to you."

His obsession with gains gave him an early death.

What has my obsession given me? A better physique, supposedly, which I somehow dislike as much as the one I had when all this madness began. No, steroids haven't given me anything at all. They've only taken away from me.

First my family and then Karina and my friends. The people I love the most. It may even take my life if I'm not careful.

After two days of being foggy-brained, my head is clear now and I know what I have to do.

I go to my room and, with a long stretch on my arm, pull out the box containing all the steroids in the house. Take it to the kitchen.

I start with the pills. Uncap the bottles and tip them over the garbage disposal. Round pills pour out. Oval pills pour out. All five bottles, completely empty. I turn on the water and hit the switch of the garbage disposal. The loud grinding makes me feel better.

I take out the growth hormone from the fridge and put it with the rest of the tiny bottles and ampoules in the box. Cover it with the lid. Then I drop the side of my fist on the box, hard and fast. Again and again. Glass cracks and breaks until it's a crushing sound.

This bullshit is the reason I lost the people who loved me, and it's what set me on the same path of destruction as Alpha.

I keep slamming my fist down on that box until splotches of oil start to soak through the lid.

I stop. My heart is racing and the bottom of my fist throbs with pain. And here I've been believing I could control my rage—another lie I've been telling myself.

Because of roid rage I hurt my dad's back, went off on Karina at the movie theater, and got my ass kicked in the lunchroom by Ricky.

This time, the only damage I've done is give myself tiny cuts on the side of my right fist. I rinse the blood off, and head to the bathroom for the first aid kit, to disinfect and wrap my hand.

30

THERE'S A MIDMORNING HUMIDITY, and overhead a few motionless, wispy clouds look extra white against a bright blue sky. Not a single breeze has rustled the leaves since I've gotten here. The weather is the same as it was for Mom's funeral almost two years ago.

Mom's grave is about eighty yards away, across the road that cuts through the cemetery. I can spot the tall tree with the lush, sprawling branches that provides shade. We chose it because the sites where sunlight never touches are cheaper.

More people have arrived, bringing the number close to sixty. The casket is set up on two thick pedestals, under a large white tarp set up like the ones at a fair.

It's never been easier to tell the family apart from the friends. Just look at the eight guys on this side of the casket, bulky under black clothes, the long sleeves stretched by muscle.

Most mourners arrivering give us a nod, if any recognition at all, before going to console Alpha's mom, who can't stop crying and pressing tissues against her eyes. His dad stands slumped, sort of off to the side of her, receiving mostly handshakes and back pats.

"We lost a good one," Launch announces after a long silence.

The others nod, dark sunglasses moving up and down. I forgot mine. When I start crying, it will be all out in the open.

The gearheads are all in collars and ties. Except for Jake wearing a plain black T-shirt—no Superman logo for a change—over black slacks.

They could all be high-salaried security guards.

"He gave it his all, though," Tower says, "and lived a great life."

More nods. Not from me though.

Was it really a great life? How? Sure, he gave it his all— *it* being huge muscles. That's precisely why his life was less than great.

They make him sound like he was some war hero, or passed away after battling a disease.

I move closer to Alpha's casket for the first time. I make it about ten feet from the casket. It's off-white with handles that might be brass. It reminds me of the last marble-and-gold trophy Alpha brought home.

I will myself to move closer, But I just can't get my legs to move.

Mindy, wearing a long black dress and oversized sunglasses, appears next to me.

She also faces the casket. "It was hard for me to get close too."

I nod.

"Alpha's parents have invited you to the reception," she says. "You can ride with me."

I need people, and being around the guys isn't helping. "Okay."

Alpha's mom made it clear in the hospital that she wanted nothing to do with Alpha's friends. She wouldn't even make eye contact with any of them. She was nice only to me, maybe because of my age. I introduced myself as Alpha's employee and roommate.

She believed me when I told her I didn't take steroids.

Mindy says, "Come over to the family side if you want. You know how Mrs. Richardson feels about Alpha's other friends, but you're welcome."

Mindy goes back with the family.

It's time to say goodbye to Alpha. I go up to the casket. I don't talk to him, because I know he can't hear me. I just close my eyes and think about him. I think of the good times I lived with him, and think back to who he was at my age. The skinny kid who felt like he wasn't enough and decided to take steroids in order to transform his body. The kid I later became.

The disappointment I felt in myself just hours ago I feel again. Because he started and couldn't stop. Because he basically killed himself so young while supposedly trying to live his best life. It's depressing as hell, so why can't I cry?

I just stand here with my eyes closed trying to focus on the good moments while the stupidity of it all keeps interrupting those thoughts.

"David," someone says behind me.

I turn to see Jake standing off to the side. I guess he's waiting for his turn.

I leave to join the others.

"Wait." Jake forces that word out with a loud whisper.

I stop.

He creeps up to me like he has a secret, glancing back at the other guys twice. Walks past me two steps and motions me over with a jerk of his head.

I join him just outside the shade of the tarp, curious at what this is about. "What's up?"

In a tight-voiced whisper he says, "I know this isn't a great time. I know that. But I wanted to talk to you before anybody else does."

Why is he being so secretive? The others are way outta earshot. I can't even hear what normally loud Tower is saying, though I can guess it's one of his braggy stories.

"Sure," I tell Jake. "What is it?"

His gelled patch of parted hair shines in the sun when he leans toward me. "What about the gear that Alpha has left over?"

My stomach turns. I inch back to see if this guy's serious. He watches me, straight-faced and patient.

"You're serious?" It might take more restraint than I have to keep my voice low. "I can't believe it. You're actually serious right now."

His eyes flick once again to the others before he says, "You know I lost my job at the packaging company and I'm low on money. *Somebody* is going to ask you for the gear, bro. That's a fact. I just want you to think of me first, in case you plan on sharing with someone."

"You're an idiot," I say. "You know that?"

Now it's his turn to be shocked. I'm not afraid of his reaction. Maybe it's because we're at a funeral. Maybe it's because I didn't actually insult the guy by calling him an idiot. It's an observation. He *is* an idiot.

"I get it, bro," he says. "I don't expect it for free or nothing. But what about a discount? I'm unemployed. That's the only reason I'm asking."

I wish I could slap this guy. Not from rage—I'm totally calm. I just think a good hard slap might rearrange his brain and make him less stupid. Make him realize, at least, where we are and how inappropriate this is.

"There's nothing to give away or sell. It's gone."

"What do you mean?" he asks with a dumb stare.

"I destroyed all the gear because I won't be using it again. You shouldn't use it again either."

"You actually threw it away? That's . . ." He looks at me, horrified. "What all was there? What did you throw away?"

Just one slap. A really good one. I swear to God.

"Our friend just died, Jake. Because of *steroids*. You're at that friend's *funeral* asking for drugs that killed your *friend*. Think about that."

I leave him there.

I walk around the grave and casket to the other side, close to where the family is mourning. This is the side where I'll be hanging out during the service.

After the second time the white-haired priest pronounced it *Alfonse* instead of *Alfonso*, I lost interest in what he was saying. Why is this old man, who didn't know Alpha, the only one who's going to talk about him?

This priest turns pages in the Bible to read something you'd think he'd have memorized by now. He talks super fast, as if he wants to hurry home for a nap.

I haven't shed a single tear yet today. I feel sad about my friend Alpha, I really do, but I'm feeling more lonely than anything—in a way that has nothing to do with him. I can't explain it.

I try not to look at the group of Alpha's friends on the other side of the casket, standing still and serious like they're Secret Service. Like they're trying not to cry.

They're not bad guys. I still like them all, even Jake with his dumb questions. I just don't wanna be like them anymore.

A shiny gray Nissan pulls up to park behind the last car in the row. Rogelio gets out, black suit and tie, and closes the door lightly.

He's the third gym member to show up who wasn't a close friend. I'm glad to see him. Not sure why.

The priest steps away from the podium.

Rogelio walks quickly, cutting through the two large trees, and makes his way to us as the priest recites a passage from the Bible. Rogelio acknowledges the gym guys with a nod and walks over to me.

As the casket is lowered into the grave, the sobs coming from Alpha's family get louder.

"I couldn't get here sooner," Rogelio says. "Are you doing okay, buddy?"

I nod.

The question makes me feel good. Nobody has asked me anything like that for months.

To think that Rogelio used to get on my nerves. Just like Dad and Karina.

Some guy I barely know cared enough to try to help me. All of a sudden I realize something. I've been so lonely among all these people because I don't care about them all that much. They can't console me. At Mom's funeral there was lots of family. Dad and Gaby, and relatives from Texas, California, and Mexico.

Here there's nobody for me to lean on. I don't love anybody here. Besides Alpha, of course, who's dead and doesn't need me around.

The casket creaks when it settles on the dirt six feet under. I feel Rogelio's arm go around my shoulders. He gives me a side-squeeze before letting go. That sort of hug makes me feel better than I have in days.

Alpha's mom lets out an anguished sob. Nearly falls when the priest hands her the saltshaker thing full of dry soil. Her husband holds her tightly as they step to the grave.

This is it. The final acceptance of death. You sprinkle some dirt over the casket. We had the same thing at Mom's funeral.

I also lost it when the priest handed that dirt shaker to Dad.

I tried to be strong for Gaby, but I was completely lost in tears, barely able to lift that shaker for my turn. My tío Chano had to hold me up and help.

I had lots of family that day to help me through the most difficult moment of my life. Days later they were gone, but I still had Dad and Gaby. Only two members of my family, but they were so great, and we were so close, that it was enough.

And I fucked it all up. So quickly and so easily. I didn't realize how fragile my life was. That by selfishly building a new me I was tearing down everything I loved the most.

I was planning on making things right with Dad soon. But I can't wait until the weekend. I don't even wanna wait until this service is over.

"Rogelio," I say, turning to him.

"Yeah?"

"This might sound crazy right now," I say, "but could you give me a ride?"

31

ROGELIO IS driving me to the auto shop. Besides asking me for the address where we were going, he hasn't said a word. Which was great. I wanted to focus on what exactly to say to Dad.

A lot of good all that thinking has done me. Every second we're getting closer to the auto shop, and I still haven't figured out what to say after the apology. Will Dad even be willing to listen?

I knocked him down and hurt his back. My own dad. Even before that day I disrespected him, snuck out and left my little sister all alone at home.

Also, why haven't I apologized sooner? If there's stuff I don't understand myself, how am I going to explain it to Dad?

Rogelio turns onto Bautista Street, and there it is three blocks away—Espinoza Auto Repair. The rows of streamers across the front, and the two-tiered rack of used tires. That's the family business where I used to work alongside Dad for two years. It's where Dad taught me all that he knew about cars, and gave me some money for my work.

Money I spent on steroids.

Rogelio doesn't pull all the way to where the tires are, like customers do. He barely pulls into the lot before stopping.

"Thanks," I tell him, and shake his hand with my bandaged one. "I really appreciate it."

"No problem." He takes out a card from his wallet—Bayview Realty—and hands it to me. "My cell phone is on there, in case you ever need it."

"Pull up closer!" a familiar voice shouts.

I turn my head. It's Dad smiling all friendly. The windows on this Nissan are tinted too dark for him to see who's inside.

"Is that your dad?" Rogelio asks.

"Yep, that's him," I say, still looking at Dad.

He's wiping his hands with a small towel. He takes a step into the sun, and motions for us to pull up closer.

That smile is going to fade soon. Here we go.

I take a deep breath and get outta the car. Close the door as my pulse quickens. Rogelio drives away. When I turn to Dad, his smile is gone.

He's standing there like a statue. I do the same thing.

As I look at him, my nervousness evaporates. Even

though I have tons to say and still don't know how to express it. I just need to be near him now.

I start walking over there. Or maybe he's the one who starts walking first. All I know is that we're moving toward each other, closing the distance between us.

And I don't know who opens their arms first but we lock into a tight embrace. Right here in the lot of Espinoza Auto Repair, with the sun blazing down on us, he holds me in his arms as I jerk with sobs.

The tears come down hard, like on the day of Mom's funeral. Big, fat tears.

My own neck gets wet from Dad's tears.

I try to say the words "I'm sorry" but he's squeezing me too hard for them to come out.

Eventually the jerking becomes a steady trembling as I keep weeping. I don't know how long this hug has gone on, and I don't care either.

I'm not letting my dad go. Not ever again.

32

TWO DAYS LATER Gaby the birthday girl is standing on a plastic fruit crate in the kitchen. She's a miniature chef mixing up the chocolate chip cookie dough. Dad will be back from the auto shop by noon with the cake he ordered, and after the kids show up we'll be ordering pizza.

None of it is muscle food. But I'm going to try to eat some and enjoy it. I want my life back, to think and feel all sorts of different things again.

Miguel comes back from the living room after putting up the last of the streamers and balloons in there. The party theme is My Little Pony.

"All done," he tells Gaby. "This looks like it's gonna be the best party in Tampa. Too bad I didn't get an invitation."

"Of course you're invited," Gaby says. "If you're my friend, you're invited."

She stops mixing to look at me. "Karina! Tell Karina to come!"

I take out my phone and pretend to do just that. The truth is that Karina knows about it and will be coming for a little while.

I ended up mentioning Gaby's birthday after I sent an apology text last night.

Hi Karina. This is David. Do you hate me? Maybe you do, but I want you to know that I'm SO SORRY about everything. I was on steroids. You were right about that. I got obsessed with getting big. I recently discovered I was dealing with muscle dysmorphia (you can look it up). I'll be starting some treatment for that. I'm just writing to say I hope you forgive me. Maybe I don't deserve your forgiveness, but I didn't mean to hurt you. You have to understand that. In fact, I'd like to see you so I can apologize in person. I'll be back in school at Culler High on Monday, but I could drop by your house before then. I've moved back home, living in the neighborhood again. Trying to piece my life together. I hope you don't hate me so much that you don't respond.

I didn't tell her how much I still think about her or that I still love her. It didn't seem like a good idea to include that in a first message.

She responded about ten minutes later:

I'm happy you're doing better.

When I mentioned Gaby's birthday party, she said

she'd drop by. *I've been wanting to see Gaby and your dad anyway.*

"Like that?" Gaby asks when she's done putting lumps of cookie dough on the tray.

"Perfect," I say, and slide it into the oven. I took my bandage off this morning and it looks like those tiny cuts on the side of my hand won't scar.

"I'll probably be able to stop by later, birthday girl," Miguel says. Then to me: "But if not I'll see you tomorrow night."

We're going to see the new Van Nelson movie. The regular-sized Van Nelson who's starring in a comedy—a new genre for him. He looks fine, I told myself when I saw the trailer. And it's true. Just like I know I look fine and will continue to look fine when my body gets smaller. It's something I know deep down though. Those negative thoughts keep invading my brain, and I gotta keep kicking them out. It's not easy.

It *won't be* easy, but I can and will beat this messed-up disorder. I can overcome anything. Even my fear of facing those kids at Culler High on Monday. It will make me into a better person.

That which does not kill me makes me stronger.

I read up on that quote and a theory that explains what Nietzsche might have meant. Basically, when life deals you a blow, you confront it. You don't run away or try some cheap fix like I did. You own it, and by dealing with it, you become stronger than you were before.

That's the kind of strength I want. The real kind that can help me deal with the unpredictable and difficult life ahead of me.

"I'm outta here," Miguel says. He pounds his chest twice and flashes the peace sign.

Gaby does the same, and accidentally smears the top of her apron with cookie goo. She looks down at it. "Dang it!"

I open the door for Miguel, sort of sad he's leaving. I know I'll probably see him in a few hours. And if not, then tomorrow. It's just that I've missed him so much these past months.

"I want to thank you for being so cool about everything," I tell him.

"Dude, I totally understand. It all makes sense now. Don't worry about it."

"I explained, sure, but I didn't apologize. I want you to know I'm sorry. I basically ditched you, fucked off for all these months, and I'm sorry about that."

"Dude," he says, and opens his arms. "We're good."

Miguel is the absolute best. I hug him.

About a half hour later the first cookies are cooling on the rack and the second tray is baking when there's a knock at the door.

"Who is it?" Gaby shouts from her bedroom, and keeps shouting as she runs past the kitchen.

"It's me!" Karina shouts from behind the closed door.

I feel myself go warm all over, just from that sweet voice. I wasn't expecting her until everybody else showed up.

Gaby swings the front door open and lets out a joyous scream so loud you'd think the actual My Little Ponies, all six, were on the lawn.

Karina sets down a present wrapped with a green bow to give Gaby a hug. "Happy birthday, Gaby!"

I've forgotten how beautiful Karina is.

"You've gotten so big!" Karina tells Gaby. "I've missed you."

"I've missed you too."

"Let me say hi to your brother."

Karina gets up and gives me a quick, but still nice, hug.

I tell Gaby to give us a minute and head outside with Karina—to the first step on the porch, where we used to sit for hours.

When she takes a seat next to me, I say, "I'm sorry, Karina. You have no idea how sorry I am."

"I know. I believe you." She meets my gaze and says, "Muscle dysmorphia makes sense. I looked it up. It sucks that you've been dealing with that."

"It's like having an irrational voice in my head that I have to get to shut up."

"How are you going to do that?"

"I'll be learning how to do it. There's a support group at the Linden Community Center that meets every Tuesday."

It felt so new and magical just moments ago, when Karina walked into the house. Now there's the old familiarity. Like no time has passed at all. I wanna reach over and hold her hand, but then I remember.

"Um, let me ask you a question," I say, and pause, wondering how to ask it. "I was at the downtown music concert and saw you with a guy."

She gives a small nod. Her face keeps the same calm expression. "What's the question?"

"Right. Yeah. Okay. So . . . is that your boyfriend or something?"

"Not that it's any of your business . . ."

I hold my breath, feeling empty and fragile. Like if I were to slip off this step I'd shatter to pieces.

". . . but no, he's not my boyfriend."

I release that breath. All the horrible nerves of the last three seconds drain from me.

She says, "It's just sex."

That knocks the last bit of oxygen outta me. I'm stunned, unable to think or say a word. I remember that guy and imagine them together. I catch the rage that starts to form in me, breathe slowly to cool it. If I'm going to be angry, it has to be at myself.

I turn to face her. A smile seems to be curling the sides of her lips. She busts out laughing.

"You're the worst, Karina."

I let her enjoy the moment while I decide the guy I

wanted to kill a few seconds ago isn't too bad. In fact, he might be cool.

When she finally stops laughing, she says, "I work at Burger King part-time now. The guy you saw me with works the drive-through. He's okay, I guess, but we didn't go out a second time."

She's single!

This love I feel for her, which I've been holding so close, doesn't scare me so much anymore. I can be open with it.

I offer my hand, palm up, so she can put hers in it.

She looks at my hand then turns her gaze directly in front of her again. "No, David. You hurt me. You can't just pop back into my life and fix everything with an apology."

I take back my hand. The rejection doesn't feel great, but I guess I don't deserve to feel great. In fact, she's being super nice with me if I really think about it.

"I totally understand," I say. "I just want you to know that I'll do anything to regain your trust. Anything at all."

She needs time. I get that. I turn my body so it's easy to face her. "I love you, Karina." I haven't said it to her in months but the words feel normal coming out. "And I want you to know I didn't deliberately hurt you and that I won't hurt you again in any way."

Her eyes fall on me, so intense and warm. "I can forgive you, David. But it doesn't mean that will make everything okay now. And it doesn't mean we'll go out again."

My gut twists and twists. Why wouldn't we get back

together? Somehow, I've missed something. "What are you saying?"

"I'd given up on you, David. Cut you outta my life for good. I wasn't expecting you to enter again. Now I gotta deal with all these feelings and stuff. Do a lot of thinking. You also have to deal with a lot yourself. You should really be focused on *that* right now."

It's hard to argue with that. I need to focus on myself right now instead of on us getting back together. She's making tons of sense.

I run everything she's said through my brain again, because I want to make sure I understand.

"Let me get this straight. Are you saying we can at least try to hang out as friends?"

"Exactly." She smiles. "Let's take things slow and mark us down as a *maybe*."

I smile too. Because I want us back together again, more than anything, and there's a possibility that it will happen.

But if it doesn't, I know it won't destroy me. Not permanently anyway. I'll deal with those feelings like the tough person I want to be. This time I won't pull another weakass stunt and try a quick fix or run away from sadness. And one day, once I get through the sadness about it, I'll be stronger than ever.

"Maybe is good," I say. "I can live with maybe."

AUTHOR'S NOTE

Back in high school my friends and I wanted to be more muscular. We lifted weights, some with more dedication than others, though we would never go so far as to take steroids.

In health class we had learned about the health problems that steroids caused: to the heart, the liver, the kidneys, the reproductive system, not to mention the negative mental effects. So why, at the age of eighteen, did I end up taking them?

We have to go back to when I was a sixteen-year-old cook at the local pizzeria. That's where I met Jake (let's call him that).

He was a twenty-year-old delivery driver and surprisingly open about using steroids. Not that he could deny it. His bodybuilding results were *staggering*, unachievable without drug enhancement. In two years I witnessed him transform from a fit college student to a muscular wonder that children would point at.

I was also impressed. By the time I turned eighteen, the pressure to have a better physique, one I associated with masculinity, became much stronger. I decided to get serious about weightlifting. I gave up basketball, got rid of the barbell set I had at home, and started training with Jake and his friends at the local gym. With all that fitness equipment, and thanks to carefully planned workouts and meals, I made great progress in the first two months, though I didn't think so at the time.

The steroid users I trained among were packing on muscle at a much faster rate. I thought I could use a boost. Just one three-month cycle of steroids to give me a push, and after that I would keep growing the natural way. That was how my thinking went. After all, what was the worst that could happen in that short time? The gym guys had been taking steroids for years, some for decades, and they seemed fine.

So I went for it, not fully understanding how my body and personality would change with all that extra testosterone in my system. What used to be the occasional blemish on my face became full-on acne, covering both cheeks and dotting my upper back. Worse were my mood swings, how I quickly flew into a rage over annoyances, no matter how small.

But I stuck with my plan. Every time I noticed my body filling out my shirt more, the side effects seemed worth it.

When I got off the steroids my symptoms actually got worse as my body's testosterone productions struggled to ramp up to normal. No more mood swings because the depression was steady, my energy at a low most of the day.

I could not believe the gym guys played with their hormones this way, switching their testosterone off and then on blast several times per year.

A couple of months later my acne and depression were done. Soon after, to my shock, so were the results. I lost all the gains I had made.

No wonder those other guys kept taking steroids. To stop meant reversing the progress, which, for them, didn't seem like much progress to begin with. Because they had a specific body image issue, one which didn't have a name yet.[1]

Muscle dysmorphia: a psychological disorder marked by a negative body image and an obsessive desire to have a muscular physique.

It is sometimes referred to as "manorexia" because it affects mostly boys and men and is quite similar to anorexia

---

[1] Before 1997 it was called reverse anorexia nervosa, because researchers didn't understand it well. Subsequently, Pope et al. (1997) described additional cases and proposed to rename the syndrome "muscle dysmorphia."
https://www.ncbi.nlm.nih.gov/pmc/articles/PMC1627897/

nervosa. Rather than try to get as thin as possible, the people affected by muscle dysmorphia try to get as muscular as possible.

The struggle boys face with body image issues often feel lesser known or discussed, though many boys feel insecurity about their bodies and take dangerous measures to improve their appearance.

The pressures for boys keep increasing. Every year the physiques of bodybuilders, actors, superheroes, video game characters, and action figures become more muscular than their predecessors.

Some experts believe that the rates for muscle dysmorphia in men may be similar to the rates of anorexia in women, but that it is more likely to go undiagnosed because of a lack of awareness.[2]

With David Espinoza's story I hope to highlight this issue that affects many boys. It is a work of fiction, inspired by people I have known and by teens and men I interviewed during my research.

I would like to thank them for taking time to share their stories with me.

To learn more or to get help if you are struggling with muscle dysmorphia, body dysmorphia, or any other body/eating disorder, here are some resources:

---

[2] https://www.sciencedirect.com/science/article/abs/pii/S1740144512000125

National Eating Disorders Association:
https://www.nationaleatingdisorders.org/

The BDD Foundation: https://bddfoundation.org/
https://bddfoundation.org/muscle-dysmorphia-body
-image-in-men/

Mental Health America:
http://www.mentalhealthamerica.net/conditions
/body-dysmorphic-disorder-bdd
http://www.mentalhealthamerica.net/conditions
/body-dysmorphic-disorder-bdd-and-youth

Pope, Jr., Harrison G., Katharine A. Phillips, and
Roberto Olivardia. *The Adonis Complex: The Secret Crisis
of Male Body Obsession.* Simon and Schuster, 2000.

ACKNOWLEDGMENTS

Thanks to my talented and supportive team at Harper-Collins. Rosemary Brosnan, your first yes changed my life, and your belief that I could write this second book propelled me. Thanks to my astute editor, Jessica MacLeish, who helped this story come together. Thanks also to editor Alexandra Cooper for helping with the final changes.

Thanks to the Bent Agency and my agent, Louise Fury, who not only takes care of the behind-the-scenes stuff, but also stepped in to read my work when I was struggling the most. Your insight and enthusiasm gave me the push I needed.

Thanks to my early readers. Marcelo Asher Quarantotto gave me excellent feedback in the early stages, and Joy L. Smith combed through the plot and assured me I had one.

Thanks to the librarians, teachers, bloggers, booksellers, reviewers, and all publishing pros helping get my story into the hands of readers.

Thanks to all my family who have consistently supported me, no matter how far away I happen to be living. My Tío Pedro believed in me when few people did. The infectious excitement of my sisters, Yesmin and Stefany, constantly rubs off on me and keeps me going. And a very big thanks to Mom, whose support keeps me sane, and who lives as though her main purpose on this planet is to lift others up.

The biggest thank you of all is for you, reader. It's because of you that I'm fortunate enough to do what I love.

Keep reading for a peek at
THE CLOSEST I'VE COME by Fred Aceves,
a book about potential and discovering yourself.

AT SCHOOL I'm a boss. In baggy jeans and a tee, with swaggy slowness and an icy stare, I roam the halls with my boys.

Other kids shoulder backpacks, talk in twos or threes. Some thumb at cell phones, rocking new clothes they got over Christmas break: sneakers with that store gleam, no fuzz on their sweaters and hoodies.

Guys call out to their friends, giving quick chin raises, while the girls shriek and run smiling to each other's arms, squeezing like twin sisters reunited after war.

What I notice most are the couples. Ain't many holding hands and ain't none kissing so far but you can spot them, their side-by-side walk with that matching rhythm or how they stand super close to talk.

When's *my* turn? Never had me a girlfriend and seems like I never will, which has at least something to do with being broke.

Today I'm looking less ratty than normal with my new solid black tee, a Christmas present. With four tees I used to repeat the same one on Monday and Friday. Now, for my final sophomore semester, I got five in rotation.

Coming up on us is a suited man, fiftyish and lean, the smoke-colored hair from the sides plastered over the bald spot.

"Hello there." He comes to a stop and smiles, hands in his pockets. His breezy way tells me he might be the one actually running things here. Probably the new principal.

"Hi," I say, with two friends joining in.

The man nods. "You guys look dangerous."

I thank him and we keep moving.

In homeroom I dig into my pocket for some pebbles and start plinking them against a side window. Whenever old and half-deaf Mrs. Howard notices, she asks for the "disruptive activity" to stop.

Uppercut in front of me is checking out the kid who screwed up bad last year and wore an Iron Man tee, freshman mistake, and has been "Virginboy" ever since. "Hey, Virginboy," he says now, and laughs when the kid looks over.

Uppercut lives in my hood and I guess we sorta friends. He's down for me, like when I got jumped behind the Sweetbay, and joined my boys in our search for the guys who did it. But I don't trust him, don't actually like him.

This is a guy who slams into others in the halls on purpose.

With nothing but roll call during homeroom he's got time to make fun of people.

Skinny Tim, who sits in front of Uppercut, is "Whiney-bitch." Whenever Uppercut punches him during the Pledge of Allegiance, the kid lets out a low groan.

Areli with the horse pencil case, who's nice to every-body, is "Churchgirl."

Super-smart Melissa is "Fatfuck."

Amy, a punk girl who sticks out more than anybody—blue streaks in her brown hair, eye-catching clothes—is safe way on the other side of the classroom.

I gotta admit she looks cool with that hair, the tagged-up green Chucks, the jangly bracelets and slashed jeans she sometimes wears. Other rocker-type girls here seem to be all image, like last week they was still into Bar-bies and cartoons.

Uppercut, pimpled and with a broken front tooth, sporting ATR kicks and that Puerto Rican flag shirt, is an easy target. And dissing him is a great idea if you love catching a beatdown in public.

Lucky me Uppercut's my sorta friend.

SLAP! Right on my forehead.

"Stop spacing, Marcos," Uppercut says.

I rub the spot and remind myself that slaps ain't no reason to get pissed, even if they do hurt like hell. Girls can nice each other to death all day, give out compliments and hugs, snap group selfies everywhere they go, but boys gotta take swings and call each other bitches.

Don't ask me. I don't make the rules.

The prehistoric loudspeaker over the whiteboard crackles and hums. Then comes the electric screech, warning that somebody in the front office is about to talk.

"Attention, Hanna High students." It's the man from the hall. He introduces himself as Principal Perry, and though we want to hear more about last semester's scandal—the sexts the last principal sent to at least three girls—he just welcomes us back like it's normal to switch principals mid-school year.

The secretary handles the yawnfest announcements, the date and time of open house, PTA meetings, and spelling bees. When the principal's on we all ears.

After telling us how happy he is to be here, he says, "Anyone in violation of the dress code be warned . . ."

We know the dress code. No short skirts or shorts (for the girls) and no sagging pants or shirts with drug references (for the boys).

A few guys sport marijuana leaf tees. If caught, you gotta wear the shirt inside out, 'cause in this school a leaf's distracting but clothes worn the wrong way ain't.

"Let me be clear," Principal Perry says. "Clothing or jewelry with suggestive or questionable language or drawings may not be worn. Examples include, but are not limited to: gang-related symbols; racial, ethnic, or sexual slogans or innuendoes; images or language about drugs, alcohol, or tobacco. Also, anyone wearing sagging pants will be immediately punished from now on."

Me and Uppercut eye each other.

An emo kid pounds a fist on his desk. "Fucking shit!"

Principal Perry clears his throat like he heard. "Dresses, skirts, and shorts must extend beyond the students' fingertips when their arms are held to the sides."

I check out Amy on the other side of the room, at what I can see of her short black skirt. Everybody's looking at her.

Though her stick legs ain't nothing to whistle at, she's cuter than some of the other girls around here.

I ain't never had sex, which has me crazy horny and thinking about it nonstop. Mall mannequins can excite me and surprise boners pop up during class, making me wonder what the hell's going on down there.

But I swear sex ain't the most important thing. It'd be dope just kicking it with a girl. Ain't females the greatest ever? Tell your problems to a girlfriend and she don't make fun of you. A girlfriend means you ain't alone.

"Have a wonderful day, Hanna High students," Perry says, his voice getting swallowed up by the ear-shattering screech. They tell us our loud headphones will damage our hearing and then make us sit through this noise.

The last principal also signed off the same way, called us "Hanna High students" like we a sports team or fan club, not a bunch of kids herded together 'cause we live close by. What else we got in common besides the same teachers, lunch food, and homework? What do I share with perfect-life Kyle Benson sitting up front?

I used to get on the school computer to sorta stalk him. Checked out his pages, his posts and pics, read the comments—blond Kyle who goes out with Tina. He's such a pretty boy you wanna punch him in the face, and she's such a hottie you wanna punch yourself in the face.

A search brought up lots of pics, even an old baseball one, small Kyle uniformed at home plate, ready to swing, bat pointing to the sun. Newer pics were taken in restaurants, a paintball field, outside the AMC theater.

That kid don't kick it like me and my boys. He's got *activities*. One thousand, eight hundred and eighty-five pics of proof on his Instagram, last I checked, while my no-credit phone don't even got a camera.

Ask me if his posts make me jealous and I gotta admit that yeah, just a little. Even the stuff he complained about was dope. Once he posted, *stuck @ fam reunion*.

Done with attendance, Mrs. Howard now calls Amy's name again. "Come here, please."

Amy shifts in her seat, hands tugging and wiggling the skirt down. When she stands up you can see her skirt's gone longer, the top hugging the bottom of her butt, and her Misfits tee covering up the trick. We watch her skinny legs move toward the teacher's desk.

Mrs. Howard sets her reading glasses halfway down her nose. "Extend your arms and no shrugging."

As Amy stands there, fingers reaching down to touch her skirt, she turns her head to smile at us.

That confidence in front of twenty-plus pairs of eyes could be real. Though we sophomores here, Amy rolls with some juniors and seniors, which tops the cool meter. Rockers, artsy kids, and other weirdos, a tiny but rowdy group that share a table in the cafeteria and cigarettes behind the gym.

I ain't never seen her smile before now. It's a nice smile.

Mrs. Howard removes her glasses. "Very well."

As we all try not to laugh, Amy's grin goes wider on the way to her seat. We all sharing a moment for the first time. If our teacher's ears were better she'd hear the snorts and giggles escaping us.

Amy's trick was even better than most of the stuff I get away with.

When Uppercut's head turns to me, I know it's coming. I just hope Amy don't hear it.

He says, "That bitch is skinnier than a crack whore."

Two girls giggle.

Amy backs up a few steps to stand in front of the classroom again, hands on hips. A straight mouth has replaced the grin. "You got something to say?"

All heads turn to us in back. Mrs. Howard slides her

eyes from Amy to Uppercut and back, not getting it.

Just one word comes outta Uppercut—"What?"

"Don't *even*. Unlike you, I spoke up, you chickenshit."

Damn! Amy's as fearless as the girls who live in my hood, Maesta.

Uppercut glances around all slow like he's about to lean forward to look at someone's test answers. "Sit down and shut the hell up."

Still in front of the class she says, "You talk and talk, dude, but you never say anything."

Sitting behind him, there ain't no way to see his face. Is he pissed? Embarrassed? I'm expecting some sorta comeback, but punk girl's on a roll.

"Forever talking about who's fat or skinny or dorky, but what's so great about *you*?"

Nothing, I answer in my head, feeling a combo of excited and scared. I want Amy to stand up there forever, to never stop talking. Someone please give her a megaphone! Her own TV show! I also sorta hope she sits down and shuts up so Uppercut don't start dissing her. Or worse.

I *could* tell Uppercut to chill but he's thick from lifting weights, could snap me like a toothpick. Once he knocked out his own cousin for trying to stop a fight. One punch was all it took.

"Young lady, you need to sit down!" Mrs. Howard's pointing in case Amy forgot which seat. "Sit down this moment!"

Amy's eyes stay locked on Uppercut. "You're a shitbag, making fun of others to make yourself feel better."

He says, "Shut up, bitch."

A few girly gasps fly through the air but the guys' faces just hang there.

Dammit! Amy's walking over here! Such a dumb move. I could get up, keep her away from Uppercut, or tell him to leave her alone. I know I should, but the truth is, I ain't tough. Even with guys my age and size who start shit. I'd rather walk away. It's why I only been in seven fights my whole life.

Amy comes down our row and right up to Uppercut who gets on his feet. He's half a head taller. They practically breathing on each other.

"Wanna make me?" A gangster stare like she's ready for all-out war.

My heart speeds up even more.

"Both of you take your seats this moment!" Mrs. Howard shuffles to the red button as fast as she can.

Something about Amy, those big brown eyes, intense with confidence, puts a warm glow inside me. I hop up real quick and sorta face Uppercut at an angle, my shoulder grazing his.

"Chill," I tell him. A "bro" or "man" at the end would soften that, but then she might think me and him is tight.

Still staring at her, Uppercut tells me, "Mind. Your. Business."

"You're scared," Amy says. "You're not gonna do anything."

She's got me figured out. Can she hear my heart banging in my chest? But wait—she wasn't talking to me. She's still looking at Uppercut.

He pushes me away and I surprise myself by getting back in the same position. I inch even closer.

"Yes?" It's the secretary's voice over the speaker.

"Please hurry!" Mrs. Howard shouts. "Two students are about to get physical with each other!"

Which is a gift dropped into my hands. "For real?" I ask, looking at each of them. "You two about to *get physical* with each other?"

Laughs all around. Even Uppercut turns his head to show me his busted smile. Nothing from Amy though. She keeps staring down Uppercut for what feels like forever.

"Chickenshit," she finally says, and takes her time walking back to her seat.

For the last few minutes of homeroom I look across the room to Amy again and again. Can't stop checking her out. She's sitting there like the coolest thing ever didn't just happen. I gotta meet this Amy, learn everything about her.

But her interested in a Maesta kid? Even strangers seem to know us. At Florida Palms Mall last weekend me and my boys checked out three cute girls and dared each other to go up to them. After a few rounds of rock, paper, scissors

I walked over all nervous. Even before I opened my mouth the hottest one said, "I don't think so," and the other two laughed more than you'd expect.

Can I fake my way into bravery again? Can I talk to Amy if I pass her alone in the halls? It's gotta be alone. In front of her friends would make me too jittery to talk and in front of my own friends . . . they wouldn't understand.

First-talk scenarios run through my head, good ones like her super thrilled to meet me, her eyes lighting up like some Disney princess. But most of them bad, like her giving me a grossed-out face before hurrying away or laughing like the mall girls.

Then I'm picturing our first date, pizza at DeLucia's in the mall, an outside table, and afterward some hand-holding in a dark movie theater. We a regular perfect-life Kyle and Tina.

Sure, no sweat. I'll just rob a bank first.

How about doing free stuff? We could meet in Brewster Park, go for walks, or just kick it at her place 'cause I'm imagining her parents are cool.

Super cheesy, I know. I'm supposed to be all about hitting it, sex without the love or friendship, but that cheeseball stuff pops into my head all the time. I can't help it.

The thing is, a girlfriend can fix you in a snap. I've seen it. Even short-fuse Kevin who'd swing on anybody over a basketball foul has been chill since Shanice. Guys now call him soft, pussy-whipped for always being with his girl, but all we ever do is talk about girls anyway. Why talk about them when you could *be* with one?

I know loneliness is supposed to be some guy on a desert island, or maybe an old lady knitting and hoping the phone will ring, but loneliness can also be a kid like me, surrounded by tons of people, friends who say "Wassup?" when I see them in the halls or walk through Maesta, friends who kick it with me all the time but only go on about who won the game last night or how some girl's got a sweet ass.

With a girlfriend I wouldn't feel so alone. Maybe Amy, so cool and tough, could be that girl.